William Shakespeare'

King Richard III

In Plain and Simple English

BookCaps™ Study Guides

www.bookcaps.com

Table of Contents

ABOUT THIS SERIES..3

CHARACTERS..4

ACT I...6

SCENE 1..7
SCENE 2..17
SCENE 3..36
SCENE 4..60

ACT II...**80**

SCENE 1..81
SCENE 2..91
SCENE 3..101
SCENE 4..106

ACT III..**113**

SCENE 1..114
SCENE 2..130
SCENE 3..140
SCENE 4..142
SCENE 5..150
SCENE 6..157
SCENE 7..158

ACT IV...**173**

SCENE 1..174
SCENE 2..182
SCENE 3..193
SCENE 4..197
SCENE 5..236

ACT V..**238**

SCENE 1..239
SCENE 2..241
SCENE 3..243
SCENE 4..266
SCENE 5..268

About This Series

The "Classic Retold" series started as a way of telling classics for the modern reader—being careful to preserve the themes and integrity of the original. Whether you want to understand Shakespeare a little more or are trying to get a better grasps of the Greek classics, there is a book waiting for you!

The series is expanding every month. Visit BookCaps.com to see all the books in the series, and while you are there join the Facebook page, so you are first to know when a new book comes out.

Characters

EDWARD THE FOURTH

Sons to the King
EDWARD, PRINCE OF WALES afterwards KING EDWARD V
RICHARD, DUKE OF YORK,

Brothers to the King
GEORGE, DUKE OF CLARENCE,
RICHARD, DUKE OF GLOUCESTER, afterwards KING RICHARD III

A YOUNG SON OF CLARENCE (Edward, Earl of Warwick)

HENRY, EARL OF RICHMOND, afterwards KING HENRY VII

CARDINAL BOURCHIER, ARCHBISHOP OF CANTERBURY

THOMAS ROTHERHAM, ARCHBISHOP OF YORK

JOHN MORTON, BISHOP OF ELY

DUKE OF BUCKINGHAM

DUKE OF NORFOLK

EARL OF SURREY, his son

EARL RIVERS, brother to King Edward's Queen

MARQUIS OF DORSET and LORD GREY, her sons

EARL OF OXFORD

LORD HASTINGS

LORD LOVEL

LORD STANLEY, called also EARL OF DERBY

SIR THOMAS VAUGHAN

SIR RICHARD RATCLIFF

SIR WILLIAM CATESBY

SIR JAMES TYRREL

SIR JAMES BLOUNT

SIR WALTER HERBERT

SIR WILLIAM BRANDON

SIR ROBERT BRAKENBURY, Lieutenant of the Tower

CHRISTOPHER URSWICK, a priest

LORD MAYOR OF LONDON

SHERIFF OF WILTSHIRE

HASTINGS, a pursuivant

TRESSEL and BERKELEY, gentlemen attending on Lady Anne

ELIZABETH, Queen to King Edward IV

MARGARET, widow of King Henry VI

DUCHESS OF YORK, mother to King Edward IV

LADY ANNE, widow of Edward, Prince of Wales, son to King
Henry VI; afterwards married to the Duke of Gloucester

A YOUNG DAUGHTER OF CLARENCE (Margaret Plantagenet,
Countess of Salisbury)

Ghosts, of Richard's victims
Lords, Gentlemen, and Attendants; Priest, Scrivener, Page,

Bishops,
Aldermen, Citizens, Soldiers, Messengers, Murderers, Keeper

ACT I

SCENE 1.

London. A street

Enter RICHARD, DUKE OF RICHARD, solus

RICHARD.
Now is the winter of our discontent
Made glorious summer by this sun of York;
And all the clouds that lour'd upon our house
In the deep bosom of the ocean buried.
Now are our brows bound with victorious wreaths;
Our bruised arms hung up for monuments;
Our stern alarums chang'd to merry meetings,
Our dreadful marches to delightful measures.
Grim-visag'd war hath smooth'd his wrinkled front,
And now, instead of mounting barbed steeds
To fright the souls of fearful adversaries,
He capers nimbly in a lady's chamber
To the lascivious pleasing of a lute.
But I-that am not shap'd for sportive tricks,
Nor made to court an amorous looking-glass-
I-that am rudely stamp'd, and want love's majesty
To strut before a wanton ambling nymph-
I-that am curtail'd of this fair proportion,
Cheated of feature by dissembling nature,
Deform'd, unfinish'd, sent before my time
Into this breathing world scarce half made up,
And that so lamely and unfashionable
That dogs bark at me as I halt by them-
Why, I, in this weak piping time of peace,
Have no delight to pass away the time,
Unless to spy my shadow in the sun
And descant on mine own deformity.
And therefore, since I cannot prove a lover
To entertain these fair well-spoken days,
I am determined to prove a villain
And hate the idle pleasures of these days.
Plots have I laid, inductions dangerous,
By drunken prophecies, libels, and dreams,

To set my brother Clarence and the King
In deadly hate the one against the other;
And if King Edward be as true and just
As I am subtle, false, and treacherous,
This day should Clarence closely be mew'd up-
About a prophecy which says that G
Of Edward's heirs the murderer shall be.
Dive, thoughts, down to my soul. Here Clarence comes.

Enter CLARENCE, guarded, and BRAKENBURY

Brother, good day. What means this armed guard
That waits upon your Grace?

Now this miserable time
has been made wonderful by Edward;
and all the clouds that were hanging over our family
have sunk back into the sea.
Now our foreheads carry victorious wreaths,
our battered weapons are hung up as memorials,
great chaos has been changed to pleasant greetings,
grim marches to delightful music.
The terrible face of war has been smoothed over:
and now, instead of mounting armoured horses
to terrify his fearful enemies,
he dances lightly in a lady's bedroom
to the sexy music of a lute.
But I was not made for those flirtatious games,
or to look in the mirror of love;
I am poorly made and don't have the
wherewithal to dance in front of a amorously inclined lass:
I, who haven't been given the correct proportions,
who has been cheated of looks by deceitful Nature,
deformed, unfinished, sent into the world only
half made, before my time–
and I am so lame and unfashionable
that dogs bark at me if I stopnear them–
why, I, in this time of songs of peace,
have no pleasure to pass away the time,
unless it is to see my shadow on the ground,
and sing a song about my own deformities.
And therefore, since I cannot be a lover
to suit these pleasant days,
I am determined I will be a villain,

and despise the idle pleasures of others.
I have constructed a plot, with a dangerous beginning,
through drunken prophesies, lies, and dreams,
to make my brother Clarence and the King
develop a deadly hatred for each other:
and if King Edward is as true and just
as I am cunning, lying, and treacherous,
then today Clarence should be imprisoned
due to a prophecy, which says that 'G'
will murder Edward's heirs–
I will bury my thoughts deep in my soul: here comes Clarence.

Good day, brother; why are you accompanied
by this armed guard?

CLARENCE.
His Majesty,
Tend'ring my person's safety, hath appointed
This conduct to convey me to th' Tower.

His Majesty,
out of concern for my safety, has appointed
this escort to take me to the Tower.

RICHARD.
Upon what cause?

For what reason?

CLARENCE.
Because my name is George.

Because my name is George.

RICHARD.
Alack, my lord, that fault is none of yours:
He should, for that, commit your godfathers.
O, belike his Majesty hath some intent
That you should be new-christ'ned in the Tower.
But what's the matter, Clarence? May I know?

Alas, my lord, that's no fault of yours:
he should imprison your godfathers for that.
Perhaps his Majesty has some plan

for you to be newly christened in the Tower.
But what's the problem, Clarence? May I know?

CLARENCE.
Yea, Richard, when I know; for I protest
As yet I do not; but, as I can learn,
He hearkens after prophecies and dreams,
And from the cross-row plucks the letter G,
And says a wizard told him that by G
His issue disinherited should be;
And, for my name of George begins with G,
It follows in his thought that I am he.
These, as I learn, and such like toys as these
Hath mov'd his Highness to commit me now.

You shall know, Richard, when I do; for I tell you
that at the moment I don't; all I can discover is that
he has been listening to prophecies and dreams,
and out of the alphabet he has picked the letter G,
and says that a wizard told him that G
would disinherit his children;
and, as my name George begins with G,
he thinks that I must be that person.
It's this, and things like this, so I hear,
that has made his Highness imprison me now.

RICHARD.
Why, this it is when men are rul'd by women:
'Tis not the King that sends you to the Tower;
My Lady Grey his wife, Clarence, 'tis she
That tempers him to this extremity.
Was it not she and that good man of worship,
Antony Woodville, her brother there,
That made him send Lord Hastings to the Tower,
From whence this present day he is delivered?
We are not safe, Clarence; we are not safe.

Why, this is what happens when men are ruled by women:
it's not the king who's sending you to the Tower;
it's his wife, Lady Grey, Clarence, it's her
who has encouraged this absurdity.
Wasn't it her and that good holy man,
Antony Woodville, her brother,
that made him send Lord Hastings to the Tower,

from which he was released today?
We are not safe, Clarence; we are not safe.

CLARENCE.
By heaven, I think there is no man is secure
But the Queen's kindred, and night-walking heralds
That trudge betwixt the King and Mistress Shore.
Heard you not what an humble suppliant
Lord Hastings was to her, for her delivery?

By heaven, I don't think anyone's safe
apart from the Queen's family and the nightly messengers
who go between the King and Mistress Shore.
Haven't you heard how humbly Lord Hastings
begged her for her forgiveness?

RICHARD.
Humbly complaining to her deity
Got my Lord Chamberlain his liberty.
I'll tell you what-I think it is our way,
If we will keep in favour with the King,
To be her men and wear her livery:
The jealous o'er-worn widow, and herself,
Since that our brother dubb'd them gentlewomen,
Are mighty gossips in our monarchy.

Humbly begging to her
got the Lord Chamberlain his freedom.
I tell you what, I think the best way for us
to keep the goodwill of the King
is to put ourselves at her service:
the jealous queen and her,
since our brother made them gentlewomen,
are great influences on the King.

BRAKENBURY.
I beseech your Graces both to pardon me:
His Majesty hath straitly given in charge
That no man shall have private conference,
Of what degree soever, with your brother.

I must ask your Graces to both excuse me:
his Majesty has given strict orders
that nobody is to speak privately with

your brother under any circumstances.

RICHARD.
Even so; an't please your worship, Brakenbury,
You may partake of any thing we say:
We speak no treason, man; we say the King
Is wise and virtuous, and his noble queen
Well struck in years, fair, and not jealous;
We say that Shore's wife hath a pretty foot,
A cherry lip, a bonny eye, a passing pleasing tongue;
And that the Queen's kindred are made gentlefolks.
How say you, sir? Can you deny all this?

Very well; if you want to, Brakenbury,
you can listen to anything we say:
we are not discussing treason, man; we say the King
is wise and virtuous, and his noble Queen
nicely mature, fair and not jealous;
we say that Shore's wife is graceful,
with red lips, merry eyes, and she speaks well;
and that the Queen's relatives are made into gentlefolk.
What do you say to that, sir? Can you deny all this?

BRAKENBURY.
With this, my lord, myself have naught to do.

This is nothing to do with me, my lord.

RICHARD.
Naught to do with Mistress Shore! I tell thee,
fellow,
He that doth naught with her, excepting one,
Were best to do it secretly alone.

Nothing to do with Mistress Shore! I tell you, fellow,
that anyone doing 'nothing' with her, apart from one,
would be well advised to do it in secret.

BRAKENBURY.
What one, my lord?

Who is the one, my lord?

RICHARD.

Her husband, knave! Wouldst thou betray me?

Her husband, scoundrel! Do you want to get me into trouble?

BRAKENBURY.
I do beseech your Grace to pardon me, and
withal
Forbear your conference with the noble Duke.

*I beg your Grace to excuse me, and also
to stop talking with the noble duke.*

CLARENCE.
We know thy charge, Brakenbury, and will
obey.

We know your orders, Brakenbury, and will obey.

RICHARD.
We are the Queen's abjects and must obey.
Brother, farewell; I will unto the King;
And whatsoe'er you will employ me in-
Were it to call King Edward's widow sister-
I will perform it to enfranchise you.
Meantime, this deep disgrace in brotherhood
Touches me deeper than you can imagine.

*Everybody must submit to the Queen.
Brother, farewell; I will go to the king;
and whatever service you want from me—
if you asked me to call King Edward's widow my sister—
I will do it to win your freedom.
In the meanwhile, this insult to our family
affects me more than you can imagine.*

CLARENCE.
I know it pleaseth neither of us well.

I know neither of us are happy about it.

RICHARD.
Well, your imprisonment shall not be long;
I will deliver or else lie for you.
Meantime, have patience.

Well, you won't be locked up for long;
I will free you or I'll take your place.
In the meantime, be patient.

CLARENCE.
I must perforce. Farewell.
Exeunt CLARENCE, BRAKENBURY, and guard

I have no choice. Farewell.

RICHARD.
Go tread the path that thou shalt ne'er return.
Simple, plain Clarence, I do love thee so
That I will shortly send thy soul to heaven,
If heaven will take the present at our hands.
But who comes here? The new-delivered Hastings?

Go and walk the path from which you will never return.
Plain, simple Clarence, I love you so
that I will shortly send your soul to heaven,
if heaven will take the gift from me.
But who is this? The newly freed Hastings?

Enter LORD HASTINGS

HASTINGS.
Good time of day unto my gracious lord!

A very good day to my gracious lord!

RICHARD.
As much unto my good Lord Chamberlain!
Well are you welcome to the open air.
How hath your lordship brook'd imprisonment?

And the same to my good Lord Chamberlain!
I'm pleased to welcome you to freedom.
How did your lordship cope with imprisonment?

HASTINGS.
With patience, noble lord, as prisoners must;
But I shall live, my lord, to give them thanks
That were the cause of my imprisonment.

Patiently, noble lord, as prisoners have to;
but I shall make sure I repay those, my lord,
who caused my imprisonment.

RICHARD.
No doubt, no doubt; and so shall Clarence too;
For they that were your enemies are his,
And have prevail'd as much on him as you.

No doubt, no doubt; and Clarence will as well;
for those who were your enemies are his,
and have treated him just as badly as you.

HASTINGS.
More pity that the eagles should be mew'd
Whiles kites and buzzards prey at liberty.

It's a great shame that eagles get locked up
while kites and buzzards are free to prey.

RICHARD.
What news abroad?

What news is there abroad?

HASTINGS.
No news so bad abroad as this at home:
The King is sickly, weak, and melancholy,
And his physicians fear him mightily.

There's no news as bad as the news at home:
the King is sickly, weak and depressed,
and his doctors are very worried for him.

RICHARD.
Now, by Saint John, that news is bad indeed.
O, he hath kept an evil diet long
And overmuch consum'd his royal person!
'Tis very grievous to be thought upon.
Where is he? In his bed?

Now, by St John, that news is certainly bad.
His lifestyle has been poor for too long,

he's worn out his royal body with excess!
It's very sad to think of.
Where is he? In his bed?

HASTINGS.
He is.

He is.

RICHARD.
Go you before, and I will follow you.
Exit HASTINGS
He cannot live, I hope, and must not die
Till George be pack'd with posthorse up to heaven.
I'll in to urge his hatred more to Clarence
With lies well steel'd with weighty arguments;
And, if I fail not in my deep intent,
Clarence hath not another day to live;
Which done, God take King Edward to his mercy,
And leave the world for me to bustle in!
For then I'll marry Warwick's youngest daughter.
What though I kill'd her husband and her father?
The readiest way to make the wench amends
Is to become her husband and her father;
The which will I-not all so much for love
As for another secret close intent
By marrying her which I must reach unto.
But yet I run before my horse to market.
Clarence still breathes; Edward still lives and reigns;
When they are gone, then must I count my gains.

You go on ahead, and I will follow you.

I hope he will not live, but he must not die
before George has been hastened up to heaven.
I'll encourage Clarence's hatred of him
with lies backed up with stern arguments;
and, if my cunning plans succeed,
Clarence does not have another day to live;
once that's done, may God take King Edward also
and leave the world free for me.
Then I will marry Warwick's youngest daughter—
who cares if I killed her husband and her father?
The best way to make it up to the girl

would be to become her husband, and her father:
which I will, not so much for love
as for another secret plan,
which I need to marry her to fulfil.
But I'm getting ahead of myself:
Clarence is still alive, so is Edward and he is still king;
I must count my gains when they are gone.

Exit

SCENE 2.

London. Another street

Enter corpse of KING HENRY THE SIXTH, with halberds to guard it;
LADY ANNE being the mourner, attended by TRESSEL and BERKELEY

ANNE.
Set down, set down your honourable load-
If honour may be shrouded in a hearse;
Whilst I awhile obsequiously lament
Th' untimely fall of virtuous Lancaster.
Poor kcy-cold figure of a holy king!
Pale ashes of the house of Lancaster!
Thou bloodless remnant of that royal blood!
Be it lawful that I invocate thy ghost
To hear the lamentations of poor Anne,
Wife to thy Edward, to thy slaughtered son,
Stabb'd by the self-same hand that made these wounds.
Lo, in these windows that let forth thy life
I pour the helpless balm of my poor eyes.
O, cursed be the hand that made these holes!
Cursed the heart that had the heart to do it!
Cursed the blood that let this blood from hence!
More direful hap betide that hated wretch
That makes us wretched by the death of thee
Than I can wish to adders, spiders, toads,
Or any creeping venom'd thing that lives!
If ever he have child, abortive be it,
Prodigious, and untimely brought to light,
Whose ugly and unnatural aspect
May fright the hopeful mother at the view,
And that be heir to his unhappiness!
If ever he have wife, let her be made
More miserable by the death of him
Than I am made by my young lord and thee!
Come, now towards Chertsey with your holy load,
Taken from Paul's to be interred there;
And still as you are weary of this weight
Rest you, whiles I lament King Henry's corse.

[The bearers take up the coffin]

Put down your honourable burden
(if one can be found on a hearse)
while I set the example of mourning
for the untimely death of virtuous Lancaster.
Poor stone dead image of a holy King,
the pale ashes of the house of Lancaster,
you bloodless remains of that royal line:
May it be lawful for me to plead with your ghost
to hear the sorrowing of poor Anne,
the wife of your Edward, your slaughtered son,
stabbed by the same hand that wounded you.
Into these wounds that killed you
I pour my useless tears.
Curses on the hand that made these wounds;
cursed be the heart that could bring itself to do it;
May the blood of the bloodletter be cursed.
I wish for worse to happen to that horrible wretch,
who has made us wretched with your death,
than I wish to adders, spiders, toads,
or any creeping poisonous thing alive.
If he ever has a child, may it be an abortion:
monstrous, born too early,
with an ugly unnatural look
which terrifies the mother to see it,
and may it inherit his unhappiness.
If he ever marries, let his death
make her more miserable than
I am made by that of my young lord, and you.
Come, bring your holy burden to Chertsey,
taken from St Paul's to be buried there;
and whenever you get tired of the weight
you can rest, while I lament for King Henry's body.

Enter RICHARD

RICHARD.
Stay, you that bear the corse, and set it down.

Wait, you carrying that corpse, put it down.

ANNE.
What black magician conjures up this fiend

To stop devoted charitable deeds?

What black magician has summoned up this devil
to stop kind and devoted deeds?

RICHARD.
Villains, set down the corse; or, by Saint Paul,
I'll make a corse of him that disobeys!

Villains, put down the corpse; or, I swear by St Paul,
I'll make a corpse of the one who disobeys!

FIRST GENTLEMAN.
My lord, stand back, and let the coffin
pass.

My Lord, stand back and let the coffin pass.

RICHARD.
Unmannerd dog! Stand thou, when I command.
Advance thy halberd higher than my breast,
Or, by Saint Paul, I'll strike thee to my foot
And spurn upon thee, beggar, for thy boldness.

Rude dog! You stop when I order.
Stop pointing your spear at me,
or, by St Paul, I'll knock you to the ground
and grind you with my heel, beggar, for your impudence.

[The bearers set down the coffin]

ANNE.
What, do you tremble? Are you all afraid?
Alas, I blame you not, for you are mortal,
And mortal eyes cannot endure the devil.
Avaunt, thou dreadful minister of hell!
Thou hadst but power over his mortal body,
His soul thou canst not have; therefore, be gone.

What, are you trembling? Are you all afraid?
Alas, I do not blame you, for you are mortal,
and the eyes of mortals cannot bear the sight of the devil.
Away with you, you foul Minister of hell!
You only have power over his mortal body,

you cannot have his soul; so, go.

RICHARD.
Sweet saint, for charity, be not so curst.

Sweet saint, be kind, don't be so harsh.

ANNE.
Foul devil, for God's sake, hence and trouble us not;
For thou hast made the happy earth thy hell
Fill'd it with cursing cries and deep exclaims.
If thou delight to view thy heinous deeds,
Behold this pattern of thy butcheries.
O, gentlemen, see, see! Dead Henry's wounds
Open their congeal'd mouths and bleed afresh.
Blush, blush, thou lump of foul deformity,
For 'tis thy presence that exhales this blood
From cold and empty veins where no blood dwells;
Thy deeds inhuman and unnatural
Provokes this deluge most unnatural.
O God, which this blood mad'st, revenge his death!
O earth, which this blood drink'st, revenge his death!
Either, heav'n, with lightning strike the murd'rer dead;
Or, earth, gape open wide and eat him quick,
As thou dost swallow up this good king's blood,
Which his hell-govern'd arm hath butchered.

Foul devil, for God's sake, go away and don't bother us;
you have turned the happy earth into hell,
filling it with screams and curses.
If you enjoy seeing your horrible deeds,
look at this example of your butchery.
Oh gentlemen, look, look! The wounds of dead Henry
have reopened and are bleeding again.
Blush, blush, you foul twisted lump,
it's your presence that makes this blood run
from cold and empty veins where there is no blood;
your inhuman and unnatural deeds
have caused this unnatural flood.
O God, who made this blood, revenge his death!
O Earth, which drinks this blood, revenge his death!
Let either heaven strike the murderer dead with lightning,
or let the Earth open wide and consume him as quickly
as you have swallowed up the blood of this good king,

whom his devilish hand butchered.

RICHARD.
Lady, you know no rules of charity,
Which renders good for bad, blessings for curses.

Lady, you are not being kind,
you should give back good for bad, blessings for curses.

ANNE.
Villain, thou knowest nor law of God nor man:
No beast so fierce but knows some touch of pity.

Villain, you don't obey the laws of God or man:
there is no animal so fierce that he doesn't feel some pity.

RICHARD.
But I know none, and therefore am no beast.

But I feel no pity, and so I am not an animal.

ANNE.
O wonderful, when devils tell the truth!

Amazing, when devils tell the truth!

RICHARD.
More wonderful when angels are so angry.
Vouchsafe, divine perfection of a woman,
Of these supposed crimes to give me leave
By circumstance but to acquit myself.

More amazing when angels are so angry.
Explain, you heavenly perfect woman,
what crimes I'm supposed to have committed,
so that I can give you proof of my innocence.

ANNE.
Vouchsafe, diffus'd infection of a man,
Of these known evils but to give me leave
By circumstance to accuse thy cursed self.

I will explain, you disease of a man,
the well-known facts of the matter just to

22

give myself permission to accuse you.

RICHARD.
Fairer than tongue can name thee, let me have
Some patient leisure to excuse myself.

Lady more beautiful than words can say,
give me a chance to excuse myself.

ANNE.
Fouler than heart can think thee, thou canst make
No excuse current but to hang thyself.

Man uglier than the heart could imagine,
the only way you could excuse yourself this is by hanging yourself.

RICHARD.
By such despair I should accuse myself.

If I did such a thing I would be accusing myself.

ANNE.
And by despairing shalt thou stand excused
For doing worthy vengeance on thyself
That didst unworthy slaughter upon others.

And by doing it you would be acquitted
for taking proper revenge on yourself
who unjustly slaughtered others.

RICHARD.
Say that I slew them not?

What if it wasn't me who killed them?

ANNE.
Then say they were not slain.
But dead they are, and, devilish slave, by thee.

Then they wouldn't be dead.
But they are dead, and, devil's slave, you killed them.

RICHARD.
I did not kill your husband.

I didn't kill your husband.

ANNE.
Why, then he is alive.

Well then, he must still be alive.

RICHARD.
Nay, he is dead, and slain by Edward's hands.

No, he is dead, and killed by Edward.

ANNE.
In thy foul throat thou liest: Queen Margaret saw
Thy murd'rous falchion smoking in his blood;
The which thou once didst bend against her breast,
But that thy brothers beat aside the point.

You're lying through your foul throat: Queen Margaret saw
your murderous sword covered with his warm blood;
the same sword that you tried to stab her with,
but your brothers pushed the point away.

RICHARD.
I was provoked by her sland'rous tongue
That laid their guilt upon my guiltless shoulders.

I was provoked by the lies she told,
which placed guilt upon my guiltless shoulders.

ANNE.
Thou wast provoked by thy bloody mind,
That never dream'st on aught but butcheries.
Didst thou not kill this king?

You were provoked by your vicious mind,
that never thinks of anything but murder.
Did you not kill this king?

RICHARD.
I grant ye.

I grant you that.

ANNE.
Dost grant me, hedgehog? Then, God grant me to
Thou mayst be damned for that wicked deed!
O, he was gentle, mild, and virtuous!

You grant me that, hedgehog? Then, may God grant me
that you will be dammed for that wicked deed!
Oh, he was gentle, mild and good!

RICHARD.
The better for the King of Heaven, that hath
him.

Then he'll be well suited to the King of Heaven,
who has him now.

ANNE.
He is in heaven, where thou shalt never come.

He is in heaven, where you will never go.

RICHARD.
Let him thank me that holp to send him
thither,
For he was fitter for that place than earth.

He should thank me for helping to send him there,
he was more suited to that place than to Earth.

ANNE.
And thou unfit for any place but hell.

And you are unsuited for any place apart from hell.

RICHARD.
Yes, one place else, if you will hear me name it.

There is one place, if you will let me name it.

ANNE.
Some dungeon.

Some dungeon.

RICHARD.
Your bed-chamber.

Your bedroom.

ANNE.
Ill rest betide the chamber where thou liest!

May there be no rest in any room where you sleep!

RICHARD.
So will it, madam, till I lie with you.

That's how it will be, madam, until I sleep with you.

ANNE.
I hope so.

That's what I hope.

RICHARD.
I know so. But, gentle Lady Anne,
To leave this keen encounter of our wits,
And fall something into a slower method-
Is not the causer of the timeless deaths
Of these Plantagenets, Henry and Edward,
As blameful as the executioner?

I know this is how it will be. But, gentle Lady Anne,
let us leave off this sharp banter,
and talk more reasonably–
hasn't the person who caused these untimely deaths
of these Plantagenets, Henry and Edward,
as much to blame as the executioner?

ANNE.
Thou wast the cause and most accurs'd effect.

You were the cause and the cursed effect.

RICHARD.
Your beauty was the cause of that effect-
Your beauty that did haunt me in my sleep

To undertake the death of all the world
So I might live one hour in your sweet bosom.

It was your beauty that caused the effect–
your beauty that haunted me in my sleep
making me want to kill the whole world
if it meant I could spend one hour with you.

ANNE.
If I thought that, I tell thee, homicide,
These nails should rend that beauty from my cheeks.

If I thought that was true, I tell you, murderer,
that I would tear my looks to bits with my nails.

RICHARD.
These eyes could not endure that beauty's wreck;
You should not blemish it if I stood by.
As all the world is cheered by the sun,
So I by that; it is my day, my life.

My eyes could not tolerate the wreck of your beauty;
if I was there you would not be allowed to damage it.
It cheers up my whole day, my whole life
in the same way the world is cheered by the sun.

ANNE.
Black night o'ershade thy day, and death thy life!

May black night overshadow your day, and death your life!

RICHARD.
Curse not thyself, fair creature; thou art both.

Do not curse yourself, beautiful creature; you are my day and my life.

ANNE.
I would I were, to be reveng'd on thee.

I wish I was, so I could get revenge on you.

RICHARD.
It is a quarrel most unnatural,
To be reveng'd on him that loveth thee.

It's most unnatural to want to
take revenge on someone who loves you.

ANNE.
It is a quarrel just and reasonable,
To be reveng'd on him that kill'd my husband.

It's entirely just and reasonable to want
to have revenge on the person who killed my husband.

RICHARD.
He that bereft thee, lady, of thy husband
Did it to help thee to a better husband.

Lady, the one who took your husband away,
did it so you could find a better husband.

ANNE.
His better doth not breathe upon the earth.

There isn't a better one alive.

RICHARD.
He lives that loves thee better than he could.

There is someone alive who loves you better than he could.

ANNE.
Name him.

Name him.

RICHARD.
Plantagenet.

Plantagenet.

ANNE.
Why, that was he.

Why, that was his name.

RICHARD.

The self-same name, but one of better nature.

The exact same name, but better made.

ANNE.
Where is he?

Where is he?

RICHARD.
Here.[She spits at him]Why dost thou spit
at me?

Here. Why are you spitting on me?

ANNE.
Would it were mortal poison, for thy sake!

I wish it was fatal poison, to get you!

RICHARD.
Never came poison from so sweet a place.

No poison ever came from such a sweet place.

ANNE.
Never hung poison on a fouler toad.
Out of my sight! Thou dost infect mine eyes.

And poison never hit a more horrible toad.
Get out of my sight! Thesight of you infects my eyes.

RICHARD.
Thine eyes, sweet lady, have infected mine.

Your eyes, sweet lady, have infected mine.

ANNE.
Would they were basilisks to strike thee dead!

I wish I had eyes like a basilisk, to strike you dead!

RICHARD.
I would they were, that I might die at once;

For now they kill me with a living death.
Those eyes of thine from mine have drawn salt tears,
Sham'd their aspects with store of childish drops-
These eyes, which never shed remorseful tear,
No, when my father York and Edward wept
To hear the piteous moan that Rutland made
When black-fac'd Clifford shook his sword at him;
Nor when thy warlike father, like a child,
Told the sad story of my father's death,
And twenty times made pause to sob and weep
That all the standers-by had wet their cheeks
Like trees bedash'd with rain-in that sad time
My manly eyes did scorn an humble tear;
And what these sorrows could not thence exhale
Thy beauty hath, and made them blind with weeping.
I never sued to friend nor enemy;
My tongue could never learn sweet smoothing word;
But, now thy beauty is propos'd my fee,
My proud heart sues, and prompts my tongue to speak.
 [She looks scornfully at him]
Teach not thy lip such scorn; for it was made
For kissing, lady, not for such contempt.
If thy revengeful heart cannot forgive,
Lo here I lend thee this sharp-pointed sword;
Which if thou please to hide in this true breast
And let the soul forth that adoreth thee,
I lay it naked to the deadly stroke,
And humbly beg the death upon my knee.
[He lays his breast open; she offers at it with his sword]
Nay, do not pause; for I did kill King Henry-
But 'twas thy beauty that provoked me.
Nay, now dispatch; 'twas I that stabb'd young Edward-
But 'twas thy heavenly face that set me on.
 [She falls the sword]
Take up the sword again, or take up me.

I wish they were, so I could die at once;
for seeing them now is a living death.
Those eyes of yours have drawn salt tears from mine,
shamed them with these childish drops;
these eyes, which never shed a tear of remorse,
not when my father York and Edward wept
to hear the terrible moans of Rutland
when black faced Clifford attacked him with his sword;

nor when your warlike father told me the
sad story of my father's death, and like a child,
twenty times had to pause and weep,
so that the cheeks of all the bystanders were soaked
like trees covered with rain. At that sad time
my manly eyes refused to shed low tears;
and your beauty has drawn out these things
which those sorrows could not, and you have made me blind with weeping.
I never begged either friend or enemy:
my tongue has never learnt how to speak smooth sweet words;
but now I am trying to gain your beauty,
my proud heart begs, and makes my tongue speak.
[She looks scornfully at him]
Don't curl your lip like that, for it was made
for kissing, lady, not to show such contempt.
If your vengeful heart can't forgive me,
here, I will lend you this sharp pointed sword,
and if you want to you can bury it into my
true heart, and release the soul of he who adores you,
I expose it here to the deadly blow,
and humbly beg for death on my knees.
[He exposes his chest and she points the sword at it]
No, do not pause, for I did kill King Henry—
but it was your beauty that inspired me.
No, do it: it was I who stabbed young Edward—
but it was your heavenly face that made me do it.
[She drops the sword]
Either pick up the sword or accept me.

ANNE.
Arise, dissembler; though I wish thy death,
I will not be thy executioner.

Get up, deceiver; although I want you dead,
I will not be your executioner.

RICHARD.
Then bid me kill myself, and I will do it.

Then tell me to kill myself, and I will do it.

ANNE.
I have already.

I have told you already.

RICHARD.
That was in thy rage.
Speak it again, and even with the word
This hand, which for thy love did kill thy love,
Shall for thy love kill a far truer love;
To both their deaths shalt thou be accessary.

That was when you were angry.
Tell me again, and as soon as you say it
this hand, which killed your love to get your love,
will, for love of you, kill a much truer love;
you will be accessory to both their deaths.

ANNE.
I would I knew thy heart.

I wish I knew what's in your heart.

RICHARD.
'Tis figur'd in my tongue.

You've heard what I have said.

ANNE.
I fear me both are false.

I fear both your heart and your tongue are false.

RICHARD.
Then never was man true.

Then no man was ever true.

ANNE.
Well, put up your sword.

Well, put away your sword.

RICHARD.
Say, then, my peace is made.

Then tell me that we are friends.

ANNE.
That shalt thou know hereafter.

You will know that afterwards.

RICHARD.
But shall I live in hope?

But can I have hopes?

ANNE.
All men, I hope, live so.

I hope that all men have hope.

RICHARD.
Vouchsafe to wear this ring.

Agree to wear this ring.

ANNE.
To take is not to give. [Puts on the ring]

Taking is not giving.

RICHARD.
Look how my ring encompasseth thy finger,
Even so thy breast encloseth my poor heart;
Wear both of them, for both of them are thine.
And if thy poor devoted servant may
But beg one favour at thy gracious hand,
Thou dost confirm his happiness for ever.

Look how my ringembraces your finger,
even as your breast embraces my poor heart;
wear both of them, as both of them are yours.
And if your poor devoted servant may
ask for just one favour from you,
you will make him happy forever.

ANNE.
What is it?

What is it?

RICHARD.
That it may please you leave these sad designs
To him that hath most cause to be a mourner,
And presently repair to Crosby House;
Where-after I have solemnly interr'd
At Chertsey monast'ry this noble king,
And wet his grave with my repentant tears-
I will with all expedient duty see you.
For divers unknown reasons, I beseech you,
Grant me this boon.

That you agree to leave these sad matters
to the one who has the most reason to be a mourner,
and go at once to Crosby House;
and after I have solemnly buried
this noble king at Chertsey monastery,
and wet his grave with my tears of repentance,
I will come to see you as soon as I can.
For many secret reasons, I beg you,
do me this favour.

ANNE.
With all my heart; and much it joys me too
To see you are become so penitent.
Tressel and Berkeley, go along with me.

With all my heart; and it pleases me very much
to see that you are being so repentant.
Tressel and Berkeley, come along with me.

RICHARD.
Bid me farewell.

Give me your good wishes.

ANNE.
'Tis more than you deserve;
But since you teach me how to flatter you,
Imagine I have said farewell already.

It's more than you deserve;
but since you are teaching me how to flatter you,

34

imagine I have said farewell already.

Exeunt two GENTLEMEN With LADY ANNE

RICHARD.
Sirs, take up the corse.

Sirs, pick up the body.

GENTLEMEN.
Towards Chertsey, noble lord?

And carry on to Chertsey, noble lord?

RICHARD.
No, to White Friars; there attend my coming.
Exeunt all but RICHARD
Was ever woman in this humour woo'd?
Was ever woman in this humour won?
I'll have her; but I will not keep her long.
What! I that kill'd her husband and his father-
To take her in her heart's extremest hate,
With curses in her mouth, tears in her eyes,
The bleeding witness of my hatred by;
Having God, her conscience, and these bars against me,
And I no friends to back my suit at all
But the plain devil and dissembling looks,
And yet to win her, all the world to nothing!
Ha!
Hath she forgot already that brave prince,
Edward, her lord, whom I, some three months since,
Stabb'd in my angry mood at Tewksbury?
A sweeter and a lovelier gentleman-
Fram'd in the prodigality of nature,
Young, valiant, wise, and no doubt right royal-
The spacious world cannot again afford;
And will she yet abase her eyes on me,
That cropp'd the golden prime of this sweet prince
And made her widow to a woeful bed?
On me, whose all not equals Edward's moiety?
On me, that halts and am misshapen thus?
My dukedom to a beggarly denier,
I do mistake my person all this while.
Upon my life, she finds, although I cannot,

Myself to be a marv'llous proper man.
I'll be at charges for a looking-glass,
And entertain a score or two of tailors
To study fashions to adorn my body.
Since I am crept in favour with myself,
I will maintain it with some little cost.
But first I'll turn yon fellow in his grave,
And then return lamenting to my love.
Shine out, fair sun, till I have bought a glass,
That I may see my shadow as I pass.

No, to Whitefriars; wait for me there.

Was a woman with these feelings ever wooed?
Was a woman with these feelings ever won?
I'll have her, but I won't keep her long.
What! I killed her husband and his father:
to win her when her hate for me is at its highest,
with curses in her mouth, tears in her eyes,
the bloody cause of her hatred close by,
with God, her conscience and these barriers
against me–
and I, with no friends to press my case
except for the devil and false looks–
and yet I can win her, and beat the world!
Ha!
Has she already forgotten that brave Prince,
Edward, her Lord, whom I, some three months ago,
stabbed at Tewkesbury in my rage?
The world will never again see
as sweet or lovely a gentleman,
a great work of nature,
Young, brave, wise, and certainly royal.
And yet she will lower her eyes to me,
who made her a widow in a bed of sorrow?
She looks at me, whom the whole of cannot equal half of Edward?
On me, who limps and has this twisted body?
I bet my dukedom against a farthing,
I have been mistaken about my looks this whole time!
I swear on my life, she thinks–although I do not–
that I am a fine figure of a man.
I shall buy a looking glass,
and have a score or two of tailors
invent fashionable clothes for my body:

since I have now decided to like myself,
I shall keep my looks up with some expense.
But first I'll put this fellow in his grave,
and then return, sorrowful, to my love.
Fair sun, shine out until I have bought a mirror,
so I can see my shadow as I go along.

Exit

SCENE 3.

London. The palace

Enter QUEEN ELIZABETH, LORD RIVERS, and LORD GREY

RIVERS.
Have patience, madam; there's no doubt his Majesty
Will soon recover his accustom'd health.

Be patient, madam: there's no doubt his Majesty
will soon be back to his normal self.

GREY.
In that you brook it ill, it makes him worse;
Therefore, for God's sake, entertain good comfort,
And cheer his Grace with quick and merry eyes.

When he sees you think things are bad, it makes him worse; therefore, for God's sake, comfort him
and cheer his Grace up by being merry.

QUEEN ELIZABETH.
If he were dead, what would betide on me?

If he dies, what will happen to me?

GREY.
No other harm but loss of such a lord.

Nothing worse than the loss of such a husband.

QUEEN ELIZABETH.
The loss of such a lord includes all harms.

The loss of such a husband is the worst thing imaginable.

GREY.
The heavens have bless'd you with a goodly son
To be your comforter when he is gone.

The heavens have blessed you with a fine son
to look after you when he's gone.

QUEEN ELIZABETH.
Ah, he is young; and his minority
Is put unto the trust of Richard Gloucester,
A man that loves not me, nor none of you.

Ah, he's young; and until he is grown he is
to be under the protection of Richard Gloucester,
a man who does not love me, nor any of you.

RIVER.
Is it concluded he shall be Protector?

Is it definite he will be the Protector?

QUEEN ELIZABETH.
It is determin'd, not concluded yet;
But so it must be, if the King miscarry.

It has been decided, but it's not definite yet;
but that's what must happen, if the king should die.

Enter BUCKINGHAM and DERBY

GREY.
Here come the Lords of Buckingham and Derby.

Here come the lords of Buckingham and Derby.

BUCKINGHAM.
Good time of day unto your royal Grace!

Good day to your Royal Highness!

DERBY.
God make your Majesty joyful as you have been.

May God give your Majesty back her happiness.

QUEEN ELIZABETH.
The Countess Richmond, good my Lord
of Derby,

To your good prayer will scarcely say amen.
Yet, Derby, notwithstanding she's your wife
And loves not me, be you, good lord, assur'd
I hate not you for her proud arrogance.

My good Lord Derby, the Countess of Richmond
would hardly agree with your prayers.
But, Derby, despite the fact that she's your wife
and does not love me, I can assure you, my good lord,
that I don't hate you on account of her arrogance.

DERBY.
I do beseech you, either not believe
The envious slanders of her false accusers;
Or, if she be accus'd on true report,
Bear with her weakness, which I think proceeds
From wayward sickness and no grounded malice.

I beg you, either don't believe
the jealous lies of false accusers;
or, if there are true accusations,
make allowances for her weakness, which I think comes
from a wandering mind, and no real hatred.

QUEEN ELIZABETH.
Saw you the King to-day, my Lord of Derby?

Did you see the King today, Lord Derby?

DERBY.
But now the Duke of Buckingham and I
Are come from visiting his Majesty.

The Duke of Buckingham and I have
just come from visiting his Majesty.

QUEEN ELIZABETH.
What likelihood of his amendment, Lords?

What chance is there of his recovery,
my Lords?

BUCKINGHAM.
Madam, good hope; his Grace speaks

cheerfully.

A good chance I hope, madam; his Grace
is speaking cheerfully.

QUEEN ELIZABETH.
God grant him health! Did you confer with him?

May God give him health! Did you speak with him?

BUCKINGHAM.
Ay, madam; he desires to make atonement
Between the Duke of Gloucester and your brothers,
And between them and my Lord Chamberlain;
And sent to warn them to his royal presence.

Yes, madam; he wants to reconcile
the Duke of Gloucester and your brothers,
and them and the Lord Chamberlain;
and has summoned them to his royal presence.

QUEEN ELIZABETH.
Would all were well! But that will never be.
I fear our happiness is at the height.

I wish all was well! But it will never happen.
I fear this is as good as it will get.

Enter RICHARD, HASTINGS, and DORSET

RICHARD.
They do me wrong, and I will not endure it.
Who is it that complains unto the King
That I, forsooth, am stern and love them not?
By holy Paul, they love his Grace but lightly
That fill his ears with such dissentious rumours.
Because I cannot flatter and look fair,
Smile in men's faces, smooth, deceive, and cog,
Duck with French nods and apish courtesy,
I must be held a rancorous enemy.
Cannot a plain man live and think no harm
But thus his simple truth must be abus'd
With silken, sly, insinuating Jacks?

They have wronged me, and I will not tolerate it.
Who is it that complains to the King
that I, by God, am harsh and do not love them?
By holy Paul, those who fill the ears of his grace
with such disloyal rumours cannot love him much.
Because I do not flatter, and look sweet,
smile to men's faces, speak smoothly and deceptively,
grotesquely copy French manners,
this makes me an angry enemy.
Can't a simple man live, thinking no harm,
without his simple truth being abused
by these silky, cunning, ingratiating upstarts?

GREY.
To who in all this presence speaks your Grace?

Who of all the people here is your Grace speaking of?

RICHARD.
To thee, that hast nor honesty nor grace.
When have I injur'd thee? when done thee wrong,
Or thee, or thee, or any of your faction?
A plague upon you all! His royal Grace-
Whom God preserve better than you would wish!-
Cannot be quiet scarce a breathing while
But you must trouble him with lewd complaints.

To you, who has neither honesty or grace.
When have I done you any harm? When I have I done you wrong,
you, or any of your party?
A plague on all of you! His royal Grace—
may God preserve him better than you would like!–
cannot lie quiet, hardly able to breathe, but
you must trouble him with your foolish complaints.

QUEEN ELIZABETH.
Brother of Gloucester, you mistake the
matter.
The King, on his own royal disposition
And not provok'd by any suitor else-
Aiming, belike, at your interior hatred
That in your outward action shows itself
Against my children, brothers, and myself-
Makes him to send that he may learn the ground.

Brother of Gloucester, you are mistaken.
The King, through his own royal inclination,
and not encouraged by anybody else–
probably intending to investigate your inner hatred
that shows itself in your outward actions
against my children, brothers and myself–
has sent for you so he can ask for your reasons.

RICHARD.
I cannot tell; the world is grown so bad
That wrens make prey where eagles dare not perch.
Since every Jack became a gentleman,
There's many a gentle person made a Jack.

I can't tell; the world has become so bad
that wrens are hunting where eagles dare not perch.
Since every vulgar person became a gentleman,
there are many gentlemen who have become vulgar.

QUEEN ELIZABETH.
Come, come, we know your meaning,
brother Gloucester:
You envy my advancement and my friends';
God grant we never may have need of you!

Come now, we know what you're talking about, brother Gloucester:
you are envious of my promotion and that of my friends;
may God grant that we never need to look for you for anything!

RICHARD.
Meantime, God grants that I have need of you.
Our brother is imprison'd by your means,
Myself disgrac'd, and the nobility
Held in contempt; while great promotions
Are daily given to ennoble those
That scarce some two days since were worth a noble.

In the meantime, God has made it so that I need you.
My brother has been imprisonmened through your schemes,
I have been disgraced, and the nobility
held in contempt; while great promotions
are given daily to make nobles out of those
who two days ago were hardly worth a noble.

QUEEN ELIZABETH.
By Him that rais'd me to this careful
height
From that contented hap which I enjoy'd,
I never did incense his Majesty
Against the Duke of Clarence, but have been
An earnest advocate to plead for him.
My lord, you do me shameful injury
Falsely to draw me in these vile suspects.

I swear by God who raised me to this onerous position
from the contented happiness I enjoyed,
I never turned his Majesty
against the Duke of Clarence, but have been
speaking on his behalf.
My Lord, these horrible suspicions of yours
do me a great injury.

RICHARD.
You may deny that you were not the mean
Of my Lord Hastings' late imprisonment.

So you will deny that you were not the reason
for the recent imprisonment of my Lord Hastings.

RIVERS.
She may, my lord; for-

She can, my lord; for–

RICHARD.
She may, Lord Rivers? Why, who knows
not so?
She may do more, sir, than denying that:
She may help you to many fair preferments
And then deny her aiding hand therein,
And lay those honours on your high desert.
What may she not? She may-ay, marry, may she-

She can, Lord Rivers? Why, everybody knows that.
She may do more than deny that, sir:
she may help you to get many fine promotions
and then deny that she gave you a helping hand,

and say that you earned all those honours yourself.

RIVERS.
What, marry, may she?

May she indeed?

RICHARD.
What, marry, may she? Marry with a king,
A bachelor, and a handsome stripling too.
Iwis your grandam had a worser match.

She may indeed. She can marry a King,
a bachelor, a handsome lad too.
I wish your grandmother had a lower match.

QUEEN ELIZABETH.
My Lord of Gloucester, I have too long
borne
Your blunt upbraidings and your bitter scoffs.
By heaven, I will acquaint his Majesty
Of those gross taunts that oft I have endur'd.
I had rather be a country servant-maid
Than a great queen with this condition-
To be so baited, scorn'd, and stormed at.

Enter old QUEEN MARGARET, behind

Small joy have I in being England's Queen.

My Lord of Gloucester, for too long I have tolerated
your blunt criticism and your bitter contempt.
By heaven, I shall tell his Majesty
of all those horrible taunts I have had to put up with.
I would rather be a serving maid in the country
than a great Queen, if it means having to
be treated with such angry contempt.

QUEEN MARGARET.
And less'ned be that small, God, I
beseech Him!
Thy honour, state, and seat, is due to me.

And I pray to God that he will stop!

Your honour, royalty and position are all due to me.

RICHARD.
What! Threat you me with telling of the
King?
Tell him and spare not. Look what I have said
I will avouch't in presence of the King.
I dare adventure to be sent to th' Tow'r.
'Tis time to speak-my pains are quite forgot.

What! Are you threatening me by saying you will tell the King?
Tell him, don't spare him. Everything I have says
I will swear to in the presence of the King.
I will chance being sent to the tower.
It is time to speak–my labours have been quite forgotten.

QUEEN MARGARET.
Out, devil! I do remember them to
well:
Thou kill'dst my husband Henry in the Tower,
And Edward, my poor son, at Tewksbury.

Damn you, devil! I remember my labours all too well:
you killed my husband Henry in the Tower,
and Edward, my poor son, at Tewkesbury.

RICHARD.
Ere you were queen, ay, or your husband
King,
I was a pack-horse in his great affairs,
A weeder-out of his proud adversaries,
A liberal rewarder of his friends;
To royalize his blood I spent mine own.

Before you were ever Queen, or your husband King,
I was his dogsbody in his great affairs,
I weeded out his proud enemies,
liberally rewarded his friends;
to make his blood royal I spilled my own.

QUEEN MARGARET.
Ay, and much better blood than his or
thine.

Yes, and much better blood than his or yours.

RICHARD.
In all which time you and your husband Grey
Were factious for the house of Lancaster;
And, Rivers, so were you. Was not your husband
In Margaret's battle at Saint Albans slain?
Let me put in your minds, if you forget,
What you have been ere this, and what you are;
Withal, what I have been, and what I am.

And all that time you and your husband Grey
were on the side of the house of Lancaster;
and, Rivers, so were you. Wasn't your husband
killed fighting for Margaret at St Albans?
Let me remind you, if you've forgotten,
what you were before now, and what you are now;
also, what I have been, and what I am.

QUEEN MARGARET.
A murd'rous villain, and so still thou art.

A murderous villain, and that's what you still are.

RICHARD.
Poor Clarence did forsake his father, Warwick,
Ay, and forswore himself-which Jesu pardon!-

Poor Clarence abandoned his father, Warwick,
yes, and perjured himself–may Jesus pardon him!–

QUEEN MARGARET.
Which God revenge!

May God avenge him!

RICHARD.
To fight on Edward's party for the crown;
And for his meed, poor lord, he is mewed up.
I would to God my heart were flint like Edward's,
Or Edward's soft and pitiful like mine.
I am too childish-foolish for this world.

To fight on Edward's side for the Crown;

and for his reward he is imprisoned.
I wish to God my heart was made of flint like Edward's,
or that Edward's was as soft and full of pity as mine.
I am too innocent for this world.

QUEEN MARGARET.
Hie thee to hell for shame and leave this
world,
Thou cacodemon; there thy kingdom is.

Go to hell in shame and leave this world,
you evil spirit; that's where your kingdom is.

RIVERS.
My Lord of Gloucester, in those busy days
Which here you urge to prove us enemies,
We follow'd then our lord, our sovereign king.
So should we you, if you should be our king.

My Lord of Gloucester, in those busy days
which you say caused us to be your enemies,
we followed our Lord, our sovereign king.
We should follow you, if you were king.

RICHARD.
If I should be! I had rather be a pedlar.
Far be it from my heart, the thought thereof!

If I were! I would rather be a beggar.
The thought of being king is far away from my heart!

QUEEN ELIZABETH.
As little joy, my lord, as you suppose
You should enjoy were you this country's king,
As little joy you may suppose in me
That I enjoy, being the Queen thereof.

You imagine, my lord, that you would get
little joy out of being the king of this country,
you may imagine I get the same lack of joy
from being the Queen of it.

QUEEN MARGARET.
As little joy enjoys the Queen thereof;

For I am she, and altogether joyless.
I can no longer hold me patient. [Advancing]
Hear me, you wrangling pirates, that fall out
In sharing that which you have pill'd from me.
Which of you trembles not that looks on me?
If not that, I am Queen, you bow like subjects,
Yet that, by you depos'd, you quake like rebels?
Ah, gentle villain, do not turn away!

She gets as little joy from it;
for I am her, and I have no joy at all.
I can no longer keep my patience.
Listen to me, you arguing thieves, who are falling out
in sharing what you have stolen from me.
Which of you can look upon me without trembling?
It's either because you are awed by me as my subjects
or scared of me because you are rebels.
Ah, gentle villain, do not turn away!

RICHARD.
Foul wrinkled witch, what mak'st thou in my
sight?

Foul wrinkled witch, what are you doing in my presence?

QUEEN MARGARET.
But repetition of what thou hast marr'd,
That will I make before I let thee go.

I am just explaining the damage you have done,
that I will make you pay for before I let you go.

RICHARD.
Wert thou not banished on pain of death?

Weren't you banished on pain of death?

QUEEN MARGARET.
I was; but I do find more pain in
banishment
Than death can yield me here by my abode.
A husband and a son thou ow'st to me;
And thou a kingdom; all of you allegiance.
This sorrow that I have by right is yours;

And all the pleasures you usurp are mine.

I was; but I find the punishment more painful
than any pain death could give me in my own home.
You owe me a husband and a son;
and you a kingdom; all of you loyalty.
The sorrow that I have is rightfully yours;
and all the pleasures you have stolen are mine.

RICHARD.
The curse my noble father laid on thee,
When thou didst crown his warlike brows with paper
And with thy scorns drew'st rivers from his eyes,
And then to dry them gav'st the Duke a clout
Steep'd in the faultless blood of pretty Rutland-
His curses then from bitterness of soul
Denounc'd against thee are all fall'n upon thee;
And God, not we, hath plagu'd thy bloody deed.

The curse my noble father put on you,
when you put a paper crown on his soldier's head
and with your hatred drew tears from his eyes,
and then to dry them attacked the Duke
with the murder of the good blameless Rutland–
the curses he then gave you derived from
the bitterness of his soul have now fallen upon you;
and it's God, not me, who has punished your bloody deed.

QUEEN ELIZABETH.
So just is God to right the innocent.

So God justly revenges the innocent.

HASTINGS.
O, 'twas the foulest deed to slay that babe,
And the most merciless that e'er was heard of!

Oh, it was the foulest deed to kill that baby,
the most merciless that has ever been heard of!

RIVERS.
Tyrants themselves wept when it was reported.

Tyrants wept when they heard of it.

DORSET.
No man but prophesied revenge for it.

Everybody said punishment would come for it.

BUCKINGHAM.
Northumberland, then present, wept to see it.

Northumberland, who was there, wept to see it.

QUEEN MARGARET.
What, were you snarling all before I came,
Ready to catch each other by the throat,
And turn you all your hatred now on me?
Did York's dread curse prevail so much with heaven
That Henry's death, my lovely Edward's death,
Their kingdom's loss, my woeful banishment,
Should all but answer for that peevish brat?
Can curses pierce the clouds and enter heaven?
Why then, give way, dull clouds, to my quick curses!
Though not by war, by surfeit die your king,
As ours by murder, to make him a king!
Edward thy son, that now is Prince of Wales,
For Edward our son, that was Prince of Wales,
Die in his youth by like untimely violence!
Thyself a queen, for me that was a queen,
Outlive thy glory, like my wretched self!
Long mayest thou live to wail thy children's death,
And see another, as I see thee now,
Deck'd in thy rights, as thou art stall'd in mine!
Long die thy happy days before thy death;
And, after many length'ned hours of grief,
Die neither mother, wife, nor England's Queen!
Rivers and Dorset, you were standers by,
And so wast thou, Lord Hastings, when my son
Was stabb'd with bloody daggers. God, I pray him,
That none of you may live his natural age,
But by some unlook'd accident cut off!

What? Were you all snarling at each other before I came,
ready to grab each other by the throat,
and now you turn all your hatred on me?
Did York's dreadful curse have so much influence with heaven

that the death of Henry and my lovely Edward,
the loss of their kingdom, my sorrowful exile,
all have to happen to pay for that stroppy brat?
Can curses get through the clouds and into heaven?
Well then, dull clouds, get out of the way of my vigorous curses:
may your king die of excess, not through war,
as mine did of murder, to make him a king.
Edward your son, who is now Prince of Wales,
may he die in his youth through the same untimely violence
as that which Edward my son, who was Prince of Wales.
You, a Queen, in revenge for me who was a Queen,
may you outlive your glory as I wretchedly have:
may you live long to bemoan the death of your children,
and see someone else, as I see you now,
taking your rightful place, as you have taken mine;
may your happiness die long before your death,
and after many long hours of grief may you
die neither a mother, a wife, nor the Queen of England.
Rivers and Dorset, you were bystanders,
and so were you, Lord Hastings, when my son
was stabbed with bloody daggers. I pray to God
that none of you may live to a normal age,
but will be cut off by some unexpected injury.

RICHARD.
Have done thy charm, thou hateful wither'd
hag.

Finish with your spell, you hateful withered hag.

QUEEN MARGARET.
And leave out thee? Stay, dog, for thou
shalt hear me.
If heaven have any grievous plague in store
Exceeding those that I can wish upon thee,
O, let them keep it till thy sins be ripe,
And then hurl down their indignation
On thee, the troubler of the poor world's peace!
The worm of conscience still be-gnaw thy soul!
Thy friends suspect for traitors while thou liv'st,
And take deep traitors for thy dearest friends!
No sleep close up that deadly eye of thine,
Unless it be while some tormenting dream
Affrights thee with a hell of ugly devils!

Thou elvish-mark'd, abortive, rooting hog,
Thou that wast seal'd in thy nativity
The slave of nature and the son of hell,
Thou slander of thy heavy mother's womb,
Thou loathed issue of thy father's loins,
Thou rag of honour, thou detested-

And leave you out? Wait, dog, for you will hear me.
If heaven has any terrible suffering in store
worse than that which I can wish upon you,
oh, let them keep it until your sins have reached their height,
and then let them hurl down their punishment
on you, who troubles the peace of this poor world!
May the worm of conscience gnaw away at your soul!
May you suspect your friends of treachery while you are live,
and may your dearest friends be traitors!
May you never close your murderous eyes in sleep,
unless you suffer from terrible dreams
about a hell full of awful devils.
You are marked as a devil, you abortive snuffling pig,
who was marked at birth
as the slave of nature, and the son of health;
you are an insult to your poor mother's womb,
you are a hated child of your father's blood,
stained honour, you hated–

RICHARD.
Margaret!

Margaret!

QUEEN MARGARET.
Richard!

Richard!

RICHARD.
Ha?

What?

QUEEN MARGARET.
I call thee not.

I didn't call you.

RICHARD.
I cry thee mercy then, for I did think
That thou hadst call'd me all these bitter names.

Then I must beg your pardon, for I thought
that you called me all those bitter names.

QUEEN MARGARET.
Why, so I did, but look'd for no reply.
O, let me make the period to my curse!

Why, so I did, but I don't require an answer.
Oh, let me finish my curse!

RICHARD.
'Tis done by me, and ends in-Margaret.

It's finished as far as I'm concerned, and it shall curse Margaret.

QUEEN ELIZABETH.
Thus have you breath'd your curse
against yourself.

So you have cursed yourself.

QUEEN MARGARET.
Poor painted queen, vain flourish of my
fortune!
Why strew'st thou sugar on that bottled spider
Whose deadly web ensnareth thee about?
Fool, fool! thou whet'st a knife to kill thyself.
The day will come that thou shalt wish for me
To help thee curse this poisonous bunch-back'd toad.

Poor fake Queen, false copy of my destiny!
Why are you being kind to that hunchbacked spider
whose deadly web surrounds you?
Fool, fool! You are sharpening the knife which will kill you.
The day will come when you will want me
to help you curse this poisonous hunchbacked toad.

HASTINGS.

False-boding woman, end thy frantic curse,
Lest to thy harm thou move our patience.

False prophesying woman, stop your frantic cursing,
in case you provoke us to lose our temper.

QUEEN MARGARET.
Foul shame upon you! you have all
mov'd mine.

Foul shame on you! You have made me
lose mine.

RIVERS.
Were you well serv'd, you would be taught your
duty.

If you were well advised, you would learn your place.

QUEEN MARGARET.
To serve me well you all should do me
duty,
Teach me to be your queen and you my subjects.
O, serve me well, and teach yourselves that duty!

You should properly all serve me,
and teach me to be your Queen and learn to be my subjects.
Oh, serve me well, and learn to do that!

DORSET.
Dispute not with her; she is lunatic.

Don't argue with her; she's mad.

QUEEN MARGARET.
Peace, Master Marquis, you are malapert;
Your fire-new stamp of honour is scarce current.
O, that your young nobility could judge
What 'twere to lose it and be miserable!
They that stand high have many blasts to shake them,
And if they fall they dash themselves to pieces.

Peace, Master Marquis, you are impudent;
you have only just got your title, you hardly have authority.

I wish that with your new title you could understand
what it means to lose it and be miserable!
Those who have a high position are shaken by many events,
and if they fall they are smashed to pieces.

RICHARD.
Good counsel, marry; learn it, learn it, Marquis.

Good advice indeed; learn it, learn it, Marquis.

DORSET.
It touches you, my lord, as much as me.

It applies just as much to you, my lord, as me.

RICHARD.
Ay, and much more; but I was born so high,
Our aery buildeth in the cedar's top,
And dallies with the wind, and scorns the sun.

Yes, and more so; but I was so highborn
that our home is at the top of the cedar tree,
it plays with the wind, and ignores the sun.

QUEEN MARGARET.
And turns the sun to shade-alas! alas!
Witness my son, now in the shade of death,
Whose bright out-shining beams thy cloudy wrath
Hath in eternal darkness folded up.
Your aery buildeth in our aery's nest.
O God that seest it, do not suffer it;
As it is won with blood, lost be it so!

And covers up the sun–alas! Alas!
Look at my son, now in the shadow of death,
whose brightness has all been covered up
by the eternal darkness of your cloudy anger.
You have built your home in our nest.
Oh God who sees it, do not tolerate it;
as it was won through blood, may it be lost in the same way!

BUCKINGHAM.
Peace, peace, for shame, if not for charity!

Peace, peace, for shame, if not for kindness!

QUEEN MARGARET.
Urge neither charity nor shame to me.
Uncharitably with me have you dealt,
And shamefully my hopes by you are butcher'd.
My charity is outrage, life my shame;
And in that shame still live my sorrow's rage!

Don't tell me to be either kind or ashamed.
You have dealt with me unkindly,
and you have shamefully kills all my hopes.
My kindness is horror, my life is my shame;
and in that shame, my sorrow still rages.

BUCKINGHAM.
Have done, have done.

Enough, enough.

QUEEN MARGARET.
O princely Buckingham, I'll kiss thy
hand
In sign of league and amity with thee.
Now fair befall thee and thy noble house!
Thy garments are not spotted with our blood,
Nor thou within the compass of my curse.

Oh princely Buckingham, I shall kiss your hand
as a sign of alliance and friendship with you.
May good things come to you and your noble house!
Your clothes are not stained with my family's blood,
and you don't come within the remit of my curse.

BUCKINGHAM.
Nor no one here; for curses never pass
The lips of those that breathe them in the air.

Nor does anyone here; all curses ever do
are curse the one who utters them.

QUEEN MARGARET.
I will not think but they ascend the sky
And there awake God's gentle-sleeping peace.

O Buckingham, take heed of yonder dog!
Look when he fawns, he bites; and when he bites,
His venom tooth will rankle to the death:
Have not to do with him, beware of him;
Sin, death, and hell, have set their marks on him,
And all their ministers attend on him.

I believe that they will climb into the sky
and awake God from his peaceful sleep.
Oh Buckingham, look out for that dog there!
When he falls on you, he will bite you; and when he bites,
his poisonous teeth will give you a deadly infection:
have nothing to do with him, watch out for him;
sin, death, and hell, have all taken him for their own,
and all their ministers serve him.

RICHARD.
What doth she say, my Lord of Buckingham?

What is she saying, my Lord Buckingham?

BUCKINGHAM.
Nothing that I respect, my gracious lord.

Nothing I give any attention to, my gracious lord.

QUEEN MARGARET.
What, dost thou scorn me for my gentle
counsel,
And soothe the devil that I warn thee from?
O, but remember this another day,
When he shall split thy very heart with sorrow,
And say poor Margaret was a prophetess!
Live each of you the subjects to his hate,
And he to yours, and all of you to God's!

What, are you scorning my kind advice,
and soothing the devil I have warned you about?
Just remember this on another day,
when he will split your heart in two with sorrow,
and you will say poor Margaret was a prophetess!
May each of you suffer from his fate,
and may he suffer yours, and may all of you suffer God's!

Exit

BUCKINGHAM.
My hair doth stand an end to hear her curses.

Her curses make my hair stand on end.

RIVERS.
And so doth mine. I muse why she's at liberty.

Mine too. I and wondering why she is free.

RICHARD.
I cannot blame her; by God's holy Mother,
She hath had too much wrong; and I repent
My part thereof that I have done to her.

I can't blame her; by God's holy mother,
too many bad things have happened to her; and I am sorry
for the part I have played in that.

QUEEN ELIZABETH.
I never did her any to my knowledge.

As far as I know I never did her any wrong.

RICHARD.
Yet you have all the vantage of her wrong.
I was too hot to do somebody good
That is too cold in thinking of it now.
Marry, as for Clarence, he is well repaid;
He is frank'd up to fatting for his pains;
God pardon them that are the cause thereof!

But you have all the advantages from it.
I was too eager to help a certain person
who now is not at all eager to remember it.
Well, as for Clarence, he has been well paid;
he has been shut up in a pen to fatten for his trouble;
May God forgive those who are responsible!

RIVERS.
A virtuous and a Christian-like conclusion,
To pray for them that have done scathe to us!

A virtuous and Christian conclusion,
praying for those who have done us harm!

RICHARD.
So do I ever-[Aside]being well advis'd;
For had I curs'd now, I had curs'd myself.

I always do–[aside] it's the best thing;
for if I cursed those people, I would be cursing myself.

Enter CATESBY

CATESBY.
Madam, his Majesty doth call for you,
And for your Grace, and you, my gracious lords.

Madam, his Majesty is calling for you,
and for your grace, and you, my gracious lords.

QUEEN ELIZABETH.
Catesby, I come. Lords, will you go
with me?

Catesby, I'm coming. Lords, will you come
with me?

RIVERS.
We wait upon your Grace.

We will attend your Grace.

Exeunt all but RICHARD

RICHARD.
I do the wrong, and first begin to brawl.
The secret mischiefs that I set abroach
I lay unto the grievous charge of others.
Clarence, who I indeed have cast in darkness,
I do beweep to many simple gulls;
Namely, to Derby, Hastings, Buckingham;
And tell them 'tis the Queen and her allies
That stir the King against the Duke my brother.
Now they believe it, and withal whet me

To be reveng'd on Rivers, Dorset, Grey;
But then I sigh and, with a piece of Scripture,
Tell them that God bids us do good for evil.
And thus I clothe my naked villainy
With odd old ends stol'n forth of holy writ,
And seem a saint when most I play the devil.

Enter two MURDERERS

But, soft, here come my executioners.
How now, my hardy stout resolved mates!
Are you now going to dispatch this thing?

I'm doing wrong, I'm starting the fight.
The secret mischiefs that I begin
I shall make sure others are blamed for.
Clarence, whom I have in fact thrown into the darkness,
I pretend to these simpletons I care for him;
particularly to Derby, Hastings, and Buckingham;
and I tell them that it is the Queen and her allies
who have stirred the king up against my brother the Duke.
Now they believe it, and so prepare my revenge
against Rivers, Dorset and Grey.
But then I sigh, and, quoting scripture,
tell them that God orders us to turn the other cheek:
and so I disguise my naked evil
with bits and pieces stolen from Holy Writ,
and seem to be a saint, when I am at my most devilish.

[Enter two murderers]

But, hush, here come my executioners.
Hello there, my hardy strong resolute mates!
Are you going to do this business?

FIRST MURDERER.
We are, my lord, and come to have the
warrant,
That we may be admitted where he is.

We are, my lord, and have come to get the warrant,
so that we can gain access to him.

RICHARD.

Well thought upon; I have it here about me.
[Gives the warrant]
When you have done, repair to Crosby Place.
But, sirs, be sudden in the execution,
Withal obdurate, do not hear him plead;
For Clarence is well-spoken, and perhaps
May move your hearts to pity, if you mark him.

Good thinking; I have it on me.
[Gives the warrant]
When you have finished, go to Crosby Place.
But, sirs, kill him quickly,
be hardhearted also, don't let him plead with you;
for Clarence speaks well, and might be able
to make you pity him, if you listen.

FIRST MURDERER.
Tut, tut, my lord, we will not stand to
prate;
Talkers are no good doers. Be assur'd
We go to use our hands and not our tongues.

Tut-tut, my lord, we will not stand around talking;
talkers are no good in action. I promise you
we are going to use our hands and not our tongues.

RICHARD.
Your eyes drop millstones when fools' eyes fall
tears.
I like you, lads; about your business straight;
Go, go, dispatch.

I can see you are not softhearted fools.
I like you, lads; go about your business at once;
go, go, hurry.

FIRST MURDERER.
We will, my noble lord.

We will, my noble Lord.

Exeunt

SCENE 4.

London. The Tower

Enter CLARENCE and KEEPER

KEEPER.
Why looks your Grace so heavily to-day?

Why is your Grace looking so miserable today?

CLARENCE.
O, I have pass'd a miserable night,
So full of fearful dreams, of ugly sights,
That, as I am a Christian faithful man,
I would not spend another such a night
Though 'twere to buy a world of happy days-
So full of dismal terror was the time!

Oh, I have had a miserable night,
so full of terrible dreams, of ugly sights,
that, I swear by my faith as a Christian,
I wouldn't spend another night like it
even if it bought me a whole lifetime of happiness—
it was so miserable and terrifying!

KEEPER.
What was your dream, my lord? I pray you
tell me.

What did you dream, my lord? Please tell me.

CLARENCE.
Methoughts that I had broken from the Tower
And was embark'd to cross to Burgundy;
And in my company my brother Gloucester,
Who from my cabin tempted me to walk
Upon the hatches. Thence we look'd toward England,
And cited up a thousand heavy times,
During the wars of York and Lancaster,

That had befall'n us. As we pac'd along
Upon the giddy footing of the hatches,
Methought that Gloucester stumbled, and in falling
Struck me, that thought to stay him, overboard
Into the tumbling billows of the main.
O Lord, methought what pain it was to drown,
What dreadful noise of waters in my ears,
What sights of ugly death within my eyes!
Methoughts I saw a thousand fearful wrecks,
A thousand men that fishes gnaw'd upon,
Wedges of gold, great anchors, heaps of pearl,
Inestimable stones, unvalued jewels,
All scatt'red in the bottom of the sea;
Some lay in dead men's skulls, and in the holes
Where eyes did once inhabit there were crept,
As 'twere in scorn of eyes, reflecting gems,
That woo'd the slimy bottom of the deep
And mock'd the dead bones that lay scatt'red by.

I thought I had escaped from the Tower,
and was on board ship crossing over to Burgundy;
I had my brother Gloucester with me,
who persuaded me to come from my cabin and walk
on the deck: from there we looked towards England,
and spoke of the thousand bad things that had happened
to us during the wars of York
and Lancaster. As we walked along
on the slippery deck,
I thought that Gloucester stumbled, and as he fell
he struck me (he was trying to save him) overboard,
into the waves of the sea.
Oh Lord! I thought I felt the pain of drowning:
what a dreadful noise of water there was in my ears;
what ugly sights of death I saw with my eyes!
I thought I saw a thousand terrible wrecks;
ten thousand men gnawed on by fish;
slabs of gold, great anchors, heaps of pearls,
stones and jewels beyond price,
all scattered on the bottom of the sea.
Some were inside the skulls of dead men, and had
crept into the holes where eyes once lived–
as if they were imitating eyes–reflecting gems,
that shone in the slimy bottom of the sea,
and mocked the dead bones that were scattered all around.

KEEPER.
Had you such leisure in the time of death
To gaze upon these secrets of the deep?

You had time as you were dying
to look at all these secrets of the deep?

CLARENCE.
Methought I had; and often did I strive
To yield the ghost, but still the envious flood
Stopp'd in my soul and would not let it forth
To find the empty, vast, and wand'ring air;
But smother'd it within my panting bulk,
Who almost burst to belch it in the sea.

I thought I had; and I often tried
to give up the ghost, but the jealous water
crushed my soul and would not let it escape
into the empty vastness of the air;
it choked it within my breathless body,
which almost had to burst to let it out into the sea.

KEEPER.
Awak'd you not in this sore agony?

Didn't this awful agony wake you up?

CLARENCE.
No, no, my dream was lengthen'd after life.
O, then began the tempest to my soul!
I pass'd, methought, the melancholy flood
With that sour ferryman which poets write of,
Unto the kingdom of perpetual night.
The first that there did greet my stranger soul
Was my great father-in-law, renowned Warwick,
Who spake aloud 'What scourge for perjury
Can this dark monarchy afford false Clarence?'
And so he vanish'd. Then came wand'ring by
A shadow like an angel, with bright hair
Dabbled in blood, and he shriek'd out aloud
'Clarence is come-false, fleeting, perjur'd Clarence,
That stabb'd me in the field by Tewksbury.
Seize on him, Furies, take him unto torment!'

With that, methoughts, a legion of foul fiends
Environ'd me, and howled in mine ears
Such hideous cries that, with the very noise,
I trembling wak'd, and for a season after
Could not believe but that I was in hell,
Such terrible impression made my dream.

No, no, my dream went into the afterlife.
Oh, what a storm began in my soul!
I thought that I crossed the sad stream
with that grim ferryman whom the poets write of,
into the kingdom of perpetual darkness.
The first person to greet my foreign soul
was my great father-in-law, famous Warwick,
who said aloud, 'What penalty for perjury
can the dark ruler give to foolish Clarence?'
And so he vanished. Then a shadow like an angel
came wandering by, with bright hair
covered in blood; and he shrieked aloud,
'Clarence has come: false, fleeing, perjured Clarence,
who stabbed me in the battle at Tewkesbury!
Seize him, Furies! Take him and torture him!'
At that, I thought, a legion of horrible Demons
surrounded me, and howled such hideous cries
in my ears that the noise itself
made me wake up trembling, and for a while afterwards
I couldn't believe that I wasn't in hell,
my dream had made such a terrible impression on me.

KEEPER.
No marvel, lord, though it affrighted you;
I am afraid, methinks, to hear you tell it.

It's no wonder it frightened you, lord;
it makes me frightened just to hear you talking about it.

CLARENCE.
Ah, Keeper, Keeper, I have done these things
That now give evidence against my soul
For Edward's sake, and see how he requites me!
O God! If my deep prayers cannot appease Thee,
But Thou wilt be aveng'd on my misdeeds,
Yet execute Thy wrath in me alone;
O, spare my guiltless wife and my poor children!

Keeper, I prithee sit by me awhile;
My soul is heavy, and I fain would sleep.

Oh, jailer, jailer, I have done things
for Edward's sake that I shall pay for in the
afterlife, and see how he repays me!
O God! If my best prayers cannot appease you,
and you insist on punishing my sins,
please only punish me;
spare my guiltless wife and my poor children!
Jailer, please sit with me awhile;
my soul is heavy, and I should like to sleep.

KEEPER.
I will, my lord. God give your Grace good rest.

I will, my lord. May God give your Grace a good rest.

[CLARENCE sleeps]

Enter BRAKENBURY the Lieutenant

BRAKENBURY.
Sorrow breaks seasons and reposing hours,
Makes the night morning and the noontide night.
Princes have but their titles for their glories,
An outward honour for an inward toil;
And for unfelt imaginations
They often feel a world of restless cares,
So that between their tides and low name
There's nothing differs but the outward fame.

Sorrow breaks up the seasons and the hours of rest,
makes the night morning and midday night.
Princes only have their titles as their glory,
external honours for inner turmoil;
instead of the pleasure we imagine they feel
they often have a world of restless care,
so that when they fall low there is
often nothing different except for their outward title.

Enter the two MURDERERS

FIRST MURDERER.

Ho! who's here?

Hello! Who's this?

BRAKENBURY.
What wouldst thou, fellow, and how cam'st
thou hither?

*What do you want, fellow, and how did you
get in here?*

FIRST MURDERER.
I would speak with Clarence, and I came
hither on my legs.

*I want to speak to Clarence, and I came
here on my legs.*

BRAKENBURY.
What, so brief?

Is that it?

SECOND MURDERER.
'Tis better, sir, than to be tedious. Let
him see our commission and talk no more.

*It's better than being long-winded, sir.
Have a look at our commission and let's have no more talk.*
[BRAKENBURY reads it]

BRAKENBURY.
I am, in this, commanded to deliver
The noble Duke of Clarence to your hands.
I will not reason what is meant hereby,
Because I will be guiltless from the meaning.
There lies the Duke asleep; and there the keys.
I'll to the King and signify to him
That thus I have resign'd to you my charge.

*This orders me to hand over
the noble Duke of Clarence to you.
I will not question what this means,
because I don't want to be involved with any of it.*

There is the duke lying asleep; and here are the keys.
I'll go to the king and tell him
that I have handed my prisoner over to you.

FIRST MURDERER.
You may, sir; 'tis a point of wisdom. Fare
you well.

Do that, sir; that's very wise. Farewell.

Exeunt BRAKENBURY and KEEPER

SECOND MURDERER.
What, shall I stab him as he sleeps?

Well, shall I stab him while he's asleep?

FIRST MURDERER.
No; he'll say 'twas done cowardly, when
he wakes.

No, he'll say it was a cowardly deed, when
he wakes up.

SECOND MURDERER.
Why, he shall never wake until the great
judgment-day.

But he won't wake up until
the day of judgement.

FIRST MURDERER.
Why, then he'll say we stabb'd him
sleeping.

Well, then he'll say we stabbed him while he was asleep.

SECOND MURDERER.
The urging of that word judgment hath
bred a kind of remorse in me.

The mention of that word judgement has
made me feel kind of regretful.

FIRST MURDERER.
What, art thou afraid?

What, are you afraid?

SECOND MURDERER.
Not to kill him, having a warrant; but to
be damn'd for killing him, from the which no warrant can
defend me.

Not of killing him, we have a warrant; part of
the damnation I will get for killing him, which no warrant can
clear me of.

FIRST MURDERER.
I thought thou hadst been resolute.

I thought you were resolved.

SECOND MURDERER.
So I am, to let him live.

And I am, to let him live.

FIRST MURDERER.
I'll back to the Duke of Gloucester and
tell him so.

I'll go back to the Duke of Gloucester and tell him so.

SECOND MURDERER.
Nay, I prithee, stay a little. I hope this
passionate humour of mine will change; it was wont to
hold me but while one tells twenty.

No, please, wait a minute. I hope this
sudden passion of mine will fade; it usually
only lasts for twenty seconds.

FIRST MURDERER.
How dost thou feel thyself now?

How are you feeling now?

SECOND MURDERER.
Faith, some certain dregs of conscience
are yet within me.

I swear, there are still some dregs of conscience
within me.

FIRST MURDERER.
Remember our reward, when the deed's
done.

Think of the reward we shall get for the deed.

SECOND MURDERER.
Zounds, he dies; I had forgot the reward.

By God, he's dead; I'd forgotten about the reward.

FIRST MURDERER.
Where's thy conscience now?

Where is your conscience now?

SECOND MURDERER.
O, in the Duke of Gloucester's purse!

Oh, it's in the Duke of Gloucester's purse!

FIRST MURDERER.
When he opens his purse to give us our
reward, thy conscience flies out.

When he opens his purse to give us our
reward, your conscience will fly out.

SECOND MURDERER.
'Tis no matter; let it go; there's few or
none will entertain it.

It doesn't matter, let it go; it's not much
use to anybody.

FIRST MURDERER.
What if it come to thee again?

What if it comes back to haunt you?

SECOND MURDERER.
I'll not meddle with it-it makes a man
coward: a man cannot steal, but it accuseth him; a man
cannot swear, but it checks him; a man cannot lie with his
neighbour's wife, but it detects him. 'Tis a blushing shame-
fac'd spirit that mutinies in a man's bosom; it fills a man
full of obstacles: it made me once restore a purse of gold
that-by chance I found. It beggars any man that keeps it.
It is turn'd out of towns and cities for a dangerous thing;
and every man that means to live well endeavours to trust
to himself and live without it.

I won't bother with it—it makes a man
a coward: a man cannot steal without it accusing him; a man
cannot swear without it stopping him; a man cannot sleep with his
neighbour's wife without it finding him out. It is a blushing
shamefaced spirit that rebels in a man's heart; it makes everything difficult
for a man; it once made me give back a purse of gold that I had
found by accident. It will make any man who obeys it a beggar.
It is thrown out of towns and cities as a dangerous thing;
and every man who wants to live well tries to trust
himself and live without it.

FIRST MURDERER.
Zounds, 'tis even now at my elbow,
persuading me not to kill the Duke.

By God, it's here at my elbow even now,
trying to persuade me not to kill the Duke.

SECOND MURDERER.
Take the devil in thy mind and believe
him not; he would insinuate with thee but to make thee
sigh.

Stay faithful to the devil and don't pay it
any attention; it will only give you grief if you do.

FIRST MURDERER.
I am strong-fram'd; he cannot prevail with
me.

I'm strong-minded; it can't win me over.

SECOND MURDERER.
Spoke like a tall man that respects thy
reputation. Come, shall we fall to work?

Spoken like a brave man who cares about
his reputation. Come, shall we get to work?

FIRST MURDERER.
Take him on the costard with the hilts of
thy sword, and then chop him in the malmsey-butt in the
next room.

Run him through the head with your sword up to
the hilt, and then chuck him in the barrel of malmsey
next door.

SECOND MURDERER.
O excellent device! and make a sop of
him.

A splendid trick! Make him a piece of dipping bread.

FIRST MURDERER.
Soft! he wakes.

Quiet! He's waking up.

SECOND MURDERER.
Strike!

Strike!

FIRST MURDERER.
No, we'll reason with him.

No, we'll reason with him.

CLARENCE.
Where art thou, Keeper? Give me a cup of wine.

Where are you, jailer? Give me a cup of wine.

SECOND MURDERER.
You shall have wine enough, my lord,
anon.

You will have plenty of wine, my lord, soon.

CLARENCE.
In God's name, what art thou?

In God's name, who are you?

FIRST MURDERER.
A man, as you are.

A man, like you.

CLARENCE.
But not as I am, royal.

But not royal, as I am.

SECOND MURDERER.
Nor you as we are, loyal.

And you are not loyal, as we are.

CLARENCE.
Thy voice is thunder, but thy looks are humble.

Your voice is like thunder, but you look humble.

FIRST MURDERER.
My voice is now the King's, my looks
mine own.

I am speaking for the King, my looks are my own.

CLARENCE.
How darkly and how deadly dost thou speak!
Your eyes do menace me. Why look you pale?
Who sent you hither? Wherefore do you come?

How darkly and how terribly you speak!

Your eyes terrify me. Why are you looking pale?
Who sent you here? Why have you come?

SECOND MURDERER.
To, to, to-

To, to, to-

CLARENCE.
To murder me?

To murder me?

BOTH MURDERERS.
Ay, ay.

Yes, yes.

CLARENCE.
You scarcely have the hearts to tell me so,
And therefore cannot have the hearts to do it.
Wherein, my friends, have I offended you?

You hardly have the heart to tell me so,
and so you cannot have the heart to do it.
How have I offended you, my friends?

FIRST MURDERER.
Offended us you have not, but the King.

It's the king you have offended, not us.

CLARENCE.
I shall be reconcil'd to him again.

I shall be reconciled with him.

SECOND MURDERER.
Never, my lord; therefore prepare to die.

Never, my lord; and so prepare to die.

CLARENCE.
Are you drawn forth among a world of men

To slay the innocent? What is my offence?
Where is the evidence that doth accuse me?
What lawful quest have given their verdict up
Unto the frowning judge, or who pronounc'd
The bitter sentence of poor Clarence' death?
Before I be convict by course of law,
To threaten me with death is most unlawful.
I charge you, as you hope to have redemption
By Christ's dear blood shed for our grievous sins,
That you depart and lay no hands on me.
The deed you undertake is damnable.

Have you been chosen from the world of men
to slay the innocent? What have I done wrong?
Where is the evidence against me?
What jury has handed its evidence up
to the frowning judge, and who pronounced
the bitter sentence of death on poor Clarence?
Unless I am convicted by the courts of law
then it is most unlawful to threaten me with death.
I order you, if you hope to be saved
by the dear blood of Christ shed for our grievous sins,
that you leave and do not lay your hands on me.
The thing you are doing is damnable.

FIRST MURDERER.
What we will do, we do upon command.

What we are doing is obeying orders.

SECOND MURDERER.
And he that hath commanded is our
King.

And the orders were given by our king.

CLARENCE.
Erroneous vassals! the great King of kings
Hath in the tables of his law commanded
That thou shalt do no murder. Will you then
Spurn at his edict and fulfil a man's?
Take heed; for he holds vengeance in his hand
To hurl upon their heads that break his law.

Wrongheaded peasants! The great King of Kings
ordered in the commandments that
you shall not murder. Are you then going to
ignore his instructions and follow those of a man?
Be careful; for he has vengeance prepared
to throw down upon those who break his laws.

SECOND MURDERER.
And that same vengeance doth he hurl
on thee
For false forswearing, and for murder too;
Thou didst receive the sacrament to fight
In quarrel of the house of Lancaster.

The same vengeance he throws down on you
for perjuring yourself, and for murder too;
you took an oath to fight
against the house of Lancaster.

FIRST MURDERER.
And like a traitor to the name of God
Didst break that vow; and with thy treacherous blade
Unripp'dst the bowels of thy sov'reign's son.

And like a traitor to the name of God
you broke your promise; and with your treacherous sword
you tore open the stomach of your king's son.

SECOND MURDERER.
Whom thou wast sworn to cherish and
defend.

Whom you had sworn to love and defend.

FIRST MURDERER.
How canst thou urge God's dreadful law
to us,
When thou hast broke it in such dear degree?

How can you tell us to obey the great laws of God,
when you have broken them so badly?

CLARENCE.
Alas! for whose sake did I that ill deed?

For Edward, for my brother, for his sake.
He sends you not to murder me for this,
For in that sin he is as deep as I.
If God will be avenged for the deed,
O, know you yet He doth it publicly.
Take not the quarrel from His pow'rful arm;
He needs no indirect or lawless course
To cut off those that have offended Him.

Alas! For whom did I commit that foul deed?
For Edward, my brother, for his sake.
He has not sent you to murder me for this,
for he is as guilty of that sin as I am.
If God wants to be avenged for the deed,
you know that he will do it in public.
Do not steal his revenge from him;
he does not need secret or illegal assistance
to punish those who have offended him.

FIRST MURDERER.
Who made thee then a bloody minister
When gallant-springing brave Plantagenet,
That princely novice, was struck dead by thee?

So who made you a bloody Minister of his
when the bravely charging Plantagenet,
that novice Prince, was struck dead by you?

CLARENCE.
My brother's love, the devil, and my rage.

My brother's love, the devil, and my anger.

FIRST MURDERER.
Thy brother's love, our duty, and thy
faults,
Provoke us hither now to slaughter thee.

Your brother's love, our duty, and your sins,
have driven us to come here now to kill you.

CLARENCE.
If you do love my brother, hate not me;
I am his brother, and I love him well.

If you are hir'd for meed, go back again,
And I will send you to my brother Gloucester,
Who shall reward you better for my life
Than Edward will for tidings of my death.

If you love my brother, do not take me;
I am his brother, and I love him very much.
If you are hired for reward, go back,
and I will send you to my brother Gloucester,
who will give you a better reward for leaving me alive
than Edward will for news of my death.

SECOND MURDERER.
You are deceiv'd: your brother Gloucester
hates you.

You are wrong: your brother Gloucester hates you.

CLARENCE.
O, no, he loves me, and he holds me dear.
Go you to him from me.

Oh no, he loves me, I am special to him.
Go to him from me.

FIRST MURDERER.
Ay, so we will.

Yes, we shall.

CLARENCE.
Tell him when that our princely father York
Bless'd his three sons with his victorious arm
And charg'd us from his soul to love each other,
He little thought of this divided friendship.
Bid Gloucester think of this, and he will weep.

Tell him that when our royal father York
blessed his three sons with his victorious arm
and ordered us from the heart to love one another,
he had not considered how we might be parted.
Ask Gloucester to consider this, and he will weep.

FIRST MURDERER.

Ay, millstones; as he lesson'd us to weep.

Yes, millstones; that's what he taught us to weep.

CLARENCE.
O, do not slander him, for he is kind.

Do not tell lies about him, he is kind.

FIRST MURDERER.
Right, as snow in harvest. Come, you
deceive yourself:
'Tis he that sends us to destroy you here.

*As kind as snow at harvest time. Come, you
are deceiving yourself: it's he who sends us here to destroy you.*

CLARENCE.
It cannot be; for he bewept my fortune
And hugg'd me in his arms, and swore with sobs
That he would labour my delivery.

*That cannot be; he wept at my fate
and embraced me, and he swore, sobbing,
that he would work for my freedom.*

FIRST MURDERER.
Why, so he doth, when he delivers you
From this earth's thraldom to the joys of heaven.

*Why, he does, he plans to send you
from the troubles of earth to the joys of heaven.*

SECOND MURDERER.
Make peace with God, for you must die,
my lord.

Make your peace with God, for you must die, my lord.

CLARENCE.
Have you that holy feeling in your souls
To counsel me to make my peace with God,
And are you yet to your own souls so blind
That you will war with God by murd'ring me?

O, sirs, consider: they that set you on
To do this deed will hate you for the deed.

Are you holy enough in your souls
to advise me to make my peace with God,
and yet so unconcerned about your own souls
that you will go to war with God by murdering me?
Think about it, sirs: those who asked you to commit
this deed will hate you for it.

SECOND MURDERER.
What shall we do?

What shall we do?

CLARENCE.
Relent, and save your souls.

Refuse, and save your souls.

FIRST MURDERER.
Relent! No, 'tis cowardly and womanish.

Refuse! No, that is cowardly and effeminate.

CLARENCE.
Not to relent is beastly, savage, devilish.
Which of you, if you were a prince's son,
Being pent from liberty as I am now,
If two such murderers as yourselves came to you,
Would not entreat for life?
My friend, I spy some pity in thy looks;
O, if thine eye be not a flatterer,
Come thou on my side and entreat for me-
As you would beg were you in my distress.
A begging prince what beggar pities not?

If you don't refuse you are beastly, savage, devilish.
If you were the son of a prince, which of you,
being penned up here as I am now,
would not beg for life,
if two murderers like yourselves came to you?
My friend, I see some pity in your face;
if your looks are not deceiving,

join my side and beg for me,
as you would beg if you were in my place.
What beggar does not pity a begging prince?

SECOND MURDERER.
Look behind you, my lord.

Look behind you, my lord.

FIRST MURDERER.
[Stabbing him]Take that, and that. If all
this will not do,
I'll drown you in the malmsey-butt within.
Exit with the body

Take that, and that. If this hasn't done the job,
I'll drown you in the barrel of malmsey in there.

SECOND MURDERER.
A bloody deed, and desperately
dispatch'd!
How fain, like Pilate, would I wash my hands
Of this most grievous murder!

A bloody deed, horribly done!
How I would like to be like Pilate and wash my hands
of this horrible murder!

Re-enter FIRST MURDERER

FIRST MURDERER.
How now, what mean'st thou that thou
help'st me not?
By heavens, the Duke shall know how slack you have
been!

What's this, what do you think you're doing, not helping me?
By heaven, the Duke shall know how slack you have been!

SECOND MURDERER.
I would he knew that I had sav'd his
brother!
Take thou the fee, and tell him what I say;
For I repent me that the Duke is slain.

I wish he could know that I had saved his brother!
You take the reward, and tell him what I say;
for I am sorry that the duke has been killed.

Exit

FIRST MURDERER.
So do not I. Go, coward as thou art.
Well, I'll go hide the body in some hole,
Till that the Duke give order for his burial;
And when I have my meed, I will away;
For this will out, and then I must not stay.

I don't. Go, you coward.
Well, I'll go and hide the body in some hole,
until the Duke gives orders for him to be buried;
and when I have my reward, I shall disappear;
this matter will come out, and I mustn't be around when it does.

Exit

ACT II

SCENE 1.

London. The palace

Flourish. Enter KING EDWARD sick, QUEEN ELIZABETH, DORSET, RIVERS,
HASTINGS, BUCKINGHAM, GREY, and others

KING EDWARD.
Why, so. Now have I done a good day's
work.
You peers, continue this united league.
I every day expect an embassage
From my Redeemer to redeem me hence;
And more at peace my soul shall part to heaven,
Since I have made my friends at peace on earth.
Hastings and Rivers, take each other's hand;
Dissemble not your hatred, swear your love.

Well, there we are. Now I have done a good day's work.
You peers, maintain this unity.
I am expecting any day now to have a visitor
from my Saviour to take me from here;
and my soul shall leave for heaven with an easier mind,
having made peace between my friends on earth.
Hastings and Rivers, take each other's hands;
ignore your hatred: swear to your love for each other.

RIVERS.
By heaven, my soul is purg'd from grudging hate;
And with my hand I seal my true heart's love.

By heaven, there is no hate left in my soul;
and I give my hand as a sign of the true love of my heart.

HASTINGS.
So thrive I, as I truly swear the like!

I feel the same, and I swear the same truly!

KING EDWARD.
Take heed you dally not before your king;
Lest He that is the supreme King of kings
Confound your hidden falsehood and award
Either of you to be the other's end.

Make sure you really mean this;
otherwise the supreme King of Kings
might discover your hidden deceit and make
one of you be the death of the other.

HASTINGS.
So prosper I, as I swear perfect love!

All is well, I swear to my perfect love!

RIVERS.
And I, as I love Hastings with my heart!

As do I, as I love Hastings with all my heart!

KING EDWARD.
Madam, yourself is not exempt from this;
Nor you, son Dorset; Buckingham, nor you:
You have been factious one against the other.
Wife, love Lord Hastings, let him kiss your hand;
And what you do, do it unfeignedly.

Madam, you are not exempt from this;
nor you, my son Dorset; nor you, Buckingham;
you have all formed parties against each other.
Wife, show love to Lord Hastings, let him kiss your hand;
and do this genuinely.

QUEEN ELIZABETH.
There, Hastings; I will never more
remember
Our former hatred, so thrive I and mine!

There, Hastings; I will now forget
our former hatred, for as long as me and mine prosper!

KING EDWARD.
Dorset, embrace him; Hastings, love Lord

Marquis.

Dorset, embrace him; Hastings, love Lord Marquis.

DORSET.
This interchange of love, I here protest,
Upon my part shall be inviolable.

I swear here that this exchange of love,
for my part, cannot be broken.

HASTINGS.
And so swear I.

And I swear the same.

[They embrace]

KING EDWARD.
Now, princely Buckingham, seal thou this
league
With thy embracements to my wife's allies,
And make me happy in your unity.

Now, princely Buckingham, confirm this alliance
by embracing my wife's confederates,
and make me happy with your unity.

BUCKINGHAM.
[To the QUEEN]Whenever Buckingham
doth turn his hate
Upon your Grace, but with all dutcous love
Doth cherish you and yours, God punish me
With hate in those where I expect most love!
When I have most need to employ a friend
And most assured that he is a friend,
Deep, hollow, treacherous, and full of guile,
Be he unto me! This do I beg of God
When I am cold in love to you or yours.

If Buckingham ever turns his hate
upon your Grace, if he does not cherish you
and yours with anything but loyal love, may God punish me
by making those who love me most hate me!

When I am in most need of a friend,
and certain that he is a friend, may he be
cunning, deceptive, treacherous and sly
to me! I beg that God will do this
if I am cold in my love for you and yours.

[They embrace]

KING EDWARD.
A pleasing cordial, princely Buckingham,
Is this thy vow unto my sickly heart.
There wanteth now our brother Gloucester here
To make the blessed period of this peace.

This promise is good medicine, princely Buckingham,
for my sickly heart.
All we need now is my brother Gloucester to be here
to conclude this blessed peace.

BUCKINGHAM.
And, in good time,
Here comes Sir Richard Ratcliff and the Duke.

And, right on time,
here comes Sir Richard Ratcliffe and the Duke.

Enter RICHARD, and RATCLIFF

RICHARD.
Good morrow to my sovereign king and
Queen;
And, princely peers, a happy time of day!

Good day to my sovereign king and Queen;
and, princely peers, good day to you!

KING EDWARD.
Happy, indeed, as we have spent the day.
Gloucester, we have done deeds of charity,
Made peace of enmity, fair love of hate,
Between these swelling wrong-incensed peers.

It has indeed been a happy day.
Gloucester, we have done kind deeds,

made peace out of conflict, love from hate,
between these haughty wrongly angry peers.

RICHARD.
A blessed labour, my most sovereign lord.
Among this princely heap, if any here,
By false intelligence or wrong surmise,
Hold me a foe-
If I unwittingly, or in my rage,
Have aught committed that is hardly borne
To any in this presence, I desire
To reconcile me to his friendly peace:
'Tis death to me to be at enmity;
I hate it, and desire all good men's love.
First, madam, I entreat true peace of you,
Which I will purchase with my duteous service;
Of you, my noble cousin Buckingham,
If ever any grudge were lodg'd between us;
Of you, and you, Lord Rivers, and of Dorset,
That all without desert have frown'd on me;
Of you, Lord Woodville, and, Lord Scales, of you;
Dukes, earls, lords, gentlemen-indeed, of all.
I do not know that Englishman alive
With whom my soul is any jot at odds
More than the infant that is born to-night.
I thank my God for my humility.

Very blessed work, my sovereign lord.
Amongst this company of Princes–if any here
through wrong information or misapprehension
think of me as an enemy–
if I have done anything unwittingly, or in anger,
that anyone here objects to, I would like
to make my peace with him:
I would rather die than be enemies;
I hate it, and would like all good men to love me.
First, madam, I beg that you and I may have true peace,
which I will gain through my devoted service;
and with you, my noble cousin Buckingham,
if there was ever any grudge between us;
and with you, Lord Rivers, and Lord Grey, with you,
who have all taken a dislike to me without reason:
dukes, earls, lords, gentlemen: indeed with all of you.
I do not know any Englishman alive

with whom I have any quarrel
greater than I have with a newborn infant–
I thank God for my humility.

QUEEN ELIZABETH.
A holy day shall this be kept hereafter.
I would to God all strifes were well compounded.
My sovereign lord, I do beseech your Highness
To take our brother Clarence to your grace.

From now on this day shall be celebrated as a holiday.
I wish to God all arguments could be solved like this.
My sovereign lord, I beg your Highness
to accept our brother Clarence into your grace.

RICHARD.
Why, madam, have I off'red love for this,
To be so flouted in this royal presence?
Who knows not that the gentle Duke is dead?
[They all start]
You do him injury to scorn his corse.

Why, madam, have I offered my love for this,
to be mocked in the presence of the King?
Doesn't everybody know that the sweet Duke is dead?
[They all start]
It is not right to mock his corpse.

KING EDWARD.
Who knows not he is dead! Who knows
he is?

Doesn't everybody know he's dead! Who knows he is?

QUEEN ELIZABETH.
All-seeing heaven, what a world is this!

Mighty heaven, what a world this is!

BUCKINGHAM.
Look I so pale, Lord Dorset, as the rest?

Lord Dorset, do I look as pale as the rest of them?

90

DORSET.
Ay, my good lord; and no man in the presence
But his red colour hath forsook his cheeks.

Yes, my good lord; and there is no man here
whose colour has not drained from his cheeks.

KING EDWARD.
Is Clarence dead? The order was revers'd.

Is Clarence dead? I revoked the order.

RICHARD.
But he, poor man, by your first order died,
And that a winged Mercury did bear;
Some tardy cripple bare the countermand
That came too lag to see him buried.
God grant that some, less noble and less loyal,
Nearer in bloody thoughts, an not in blood,
Deserve not worse than wretched Clarence did,
And yet go current from suspicion!

But he, poor man, died as a result of your first order,
which was carried there by a swift messenger;
some lazy cripple carried the counter order
that came too late to save him.
God knows that some, less noble and less loyal,
who have worse thoughts and worse blood,
deserved to get the treatment poor Clarence got,
and yet they are thought of as genuine!

Enter DERBY

DERBY.
A boon, my sovereign, for my service done!

Grant me a favour, your Majesty, for the service I have done!

KING EDWARD.
I prithee, peace; my soul is full of sorrow.

Please, be quiet; my soul is full of sorrow.

DERBY.

I will not rise unless your Highness hear me.

I will not rise until your Highness listens to me.

KING EDWARD.
Then say at once what is it thou requests.

Then say quickly what you want.

DERBY.
The forfeit, sovereign, of my servant's life;
Who slew to-day a riotous gentleman
Lately attendant on the Duke of Norfolk.

The power, Majesty, over my servant's life;
today he killed a rowdy gentleman
who was recently a servant to the Duke of Norfolk.

KING EDWARD.
Have I a tongue to doom my brother's death,
And shall that tongue give pardon to a slave?
My brother killed no man-his fault was thought,
And yet his punishment was bitter death.
Who sued to me for him? Who, in my wrath,
Kneel'd at my feet, and bid me be advis'd?
Who spoke of brotherhood? Who spoke of love?
Who told me how the poor soul did forsake
The mighty Warwick and did fight for me?
Who told me, in the field at Tewksbury
When Oxford had me down, he rescued me
And said 'Dear Brother, live, and be a king'?
Who told me, when we both lay in the field
Frozen almost to death, how he did lap me
Even in his garments, and did give himself,
All thin and naked, to the numb cold night?
All this from my remembrance brutish wrath
Sinfully pluck'd, and not a man of you
Had so much race to put it in my mind.
But when your carters or your waiting-vassals
Have done a drunken slaughter and defac'd
The precious image of our dear Redeemer,
You straight are on your knees for pardon, pardon;
And I, unjustly too, must grant it you.[DERBY rises]
But for my brother not a man would speak;

Nor I, ungracious, speak unto myself
For him, poor soul. The proudest of you all
Have been beholding to him in his life;
Yet none of you would once beg for his life.
O God, I fear thy justice will take hold
On me, and you, and mine, and yours, for this!
Come, Hastings, help me to my closet. Ah, poor Clarence!

Can my tongue sentence my brother to death,
and be used to pardon a slave?
My brother killed no one: his only fault was his thoughts,
and yet his punishment was a bitter death.
Who pleaded to me for him? Who, when I was angry,
kneeled at my feet and told me to think carefully?
Who spoke of brotherhood? Who spoke of love?
Who reminded me that the poor soul abandoned
the mighty Warwick, and fought for me?
Who reminded me that on the battlefield at Tewkesbury,
when Oxford stood over me, that he rescued me
and said, 'Dear brother, live and be a king'?
Who reminded me that when we both lay in the battlefield
almost frozen to death, that he wrapped me
in his own clothes, and abandoned himself,
thin and naked, to the numbing cold of the night?
Brutal anger has sinfully torn all this
from my memory, and not one of you
was good enough to remind me of it.
But when your carters or your serving men
have committed a drunken murder, and insulted
the precious face of our dear Lord,
you are straight down on your knees begging for pardon,
and I, unjustly, must give it to you.
But not one man spoke out for my brother,
and I, ungraciously, did not speak to myself on his
behalf, poor soul. Even the greatest of you
were in his debt while he was alive,
yet not one of you troubled to beg for his life.
O God, I feel justice will fall
on me, and you, and our families for this.
Come on, Hastings, help me to my room.
Ah, poor Clarence!

Exeunt some with KING and QUEEN

RICHARD.
This is the fruits of rashness. Mark'd you not
How that the guilty kindred of the Queen
Look'd pale when they did hear of Clarence' death?
O, they did urge it still unto the King!
God will revenge it. Come, lords, will you go
To comfort Edward with our company?

This is what happens when things are decided in a hurry. Did you notice
how the guilty relatives of the Queen
looked pale when they heard of Clarence's death?
It was them who encouraged the King to order it!
God will take revenge. Come, Lords, will you come
with me to comfort Edward?

BUCKINGHAM.
We wait upon your Grace.

We shall come with your Grace.

Exeunt

94

SCENE 2.

London. The palace

Enter the old DUCHESS OF YORK, with the SON and DAUGHTER of
CLARENCE

SON.
Good grandam, tell us, is our father dead?

Good grandmother, tell us, is our father dead?

DUCHESS.
No, boy.

No, boy.

DAUGHTER.
Why do you weep so oft, and beat your breast,
And cry 'O Clarence, my unhappy son!"?

*Then why are you always crying, and beating your chest,
and wailing, 'Oh Clarence, my unhappy son!'?*

SON.
Why do you look on us, and shake your head,
And call us orphans, wretches, castaways,
If that our noble father were alive?

*Why do you look at us and shake your head,
calling us orphans, wretches, castaways,
if our noble father is alive?*

DUCHESS.
My pretty cousins, you mistake me both;
I do lament the sickness of the King,
As loath to lose him, not your father's death;
It were lost sorrow to wail one that's lost.

My pretty cousins, you both misunderstand me;

I am lamenting the King's illness,
as I will hate to lose him, not your father's death;
it would be a waste of sorrow to mourn for someone who's already gone.

SON.
Then you conclude, my grandam, he is dead.
The King mine uncle is to blame for it.
God will revenge it; whom I will importune
With earnest prayers all to that effect.

So you believe, grandmother, that he is dead.
My uncle the king is to blame for it.
God will take revenge; and I will beg
for him to do so in my prayers.

DAUGHTER.
And so will I.

And so will I.

DUCHESS.
Peace, children, peace! The King doth love you
well.
Incapable and shallow innocents,
You cannot guess who caus'd your father's death.

Peace, children, peace! The King loves you very much.
You are ignorant of the ways of the world,
you cannot guess who caused your father's death.

SON.
Grandam, we can; for my good uncle Gloucester
Told me the King, provok'd to it by the Queen,
Devis'd impeachments to imprison him.
And when my uncle told me so, he wept,
And pitied me, and kindly kiss'd my cheek;
Bade me rely on him as on my father,
And he would love me dearly as a child.

Grandmother, we can; my good uncle Gloucester
told me that the King, egged on by the Queen,
invented charges to have him imprisoned.
And when my uncle told me about it, he wept,
and pitied me, and affectionately kissed my cheeks;

he said to regard him as my father, and
that he would love me as dearly as his own child.

DUCHESS.
Ah, that deceit should steal such gentle shape,
And with a virtuous vizor hide deep vice!
He is my son; ay, and therein my shame;
Yet from my dugs he drew not this deceit.

How terrible that deceit should assume such a gentle form,
and hide his deep sins behind a mask of virtue!
He is my son; that is shameful to me;
but he did not learn this deceit at my breast.

SON.
Think you my uncle did dissemble, grandam?

Do you think my uncle was lying, grandmother?

DUCHESS.
Ay, boy.

Yes, boy.

SON.
I cannot think it. Hark! what noise is this?

I can't believe it. Listen! What's this noise?

Enter QUEEN ELIZABETH, with her hair about her
ears; RIVERS and DORSET after her

QUEEN ELIZABETH.
Ah, who shall hinder me to wail and
weep,
To chide my fortune, and torment myself?
I'll join with black despair against my soul
And to myself become an enemy.

Ah, who can stop me wailing and weeping,
cursing my fortune, and torturing myself?
I'll ally myself with black despair and attack my soul,
becoming my own enemy.

DUCHESS.
What means this scene of rude impatience?

What is the meaning of this vulgar hysteria?

QUEEN ELIZABETH.
To make an act of tragic violence.
 Edward, my lord, thy son, our king, is dead.
Why grow the branches when the root is gone?
Why wither not the leaves that want their sap?
If you will live, lament; if die, be brief,
That our swift-winged souls may catch the King's,
Or like obedient subjects follow him
To his new kingdom of ne'er-changing night.

I am marking an act of tragic violence.
Edward, my lord, your son, our King, is dead.
Why do the branches grow when the root is dead?
Why don't the leaves, lacking sap, die?
If you want to live, grieve; if you're going to die, do it quickly,
so that our swift winged souls may catch up with the King's,
following him like obedient subjects
into his new kingdom of eternal darkness.

DUCHESS.
Ah, so much interest have I in thy sorrow
As I had title in thy noble husband!
I have bewept a worthy husband's death,
And liv'd with looking on his images;
But now two mirrors of his princely semblance
Are crack'd in pieces by malignant death,
And I for comfort have but one false glass,
That grieves me when I see my shame in him.
Thou art a widow, yet thou art a mother
And hast the comfort of thy children left;
But death hath snatch'd my husband from mine arms
And pluck'd two crutches from my feeble hands-
Clarence and Edward. O, what cause have I-
Thine being but a moiety of my moan-
To overgo thy woes and drown thy cries?

I share as much in your sorrow
as I shared in the rights to your noble husband.
I have wept for the death of a good husband,

and spent my life looking at his images:
but now two copies of his royal appearance
have been smashed to pieces by malignant death;
and all I have to comfort me is one false copy,
that makes me sorrowful to see my shame in him.
You are widowed—but you are a mother,
and have the comfort of your children left;
but death has snatched my husband from my arms
and torn my two crutches from my feeble hands:
Clarence and Edward. Oh, what good reasons I have,
your sorrows being just a fraction of mine,
to exceed your lamenting and drown out your cries.

SON.
Ah, aunt, you wept not for our father's death!
How can we aid you with our kindred tears?

Ah, aunt, you did not weep at the death of our father!
How can we help you with similar tears?

DAUGHTER.
Our fatherless distress was left unmoan'd;
Your widow-dolour likewise be unwept!

You did not support us in our fatherless distress;
and so may the sorrow of your widowhood be unmourned in the same way!

QUEEN ELIZABETH.
Give me no help in lamentation;
I am not barren to bring forth complaints.
All springs reduce their currents to mine eyes
That I, being govern'd by the watery moon,
May send forth plenteous tears to drown the world!
Ah for my husband, for my dear Lord Edward!

I don't need your help in sorrowing;
I can do enough on my own.
The streams of all springs run into my eyes,
so that I, being under the influence of the watery moon,
can send out a flood of tears to drown the world.
Alas for my husband, for my dear lord Edward!

CHILDREN.
Ah for our father, for our dear Lord Clarence!

Alas for our father, for our dear Lord Clarence!

DUCHESS.
Alas for both, both mine, Edward and Clarence!

Alas for both, both of them mine, Edward and Clarence!

QUEEN ELIZABETH.
What stay had I but Edward? and he's
gone.

What support did I have apart from Edward? And he is gone.

CHILDREN.
What stay had we but Clarence? and he's gone.

What support did we have apart from Clarence? And he is gone.

DUCHESS.
What stays had I but they? and they are gone.

What supports did I have but those two? And they are gone.

QUEEN ELIZABETH.
Was never widow had so dear a loss.

No widow ever suffered such a grievous loss.

CHILDREN.
Were never orphans had so dear a loss.

No orphans ever suffered such a grievous loss.

DUCHESS.
Was never mother had so dear a loss.
Alas, I am the mother of these griefs!
Their woes are parcell'd, mine is general.
She for an Edward weeps, and so do I:
I for a Clarence weep, so doth not she.
These babes for Clarence weep, and so do I:
I for an Edward weep, so do not they.
Alas, you three on me, threefold distress'd,
Pour all your tears! I am your sorrow's nurse,

And I will pamper it with lamentation.

No mother ever suffered such a grievous loss.
Alas, I am the mother of these sorrows!
Their sorrows are partial, mine are overwhelming.
She weeps for Edward, and so do I:
I weep for Clarence, and she does not.
These children weep for Clarence, and so do I:
I weep for Redwood, and they do not.
Alas, you three, with your triple distress,
Pour all your tears on me! I am the nurse to your sorrow,
and I will feed it with wailing.

DORSET.
Comfort, dear mother. God is much displeas'd
That you take with unthankfulness his doing.
In common worldly things 'tis called ungrateful
With dull unwillingness to repay a debt
Which with a bounteous hand was kindly lent;
Much more to be thus opposite with heaven,
For it requires the royal debt it lent you.

Be calm, dear mother. God is very displeased
that you are ungrateful for his deeds.
In the ordinary way of the world it is called ungrateful
to be sullenly unwilling to repay a debt
which was generously and kindly lent;
it is much worse to be ungrateful to heaven,
when it reclaims this royal person it lent to you.

RIVERS.
Madam, bethink you, like a careful mother,
Of the young prince your son. Send straight for him;
Let him be crown'd; in him your comfort lives.
Drown desperate sorrow in dead Edward's grave,
And plant your joys in living Edward's throne.

Madam, consider, like a good mother,
the young Prince, your son. Sent forhim at once;
let him be crowned; that's where your comfort lies.
Bury your desperate sorrow in the grave of dead Edward,
and grow your happiness from the throne of the living Edward.

Enter RICHARD, BUCKINGHAM, DERBY,

HASTINGS, and RATCLIFF

RICHARD.
Sister, have comfort. All of us have cause
To wail the dimming of our shining star;
But none can help our harms by wailing them.
Madam, my mother, I do cry you mercy;
I did not see your Grace. Humbly on my knee
I crave your blessing.

Sister, be comforted. All of us have reason
to be sorrowful at the death of our leader;
but wailing about it won't do any good.
Madam, my mother, I beg you to forgive me;
I did not see your Grace. I humbly kneel
and ask for your blessing.

DUCHESS.
God bless thee; and put meekness in thy breast,
Love, charity, obedience, and true duty!

God bless you; may he make you meek, with
love, charity, obedience and true duty!

RICHARD.
Amen![Aside]And make me die a good old
man!
That is the butt end of a mother's blessing;
I marvel that her Grace did leave it out.

Amen! [Aside] And let me die a good old man!
That is the usual end of a mother's blessing;
I'm amazed that her grace left it out.

BUCKINGHAM.
You cloudy princes and heart-sorrowing
peers,
That bear this heavy mutual load of moan,
Now cheer each other in each other's love.
Though we have spent our harvest of this king,
We are to reap the harvest of his son.
The broken rancour of your high-swol'n hearts,
But lately splinter'd, knit, and join'd together,
Must gently be preserv'd, cherish'd, and kept.

Me seemeth good that, with some little train,
Forthwith from Ludlow the young prince be fet
Hither to London, to be crown'd our King.

You sad princes and brokenhearted peers,
who all share this great weight of sorrow,
now help each other with your love for each other.
Although we have now lost our king,
we now have the benefit of his son.
Join together your passionate hearts,
which were recently estranged, you must
keep the peace that was recently established.
It seems to me the best thing to do is for
the young prince to be fetched from Ludlow, with a small
entourage, and brought to London, to be crowned as king.

RIVERS.
Why with some little train, my Lord of
Buckingham?

Why with a small entourage, Lord Buckingham?

BUCKINGHAM.
Marry, my lord, lest by a multitude
The new-heal'd wound of malice should break out,
Which would be so much the more dangerous
By how much the estate is green and yet ungovern'd;
Where every horse bears his commanding rein
And may direct his course as please himself,
As well the fear of harm as harm apparent,
In my opinion, ought to be prevented.

Well, my lord, in case the newly healed strife
should break out again amongst the public,
which would be that much more dangerous
due to his youthful and unguided position;
every horse is carrying his own reins,
and can go wherever he pleases,
and in my opinion we must prevent
any fear of harm, as well as actual harm.

RICHARD.
I hope the King made peace with all of us;
And the compact is firm and true in me.

I hope the King brought peace to all of us;
I am certainly determined to maintain the agreement.

RIVERS.
And so in me; and so, I think, in all.
Yet, since it is but green, it should be put
To no apparent likelihood of breach,
Which haply by much company might be urg'd;
Therefore I say with noble Buckingham
That it is meet so few should fetch the Prince.

And so am I, and so, I think, is everybody.
But, since it is still young, it should not be
placed in a position where it could be breached,
which could happen in a large crowd;
therefore I agree with noble Buckingham
that it is right that only a few should fetch the Prince.

HASTINGS.
And so say I.

I agree.

RICHARD.
Then be it so; and go we to determine
Who they shall be that straight shall post to Ludlow.
Madam, and you, my sister, will you go
To give your censures in this business?

Then let it be so; and let us decide
who are the ones who shall go at once to Ludlow.
Madam, and you, my sister, will you go
to give your advice on this business?
ELIZ & DUCHESS With all our hearts.

Gladly.

Exeunt all but BUCKINGHAM and RICHARD

BUCKINGHAM.
My lord, whoever journeys to the Prince,
For God sake, let not us two stay at home;
For by the way I'll sort occasion,

As index to the story we late talk'd of,
To part the Queen's proud kindred from the Prince.

My lord, whoever travels to the Prince,
for God's sake, make sure we to do not stay at home;
for along the way I'll find a chance,
as part of the story we recently spoke of,
to separate the Queen's arrogant relatives from him.

RICHARD.
My other self, my counsel's consistory,
My oracle, my prophet, my dear cousin,
I, as a child, will go by thy direction.
Toward Ludlow then, for we'll not stay behind.

My mirror image, my Parliament,
my Oracle, my prophet, my dear cousin:
I will follow your advice like a child.
Off to Ludlow then, for we will not stay behind.

Exeunt

SCENE 3.

London. A street

Enter one CITIZEN at one door, and another at the other

FIRST CITIZEN.
Good morrow, neighbour. Whither away so
fast?

Good day, neighbour. Where are you rushing off to?

SECOND CITIZEN.
I promise you, I scarcely know myself.
Hear you the news abroad?

I can assure you, I hardly know myself.
Have you heard the news that's going round?

FIRST CITIZEN.
Yes, that the King is dead.

Yes, that the king is dead.

SECOND CITIZEN.
Ill news, by'r lady; seldom comes the
better.
I fear, I fear 'twill prove a giddy world.

I swear by the virgin, it's bad news; we don't often get good.
I fear this is going to cause chaos.

Enter another CITIZEN

THIRD CITIZEN.
Neighbours, God speed!

Neighbours, God speed!

FIRST CITIZEN.

Give you good morrow, sir.

Good day to you, sir.

THIRD CITIZEN.
Doth the news hold of good King Edward's
death?

Is the news about good King Edward's death true?

SECOND CITIZEN.
Ay, sir, it is too true; God help the while!

Yes, it is too true; God help these times!

THIRD CITIZEN.
Then, masters, look to see a troublous
world.

Then, masters, expect to see a disturbed world.

FIRST CITIZEN.
No, no; by God's good grace, his son shall
reign.

No, no; by the good grace of God, his son shall rule.

THIRD CITIZEN.
Woe to that land that's govern'd by a child.

It's an unlucky land that is ruled by a child.

SECOND CITIZEN.
In him there is a hope of government,
Which, in his nonage, council under him,
And, in his full and ripened years, himself,
No doubt, shall then, and till then, govern well.

There is plenty of promise of good government from him,
while he is a minor he can be guided by the council,
and when he comes of age he can govern himself,
and there's no doubt we will have good government both then and now.

FIRST CITIZEN.

So stood the state when Henry the Sixth
Was crown'd in Paris but at nine months old.

We were in the same position when Henry the Sixth
was crowned in Paris when he was just nine months old.

THIRD CITIZEN.
Stood the state so? No, no, good friends,
God wot;
For then this land was famously enrich'd
With politic grave counsel; then the King
Had virtuous uncles to protect his Grace.

The same position? No, no, good friends, God knows;
for at that time the country had notable quantities
of why is experienced counsellors; the King
had virtuous uncles to protect him.

FIRST CITIZEN.
Why, so hath this, both by his father and
mother.

Why, so has this one, on his father and his mother's side.

THIRD CITIZEN.
Better it were they all came by his father,
Or by his father there were none at all;
For emulation who shall now be nearest
Will touch us all too near, if God prevent not.
O, full of danger is the Duke of Gloucester!
And the Queen's sons and brothers haught and proud;
And were they to be rul'd, and not to rule,
This sickly land might solace as before.

It would be better if they were all on his father's side,
or if his father had no problems at all;
for the rivalry for the highest positions
will affect us all badly, if God does not prevent it.
The Duke of Gloucester is very dangerous!
And the Queen's sons and brothers are arrogant and proud;
if they could be ruled, and not rule,
this disturbed land might be peaceful again.

FIRST CITIZEN.

Come, come, we fear the worst; all will be
well.

Come, come, we are fearing the worst; everything will be alright.

THIRD CITIZEN.
When clouds are seen, wise men put on
their cloaks;
When great leaves fall, then winter is at hand;
When the sun sets, who doth not look for night?
Untimely storms make men expect a dearth.
All may be well; but, if God sort it so,
'Tis more than we deserve or I expect.

When clouds appear, wise men put on their cloaks;
when greatly useful, then winter is coming;
when the sun sets, we all expect nights to come.
Unseasonable storms make men predicts a famine.
All may be well; but, if God allows it to be,
it will be more than we deserve, or I expect.

SECOND CITIZEN.
Truly, the hearts of men are full of fear.
You cannot reason almost with a man
That looks not heavily and full of dread.

The hearts of men are truly full of fear.
It's almost impossible to find a man
who doesn't look serious and fearful.

THIRD CITIZEN.
Before the days of change, still is it so;
By a divine instinct men's minds mistrust
Ensuing danger; as by proof we see
The water swell before a boist'rous storm.
But leave it all to God. Whither away?

It is always the way in changing times;
men have God-given instinct to spot
oncoming danger; it's the way we see
the waters rising before Ray heavy storm.
But leave it all to God. Where are you going?

SECOND CITIZEN.

Marry, we were sent for to the justices.

Why, we were summoned to go to the justices.

THIRD CITIZEN.
And so was I; I'll bear you company.

And so was I; I'll come with you.

Exeunt

SCENE 4.

London. The palace

Enter the ARCHBISHOP OF YORK, the young DUKE OF YORK, QUEEN ELIZABETH,
and the DUCHESS OF YORK

ARCHBISHOP.
Last night, I hear, they lay at Stony Stratford,
And at Northampton they do rest to-night;
To-morrow or next day they will be here.

I hear that last night they stopped at Stony Stratford,
and they are resting tonight at Northampton;
they will be here tomorrow or the day after.

DUCHESS.
I long with all my heart to see the Prince.
I hope he is much grown since last I saw him.

I am longing with all my heart to see the Prince.
I hope he has grown up a lot since I last saw him.

QUEEN ELIZABETH.
But I hear no; they say my son of York
Has almost overta'en him in his growth.

I've heard not; they say my son York
has almost grown larger than him.

YORK.
Ay, mother; but I would not have it so.

Yes, mother; but I don't want to.

DUCHESS.
Why, my good cousin, it is good to grow.

Why, my good cousin, it's good to grow.

YORK.
Grandam, one night as we did sit at supper,
My uncle Rivers talk'd how I did grow
More than my brother. 'Ay,' quoth my uncle Gloucester
'Small herbs have grace: great weeds do grow apace.'
And since, methinks, I would not grow so fast,
Because sweet flow'rs are slow and weeds make haste.

Grandmother, one night as we were sitting at supper,
my uncle Rivers was talking about how I was growing
taller than my brother. 'Yes,' my uncle Gloucester said,
'Small herbs have Grace: great weeds grow fast.'
And since then I have not wanted to grow as fast,
because sweet flowers grow slowly and weeds quickly.

DUCHESS.
Good faith, good faith, the saying did not hold
In him that did object the same to thee.
He was the wretched'st thing when he was young,
So long a-growing and so leisurely
That, if his rule were true, he should be gracious.

Good heavens, what he said to you
didn't apply to himself.
He was the most wretched thing when he was young,
who took such a long time to grow
that if his saying was true, he would be gracious.

ARCHBISHOP.
And so no doubt he is, my gracious madam.

And I'm sure he is, my gracious madam.

DUCHESS.
I hope he is; but yet let mothers doubt.

I hope he is; but let me as a mother doubt it.

YORK.
Now, by my troth, if I had been rememb'red,
I could have given my uncle's Grace a flout
To touch his growth nearer than he touch'd mine.

Now, I swear, if I'd thought of it,
I could have my uncle a comeback
that would have insulted his growth more than he insulted mine.

DUCHESS.
How, my young York? I prithee let me hear it.

How, young York? Let me hear it.

YORK.
Marry, they say my uncle grew so fast
That he could gnaw a crust at two hours old.
'Twas full two years ere I could get a tooth.
Grandam, this would have been a biting jest.

Wife, they say my uncle grew so fast
that he could chew a crust when he was two hours old.
It was whole two years before I grew any teeth.
Grandmother, this would have been a biting joke.

DUCHESS.
I prithee, pretty York, who told thee this?

Please tell me, pretty York, who told you this?

YORK.
Grandam, his nurse.

Grandmother, his nurse.

DUCHESS.
His nurse! Why she was dead ere thou wast
born.

His nurse! Why, she was dead before you were born.

YORK.
If 'twere not she, I cannot tell who told me.

If it wasn't her, I don't know who told me.

QUEEN ELIZABETH.
A parlous boy! Go to, you are too
shrewd.

113

You're a mischievous lad! Get away with you, you're too cunning.

ARCHBISHOP.
Good madam, be not angry with the child.

Good madam, do not be angry with the child.

QUEEN ELIZABETH.
Pitchers have ears.

There are plenty of spies about.

Enter a MESSENGER

ARCHBISHOP.
Here comes a messenger. What news?

Here comes the messenger. What's the news?

MESSENGER.
Such news, my lord, as grieves me to report.

News, my lord, which it makes me sorry to have to report.

QUEEN ELIZABETH.
How doth the Prince?

How is the prince?

MESSENGER.
Well, madam, and in health.

He is well, madam, and healthy.

DUCHESS.
What is thy news?

What is your news?

MESSENGER.
Lord Rivers and Lord Grey
Are sent to Pomfret, and with them
Sir Thomas Vaughan, prisoners.

Lord Rivers and Lord Grey
have been sent to Pomfret, with
Sir Thomas Vaughan, as prisoners.

DUCHESS.
Who hath committed them?

Who sent them there?

MESSENGER.
The mighty Dukes, Gloucester and Buckingham.

The great dukes, Gloucester and Buckingham.

ARCHBISHOP.
For what offence?

For what crime?

MESSENGER.
The sum of all I can, I have disclos'd.
Why or for what the nobles were committed
Is all unknown to me, my gracious lord.

I have told you all I know.
Why or for what the nobles were sentenced
I do not know, my gracious lord.

QUEEN ELIZABETH.
Ay me, I see the ruin of my house!
The tiger now hath seiz'd the gentle hind;
Insulting tyranny begins to jet
Upon the innocent and aweless throne.
Welcome, destruction, blood, and massacre!
I see, as in a map, the end of all.

Alas, I can see the downfall of my family!
The tiger has now grabbed the gentle deer;
insulting tyranny is now hanging over
the innocent and powerless throne.
Welcome, destruction, blunt and massacre!
I can see the end of everything as clearly as if
it was drawn out for me on a map.

DUCHESS.
Accursed and unquiet wrangling days,
How many of you have mine eyes beheld!
My husband lost his life to get the crown;
And often up and down my sons were toss'd
For me to joy and weep their gain and loss;
And being seated, and domestic broils
Clean over-blown, themselves the conquerors
Make war upon themselves-brother to brother,
Blood to blood, self against self. O, preposterous
And frantic outrage, end thy damned spleen,
Or let me die, to look on death no more!

Cursed and disturbed days of struggle,
how many of you I have seen!
My husband lost his life to get the Crown;
and the fortunes of my sons often rose and fell
so that I wept and was happy with their losses and gains;
when they had got their position and the civil wars
had completely blown over, they themselves, the victors,
began to make war against each other–brother on brother,
blood on blood, self against self. Oh, appalling
and terrible outrage, and your damned anger,
or let me die, and so see no more death.

QUEEN ELIZABETH.
Come, come, my boy; we will to
sanctuary.
Madam, farewell.

Come, come, my boy; we will go to a safe place.
Madam, farewell.

DUCHESS.
Stay, I will go with you.

Wait, I will come with you.

QUEEN ELIZABETH.
You have no cause.

You have no reason to.

ARCHBISHOP.
[To the QUEEN]My gracious lady, go.
And thither bear your treasure and your goods.
For my part, I'll resign unto your Grace
The seal I keep; and so betide to me
As well I tender you and all of yours!
Go, I'll conduct you to the sanctuary.

Go, my gracious lady.
And take your treasure and your goods there as well.
As from me, I shall give to your Grace
the Royal seal I have; and so treat me
the same way I treat you and all of yours!
Come, I'll escort you to the sanctuary.

Exeunt

ACT III

SCENE 1.

London. A street

The trumpets sound. Enter the PRINCE OF WALES, RICHARD, BUCKINGHAM,
CATESBY, CARDINAL BOURCHIER, and others

BUCKINGHAM.
Welcome, sweet Prince, to London, to your
chamber.

Welcome, sweet prince, to London, to your capital.

RICHARD.
Welcome, dear cousin, my thoughts' sovereign.
The weary way hath made you melancholy.

Welcome, dear cousin, the ruler of my thoughts.
The tiring journey has made you depressed.

PRINCE.
No, uncle; but our crosses on the way
Have made it tedious, wearisome, and heavy.
I want more uncles here to welcome me.

No, uncle; but the troubles we had on the way
have made it tedious, tiresome and dull.
There should be more uncles here to welcome me.

RICHARD.
Sweet Prince, the untainted virtue of your
years
Hath not yet div'd into the world's deceit;
Nor more can you distinguish of a man
Than of his outward show; which, God He knows,
Seldom or never jumpeth with the heart.
Those uncles which you want were dangerous;
Your Grace attended to their sug'red words
But look'd not on the poison of their hearts.

God keep you from them and from such false friends!

Sweet Prince, your unblemished youthful innocence
hasn't yet plumb the depths of the world's deceit;
you can't tell anything about a man apart
from what he looks like; which, God knows,
hardly ever completely agrees with his heart.
Those uncles you are missing word dangerous;
your Grace listened to their sweet words
but didn't see the poison in their hearts.
May God save you from them and from other such false friends!

PRINCE.
God keep me from false friends! but they were
none.

God save me from false friends! But they were not.

RICHARD.
My lord, the Mayor of London comes to greet
you.

My Lord, the Mayor of London comes to greet you.

Enter the LORD MAYOR and his train

MAYOR.
God bless your Grace with health and happy days!

May God bless your grace with health and happiness!

PRINCE.
I thank you, good my lord, and thank you all.
I thought my mother and my brother York
Would long ere this have met us on the way.
Fie, what a slug is Hastings, that he comes not
To tell us whether they will come or no!

I thank you, my good lord, and thank you all.
I thought my mother and my brother York
would have met us on our journey long before this.
What a slug Hastings is, not coming
to tell us whether they are coming or not!

Enter LORD HASTINGS

BUCKINGHAM.
And, in good time, here comes the sweating
Lord.

And, right on cue, here comes the sweating Lord.

PRINCE.
Welcome, my lord. What, will our mother come?

Welcome, my lord. Is my mother coming?

HASTINGS.
On what occasion, God He knows, not I,
The Queen your mother and your brother York
Have taken sanctuary. The tender Prince
Would fain have come with me to meet your Grace,
But by his mother was perforce withheld.

For what reason God only knows, I don't,
your mother the Queen and your brother York
have gone into a sanctuary. The young Prince
intended to come with me to meet your grace,
but his mother forcefully kept him back.

BUCKINGHAM.
Fie, what an indirect and peevish course
Is this of hers? Lord Cardinal, will your Grace
Persuade the Queen to send the Duke of York
Unto his princely brother presently?
If she deny, Lord Hastings, go with him
And from her jealous arms pluck him perforce.

What deceitful and perverse course of action
is she taking? Lord Cardinal, will your Grace
persuade the Queen to send the Duke of York
to his princely brother at once?
Go with him, Lord Hastings, and if she refuses
take him by force from her jealous arms.

CARDINAL.
My Lord of Buckingham, if my weak oratory
Can from his mother win the Duke of York,

Anon expect him here; but if she be obdurate
To mild entreaties, God in heaven forbid
We should infringe the holy privilege
Of blessed sanctuary! Not for all this land
Would I be guilty of so deep a sin.

My Lord Buckingham, if my poor speech
can persuade his mother to give up the Duke of York,
expect him here soon; but if she is obstinate
in the face of our pleas, God in heaven forbid
that we would disobeyed the holy privilege
of blessed sanctuary! I would not commit
such a sin for the whole kingdom.

BUCKINGHAM.
You are too senseless-obstinate, my lord,
Too ceremonious and traditional.
Weigh it but with the grossness of this age,
You break not sanctuary in seizing him.
The benefit thereof is always granted
To those whose dealings have deserv'd the place
And those who have the wit to claim the place.
This Prince hath neither claim'd it nor deserv'd it,
And therefore, in mine opinion, cannot have it.
Then, taking him from thence that is not there,
You break no privilege nor charter there.
Oft have I heard of sanctuary men;
But sanctuary children never till now.

You are too sucking always, my lord,
too ceremonial and traditional.
Think about the manners of this time,
you won't be breaking the sanctuary by seizing him.
The benefit of sanctuary is always granted
to those whose actions make them deserving of it,
and those who have the sense to ask for it.
The Prince has neither asked for it nor deserved it,
and so, in my opinion, cannot have it.
So, by taking him away from something that does not exist,
you are not breaking any laws all regulations.
I have often heard of men in sanctuary;
but never until now of sanctuary children.

CARDINAL.

My lord, you shall o'errule my mind for once.
Come on, Lord Hastings, will you go with me?

My Lord, you shall govern my mind for once.
Come on, Lord Hastings, will you come with me?

HASTINGS.
I go, my lord.

I'm coming, my lord.

PRINCE.
Good lords, make all the speedy haste you may.
Exeunt CARDINAL and HASTINGS
Say, uncle Gloucester, if our brother come,
Where shall we sojourn till our coronation?

Good lords, go as fast as you can.
Tell me, uncle Gloucester, if my brother is coming,
where shall we stay until my coronation?

RICHARD.
Where it seems best unto your royal self.
If I may counsel you, some day or two
Your Highness shall repose you at the Tower,
Then where you please and shall be thought most fit
For your best health and recreation.

Wherever your royal self thinks it best.
If I may advise you, I suggest you spend
a day or two at the Tower,
and then where you like and wherever you think best
for your health and amusement.

PRINCE.
I do not like the Tower, of any place.
Did Julius Caesar build that place, my lord?

I dislike the tower more than any place.
Was it built by Julius Caesar, my lord?

BUCKINGHAM.
He did, my gracious lord, begin that place,
Which, since, succeeding ages have re-edified.

My gracious lord, he did begin that place,
which has been rebuilt in The Times that followed.

PRINCE.
Is it upon record, or else reported
Successively from age to age, he built it?

Is it a matter of record, or has it been handed down
from age to age, that he built it?

BUCKINGHAM.
Upon record, my gracious lord.

It's on record, my gracious lord.

PRINCE.
But say, my lord, it were not regist'red,
Methinks the truth should live from age to age,
As 'twere retail'd to all posterity,
Even to the general all-ending day.

But, my lord, if it wasn't written down,
I think the truth would still survive from age to age,
handed down through posterity,
even to Judgement Day.

RICHARD.
[Aside]So wise so young, they say, do never
live long.

Those who are so wise when so young, they say, never live long.

PRINCE.
What say you, uncle?

What are you saying, uncle?

RICHARD.
I say, without characters, fame lives long.
[Aside]Thus, like the formal vice, Iniquity,
I moralize two meanings in one word.

I was saying, that fame survives without written records.

[Aside] So, like the regular vice of iniquity,
I give one word two meanings.

PRINCE.
That Julius Caesar was a famous man;
With what his valour did enrich his wit,
His wit set down to make his valour live.
Death makes no conquest of this conqueror;
For now he lives in fame, though not in life.
I'll tell you what, my cousin Buckingham-

That Julius Caesar was a famous man;
he had intelligence as well as bravery,
and his intelligence wrote things down so his bravery lived.
Death did not triumph over this conqueror;
for now he is living through fame, though not alive.
I'll tell you what, my cousin Buckingham–

BUCKINGHAM.
What, my gracious lord?

What, my gracious lord?

PRINCE.
An if I live until I be a man,
I'll win our ancient right in France again,
Or die a soldier as I liv'd a king.

If I should live until I am a man,
I will win back our ancient lands in France,
or die as a soldier as I lived as a king.

RICHARD.
[Aside]Short summers lightly have a forward
spring.

Short summers usually have early springs.

Enter HASTINGS, young YORK, and the CARDINAL

BUCKINGHAM.
Now, in good time, here comes the Duke of
York.

Now, right on cue, here comes the Duke of York.

PRINCE.
Richard of York, how fares our loving brother?

Richard of York, how is my loving brother?

YORK.
Well, my dread lord; so must I call you now.

I am well, your Majesty; that's what I must call you now.

PRINCE.
Ay brother, to our grief, as it is yours.
Too late he died that might have kept that title,
Which by his death hath lost much majesty.

Yes brother, to my sorrow, as it is to yours.
He who could have kept that title died too recently,
and the title has lost much of its majesty by his death.

RICHARD.
How fares our cousin, noble Lord of York?

How is my cousin, noble Lord of York?

YORK.
I thank you, gentle uncle. O, my lord,
You said that idle weeds are fast in growth.
The Prince my brother hath outgrown me far.

I thank you, kind uncle. Oh, my lord,
you said that useless weeds grow fast.
The Prince my brother has far outgrown me.

RICHARD.
He hath, my lord.

He has, my lord.

YORK.
And therefore is he idle?

And so is he useless?

RICHARD.
O, my fair cousin, I must not say so.

Oh, my fair cousin, I mustn't say that.

YORK.
Then he is more beholding to you than I.

Then he has more power over you than I do.

RICHARD.
He may command me as my sovereign;
But you have power in me as in a kinsman.

He may command me as my monarch;
but you have power over me as a relative.

YORK.
I pray you, uncle, give me this dagger.

Please, uncle, give me this dagger.

RICHARD.
My dagger, little cousin? With all my heart!

Give you my dagger, little cousin? I'd love to!

PRINCE.
A beggar, brother?

Are you a beggar, brother?

YORK.
Of my kind uncle, that I know will give,
And being but a toy, which is no grief to give.

Begging from my kind uncle, whom I know will give,
and as it's just a trifle, it won't hurt him to give it.

RICHARD.
A greater gift than that I'll give my cousin.

I shall give my cousin a greater gift than that.

YORK.
A greater gift! O, that's the sword to it!

A great gift! Oh, that's the sword which goes with it!

RICHARD.
Ay, gentle cousin, were it light enough.

Yes, gentle cousin, if it was light enough.

YORK.
O, then, I see you will part but with light gifts:
In weightier things you'll say a beggar nay.

Oh, I see that you only give away small gifts:
in heavier matters you say no to the beggar.

RICHARD.
It is too heavy for your Grace to wear.

It is too heavy for your Grace to wear.

YORK.
I weigh it lightly, were it heavier.

It means nothing to me, even if it were heavier.

RICHARD.
What, would you have my weapon, little
Lord?

What, do you want my weapon, Little Lord?

YORK.
I would, that I might thank you as you call me.

I would, so I could thank you for what you call me.

RICHARD.
How?

What?

128

YORK.
Little.

Little.

PRINCE.
My Lord of York will still be cross in talk.
Uncle, your Grace knows how to bear with him.

My Lord of York is querulous.
Uncle, your Grace knows how to bear with him.

YORK.
You mean, to bear me, not to bear with me.
Uncle, my brother mocks both you and me;
Because that I am little, like an ape,
He thinks that you should bear me on your shoulders.

You mean, to bear me, not to bear with me.
Uncle, my brother is mocking both you and me;
because I am little, like an ape,
he thinks that you should carry me on your shoulders.

BUCKINGHAM.
With what a sharp-provided wit he reasons!
To mitigate the scorn he gives his uncle
He prettily and aptly taunts himself.
So cunning and so young is wonderful.

Will a quick wit he has!
To soften the insult he's giving his uncle
he cleverly and wittily mocks himself.
It's wonderful to be so cunning so young.

RICHARD.
My lord, will't please you pass along?
Myself and my good cousin Buckingham
Will to your mother, to entreat of her
To meet you at the Tower and welcome you.

My lord, can we please move along?
Myself and my good cousin Buckingham
we'll go to your mother, to ask her
to meet you at the Tower and welcome you.

YORK.
What, will you go unto the Tower, my lord?

What, are you going to the Tower, my lord?

PRINCE.
My Lord Protector needs will have it so.

My Lord Protector insists on it.

YORK.
I shall not sleep in quiet at the Tower.

I shall not sleep peacefully in the Tower.

RICHARD.
Why, what should you fear?

Why, what are you afraid of?

YORK.
Marry, my uncle Clarence' angry ghost.
My grandam told me he was murder'd there.

Well, the angry ghost of my uncle Clarence.
My grandmother told me he was murdered there.

PRINCE.
I fear no uncles dead.

I'm not afraid of any dead uncles.

RICHARD.
Nor none that live, I hope.

Nor any live ones, I hope.

PRINCE.
An if they live, I hope I need not fear.
But come, my lord; and with a heavy heart,
Thinking on them, go I unto the Tower.

If there are live, I hope I don't need to fear them.

But come, my lord; and with a heavy heart,
thinking about them, I will go to the Tower.

A sennet.
Exeunt all but RICHARD, BUCKINGHAM, and CATESBY

BUCKINGHAM.
Think you, my lord, this little prating York
Was not incensed by his subtle mother
To taunt and scorn you thus opprobriously?

Do you think, my lord, that this little chattering York
was spurred on by his cunning mother
to taunt and mock you so rudely?

RICHARD.
No doubt, no doubt. O, 'tis a perilous boy;
Bold, quick, ingenious, forward, capable.
He is all the mother's, from the top to toe.

No doubt, no doubt. Oh, that's a dangerous boy;
bold, quick, ingenious, forward, capable.
He's just like his mother in every way.

BUCKINGHAM.
Well, let them rest. Come hither, Catesby.
Thou art sworn as deeply to effect what we intend
As closely to conceal what we impart.
Thou know'st our reasons urg'd upon the way.
What think'st thou? Is it not an easy matter
To make William Lord Hastings of our mind,
For the instalment of this noble Duke
In the seat royal of this famous isle?

Well, leave them to it. Come here, Catesby.
You have sworn have solemnly to do our bidding
as you have to keep what we tell you secret.
You know are reasons, we explained on the way.
What do you think? Won't it be simple
to convince William, Lord Hastings, to support
installing this noble duke
on to the royal throne of this famous island?

CATESBY.
He for his father's sake so loves the Prince
That he will not be won to aught against him.

He loves the Prince so much for his father's sake
that he will not be persuaded to do anything against him.

BUCKINGHAM.
What think'st thou then of Stanley? Will
not he?

Then what do you think of Stanley? Will he?

CATESBY.
He will do all in all as Hastings doth.

He will follow Hastings in everything.

BUCKINGHAM.
Well then, no more but this: go, gentle
Catesby,
And, as it were far off, sound thou Lord Hastings
How he doth stand affected to our purpose;
And summon him to-morrow to the Tower,
To sit about the coronation.
If thou dost find him tractable to us,
Encourage him, and tell him all our reasons;
If he be leaden, icy, cold, unwilling,
Be thou so too, and so break off the talk,
And give us notice of his inclination;
For we to-morrow hold divided councils,
Wherein thyself shalt highly be employ'd.

Well then, only do this: go, gentle Catesby,
and subtly discover from Lord Hastings
what he thinks of our plans;
and asked him to come to the Tower tomorrow,
to help plan the coronation.
If you find him amenable towards us,
encourage him, and tell him of our plans;
if he is slow, I see, cold, I'm willing,
then you must be too, and break of the conversation,
and tell us what he thinks;
for we will hold various meetings tomorrow

in which you shall be greatly employed.

RICHARD.
Commend me to Lord William. Tell him,
Catesby,
His ancient knot of dangerous adversaries
To-morrow are let blood at Pomfret Castle;
And bid my lord, for joy of this good news,
Give Mistress Shore one gentle kiss the more.

Give my best to Lord William. Tell him, Catesby,
that his group of old enemies
will be bleeding tomorrow at Pomfret Castle;
and tell my lord to celebrate this good news
by giving Mistress Shore an extra gentle kiss.

BUCKINGHAM.
Good Catesby, go effect this business soundly.

Good Catesby, go and perform this business well.

CATESBY.
My good lords both, with all the heed I can.

My good lords, I will do it as well as I can.

RICHARD.
Shall we hear from you, Catesby, ere we sleep?

Will we hear from you, Catesby, before we sleep?

CATESBY.
You shall, my lord.

You shall, my lord.

RICHARD.
At Crosby House, there shall you find us both.

You will find us both at Crosby House.

Exit CATESBY

BUCKINGHAM.

Now, my lord, what shall we do if we
perceive
Lord Hastings will not yield to our complots?

Now, my lord, what shall we do if we discover
Lord Hastings will not join in with our plots?

RICHARD.
Chop off his head-something we will
determine.
And, look when I am King, claim thou of me
The earldom of Hereford and all the movables
Whereof the King my brother was possess'd.

Top of his head–something we'll decide on.
And, when I am king, you can claim from me
the earldom of Hereford and all thepersonal possessions
which the king my brother owned.

BUCKINGHAM.
I'll claim that promise at your Grace's hand.

I'll shake your Grace's hand on that.

RICHARD.
And look to have it yielded with all kindness.
Come, let us sup betimes, that afterwards
We may digest our complots in some form.

And you will find it gives to you kindly.
Come, let's eat early, so that afterwards
we can discuss our plots.

Exeunt

SCENE 2.

Before LORD HASTING'S house

Enter a MESSENGER to the door of HASTINGS

MESSENGER.
My lord, my lord!

My lord, my lord!

[Knocking]

HASTINGS.
[Within]Who knocks?

Who's knocking?

MESSENGER.
One from the Lord Stanley.

Someone from Lord Stanley.

HASTINGS.
[Within]What is't o'clock?

What time is it?

MESSENGER.
Upon the stroke of four.

Four o'clock exactly.

Enter LORD HASTINGS

HASTINGS.
Cannot my Lord Stanley sleep these tedious
nights?

Can't my Lord Stanley get to sleep in these long nights?

MESSENGER.
So it appears by that I have to say.
First, he commends him to your noble self.

It seems so from what I have to say.
Firstly, he sends you his greetings.

HASTINGS.
What then?

Then what?

MESSENGER.
Then certifies your lordship that this night
He dreamt the boar had razed off his helm.
Besides, he says there are two councils kept,
And that may be determin'd at the one
Which may make you and him to rue at th' other.
Therefore he sends to know your lordship's pleasure-
If you will presently take horse with him
And with all speed post with him toward the north
To shun the danger that his soul divines.

Then he informs your Lordship that this night
he dreams that a boar tour of his helmet.
Besides that, he says there will be two meetings,
and what is decided at one
may be bad for you and him at the other.
So he has sent to ask what your lordship wants to do—
if you want to join him at once in riding
as fast as possible to the north
to escape the danger he feels in his soul.

HASTINGS.
Go, fellow, go, return unto thy lord;
Bid him not fear the separated council:
His honour and myself are at the one,
And at the other is my good friend Catesby;
Where nothing can proceed that toucheth us
Whereof I shall not have intelligence.
Tell him his fears are shallow, without instance;
And for his dreams, I wonder he's so simple
To trust the mock'ry of unquiet slumbers.

To fly the boar before the boar pursues
Were to incense the boar to follow us
And make pursuit where he did mean no chase.
Go, bid thy master rise and come to me;
And we will both together to the Tower,
Where, he shall see, the boar will use us kindly.

Go, fellow, go, go back to your Lord;
tell him not to worry about the divided Council:
his honour and myself will be at one of them,
and my good friend Catesby will be at the other;
there is nothing that can happen which affects us
which I shall not hear about.
Tell him his fears are groundless;
and as for his dreams, I'm amazed he so stupid
as to believe the foolish things created by restless sleep.
To run from the boar before the boar chases us
encourages the boar to follow us
and start a chase where before he had no intention of doing so.
Go, tell your master to get up and come to me;
and we will both go together to the Tower,
where, he shall see, the boar will treat us kindly.

MESSENGER.
I'll go, my lord, and tell him what you say.

I shall go, my lord, and tell him what you say.

 Exit

 Enter CATESBY

CATESBY.
Many good morrows to my noble lord!

Many good mornings to my noble lord!

HASTINGS.
Good morrow, Catesby; you are early stirring.
What news, what news, in this our tott'ring state?

Good morning, Catesby; you are up early.
What's the news, what's the news, in our precarious country?

CATESBY.
It is a reeling world indeed, my lord;
And I believe will never stand upright
Till Richard wear the garland of the realm.

The world is certainly reeling, my lord;
I don't believe it can ever be settled again
until Richard is wearing the garland of the kingdom.

HASTINGS.
How, wear the garland! Dost thou mean the
crown?

What, wear the garland! Do you mean the crown?

CATESBY.
Ay, my good lord.

Yes, my good lord.

HASTINGS.
I'll have this crown of mine cut from my
shoulders
Before I'll see the crown so foul misplac'd.
But canst thou guess that he doth aim at it?

I'll have my head cut off my shoulders
before I see the crown put in such a foul place.
But do you think he's trying to get it?

CATESBY.
Ay, on my life; and hopes to find you forward
Upon his party for the gain thereof;
And thereupon he sends you this good news,
That this same very day your enemies,
The kindred of the Queen, must die at Pomfret.

Yes, I swear to it; and he hopes that you will
join with his party to help him;
and for that reason he is sending you this good news,
that on this very day your enemies,
the relatives of the Queen, will die at Pomfret.

HASTINGS.

Indeed, I am no mourner for that news,
Because they have been still my adversaries;
But that I'll give my voice on Richard's side
To bar my master's heirs in true descent,
God knows I will not do it to the death.

Indeed, I won't shed any tears for that,
because they have remained as my enemies;
Bart to lend my voice to Richard's side
and block the true descent of my master's heirs
is something I will not do to the day I die.

CATESBY.
God keep your lordship in that gracious mind!

May God keep your Lordship steadfast in that thought!

HASTINGS.
But I shall laugh at this a twelve month hence,
That they which brought me in my master's hate,
I live to look upon their tragedy.
Well, Catesby, ere a fortnight make me older,
I'll send some packing that yet think not on't.

But I shall still be laughing at this year from now,
that the ones who made my master hate me
are going to die while I live to see it.
Well, Catesby, before another fortnight has passed,
I shall finish off some who little suspect it at the moment.

CATESBY.
'Tis a vile thing to die, my gracious lord,
When men are unprepar'd and look not for it.

It's a terrible thing to die, my gracious lord,
for men who are not expecting it and are unprepared.

HASTINGS.
O monstrous, monstrous! And so falls it out
With Rivers, Vaughan, Grey; and so 'twill do
With some men else that think themselves as safe
As thou and I, who, as thou knowest, are dear
To princely Richard and to Buckingham.

O terrible, terrible! And that's how it is
with Rivers, Vaughan and Grave; and that's how it will be
with some men who think they are safe
as you and I, who, as you know, are dear
to the princely Richard and to Buckingham.

CATESBY.
The Princes both make high account of you-
[Aside]For they account his head upon the bridge.

The Princes both speak very highly of you–
[Aside] They shall have your head high on a spike on the bridge.

HASTINGS.
I know they do, and I have well deserv'd it.

Enter LORD STANLEY

Come on, come on; where is your boar-spear, man?
Fear you the boar, and go so unprovided?

I know they do, and I have very much earned it.

Come on, come on; where is your boar spear, man?
You are scared of the boar, and yet you go about unprepared?

STANLEY.
My lord, good morrow; good morrow, Catesby.
You may jest on, but, by the holy rood,
I do not like these several councils, I.

Good morning, my lord; good morning, Catesby.
You can joke, but, by God,
I don't like these divided councils.

HASTINGS.
My lord, I hold my life as dear as yours,
And never in my days, I do protest,
Was it so precious to me as 'tis now.
Think you, but that I know our state secure,
I would be so triumphant as I am?

My Lord, my life is as important to me as yours is to you,
and I swear it has never been in all my life

as precious to me as it is now.
Do you think that I would be as happy as I am
if I didn't know that we were quite safe?

STANLEY.
The lords at Pomfret, when they rode from
London,
Were jocund and suppos'd their states were sure,
And they indeed had no cause to mistrust;
But yet you see how soon the day o'ercast.
This sudden stab of rancour I misdoubt;
Pray God, I say, I prove a needless coward.
What, shall we toward the Tower? The day is spent.

The lords who are now at Pomfret, when they wrote from London,
were happy and thought that they were safe,
and indeed they had no reason for mistrust;
but you see how quickly the day can become overcast.
This sudden stab of anger makes me worried;
I pray to God that I am shown to be a talent for no reason.
Well, shall we go to the Tower? Dawn is breaking.

HASTINGS.
Come, come, have with you. Wot you what, my
Lord?
To-day the lords you talk'd of are beheaded.

Come along then. Do you know what, my Lord?
Today the lord's you spoke of being beheaded.

STANLEY.
They, for their truth, might better wear their
heads
Than some that have accus'd them wear their hats.
But come, my lord, let's away.

For their truthfulness they might deserve to keep their heads
more than some who accuse them deserve their hats.
But come, my lord, let's go.

Enter HASTINGS, a pursuivant

HASTINGS.
Go on before; I'll talk with this good fellow.

Exeunt STANLEY and CATESBY

How now, Hastings! How goes the world with thee?

Go on ahead; I shall talk to this good fellow.

Hello there, Hastings! How are things with you?

PURSUIVANT.
The better that your lordship please to ask.

All the better as your lordship is so kind to ask.

HASTINGS.
I tell thee, man, 'tis better with me now
Than when thou met'st me last where now we meet:
Then was I going prisoner to the Tower
By the suggestion of the Queen's allies;
But now, I tell thee-keep it to thyself-
This day those enemies are put to death,
And I in better state than e'er I was.

I tell you, man, things are better with me now
man when you last met me here:
then I was going as a prisoner to the Tower
at the suggestion of the Queen's allies;
but now, I can tell you–keep it to yourself–
that today those enemies being put to death,
and I am better than I've ever been.

PURSUIVANT.
God hold it, to your honour's good content!

May God keep you in that state, for your honour's happiness!

HASTINGS.
Gramercy, Hastings; there, drink that for me.

Great thanks, Hastings; there, have a drink on me.

[Throws him his purse]

PURSUIVANT.

I thank your honour.

I thank your honour.

Exit

Enter a PRIEST

PRIEST.
Well met, my lord; I am glad to see your honour.

Hello there, my lord; I'm glad to see your honour.

HASTINGS.
I thank thee, good Sir John, with all my heart.
I am in your debt for your last exercise;
Come the next Sabbath, and I will content you.

I thank you, good Sir John, with all my heart.
I still owe you for your loss discourse;
come next Sunday, and I will pay you.

[He whispers in his ear]

PRIEST.
I'll wait upon your lordship.

I shall attend your lordship.

Enter BUCKINGHAM

BUCKINGHAM.
What, talking with a priest, Lord
Chamberlain!
Your friends at Pomfret, they do need the priest:
Your honour hath no shriving work in hand.

What, talking to a priest, Lord Chamberlain!
Your friends at Pomfret, they're the ones who need a priest:
your honour doesn't need to make a confession.

HASTINGS.
Good faith, and when I met this holy man,
The men you talk of came into my mind.

What, go you toward the Tower?

I swear, when I met this holy man,
the men you are speaking of came to my mind.
What, are you going to the Tower?

BUCKINGHAM.
I do, my lord, but long I cannot stay there;
I shall return before your lordship thence.

I am, my lord, but I can't stay there long;
I will be back from there before your lordship.

HASTINGS.
Nay, like enough, for I stay dinner there.

Well, that's likely enough, because I'm staying there for dinner.

BUCKINGHAM.
[Aside]And supper too, although thou
knowest it not.-
Come, will you go?

[Aside] And supper too, although you don't know it.–
Come, will you go?

HASTINGS.
I'll wait upon your lordship.

I'll attend your lordship.

Exeunt

SCENE 3.

Pomfret Castle

Enter SIR RICHARD RATCLIFF, with halberds, carrying the Nobles,
RIVERS, GREY, and VAUGHAN, to death

RIVERS.
Sir Richard Ratcliff, let me tell thee this:
To-day shalt thou behold a subject die
For truth, for duty, and for loyalty.

Sir Richard Ratcliff, let me tell you this:
today you will see a subject die
for truth, for duty and for loyalty.

GREY.
God bless the Prince from all the pack of you!
A knot you are of damned blood-suckers.

God save the Prince from the whole pack of you!
The whole lot of you are damned bloodsuckers.

VAUGHAN.
You live that shall cry woe for this hereafter.

You who live shall be sorry for this in future.

RATCLIFF.
Dispatch; the limit of your lives is out.

Get moving: the time of your life has run out.

RIVERS.
O Pomfret, Pomfret! O thou bloody prison,
Fatal and ominous to noble peers!
Within the guilty closure of thy walls
 Richard the second here was hack'd to death;
And for more slander to thy dismal seat,
We give to thee our guiltless blood to drink.

O Pomfret, Pomfret! Oh you bloody prison,
dreadful and fatal to noble peers!
Within the guilty enclosure of your walls
Richard the second was hacked to death here;
and to make your horrible reputation worse,
we give you our guiltless blood to drink.

GREY.
Now Margaret's curse is fall'n upon our heads,
When she exclaim'd on Hastings, you, and I,
For standing by when Richard stabb'd her son.

Now we are suffering for Margaret's curse,
when she cursed Hastings, you and I,
for standing by when Richard stabbed her son.

RIVERS.
Then curs'd she Richard, then curs'd she
Buckingham,
Then curs'd she Hastings. O, remember, God,
To hear her prayer for them, as now for us!
And for my sister, and her princely sons,
Be satisfied, dear God, with our true blood,
Which, as thou know'st, unjustly must be spilt.

Then she cursed Richard, then she cursed Buckingham,
then she cursed Hastings. Oh, remember, God,
to make sure that they get what she asked for as we do!
And as for my sister, and her princely sons,
be happy, dear God, with our loyal blood,
which, as you know, is going to be spilt unjustly.

RATCLIFF.
Make haste; the hour of death is expiate.

Hurry up; the hour of death has come.

RIVERS.
Come, Grey; come, Vaughan; let us here embrace.
Farewell, until we meet again in heaven.

Come, Grey; come, Vaughan; let us embrace here.
Farewell, until we meet again in heaven.

Exeunt

SCENE 4.

London. The Tower

Enter BUCKINGHAM, DERBY, HASTINGS, the BISHOP of ELY, RATCLIFF, LOVEL,
with others and seat themselves at a table

HASTINGS.
Now, noble peers, the cause why we are met
Is to determine of the coronation.
In God's name speak-when is the royal day?

Now, noble peers, the reason we are meeting
is to decide on the coronation.
Speak in the name of God–when is the royal day?

BUCKINGHAM.
Is all things ready for the royal time?

Is everything ready for it?

DERBY.
It is, and wants but nomination.

It is, we just need to choose a day.

BISHOP OF ELY.
To-morrow then I judge a happy day.

Then I think tomorrow would be a good day.

BUCKINGHAM.
Who knows the Lord Protector's mind
herein?
Who is most inward with the noble Duke?

Who knows what the Lord Protector thinks about this?
Who is closest to the noble Duke?

BISHOP OF ELY.
Your Grace, we think, should soonest know
his mind.

I should imagine your Grace is most likely to know what he thinks.

BUCKINGHAM.
We know each other's faces; for our hearts,
He knows no more of mine than I of yours;
Or I of his, my lord, than you of mine.
Lord Hastings, you and he are near in love.

We know each other's faces; as for our hearts,
he knows no more about mine than I do about yours;
and I know no more of his, my lord, that you do of mine.
Lord Hastings, you and he are very close.

HASTINGS.
I thank his Grace, I know he loves me well;
But for his purpose in the coronation
I have not sounded him, nor he deliver'd
His gracious pleasure any way therein.
But you, my honourable lords, may name the time;
And in the Duke's behalf I'll give my voice,
Which, I presume, he'll take in gentle part.

I thank your Grace, I know he's fond of me;
but I have not asked him his feelings about
the Coronation, nor has he mentioned
in any way what he's thinking about it.
But you can name the day, my honourable lords;
I shall give my opinion on the Duke's behalf,
which I assume he will be happy with.

Enter RICHARD

BISHOP OF ELY.
In happy time, here comes the Duke himself.

Fortunately, here comes the Duke himself.

RICHARD.
My noble lords and cousins all, good morrow.
I have been long a sleeper, but I trust

My absence doth neglect no great design
Which by my presence might have been concluded.

My noble lords and cousins all, good morning.
I have slept for a long time, but I hope
my absence has not stopped you from making any great plans
which could have been made if I was here.

BUCKINGHAM.
Had you not come upon your cue, my lord,
William Lord Hastings had pronounc'd your part-
I mean, your voice for crowning of the King.

If you hadn't come just at the right time, my lord,
William Lord Hastings was going to speak for you—
I mean, for your opinion on the coronation.

RICHARD.
Than my Lord Hastings no man might be
bolder;
His lordship knows me well and loves me well.
My lord of Ely, when I was last in Holborn
I saw good strawberries in your garden there.
I do beseech you send for some of them.

And there is no man more suited to do so than my Lord Hastings;
his Lordship knows me well and lost me well.
My Lord of Ely, last time I was in Holborn
I saw some good strawberries in your garden.
I would very much like you to send for some of them.

BISHOP of ELY.
Marry and will, my lord, with all my heart.

I certainly shall, my lord, it will be a pleasure.

Exit

RICHARD.
Cousin of Buckingham, a word with you.
[Takes him aside]
Catesby hath sounded Hastings in our business,
And finds the testy gentleman so hot
That he will lose his head ere give consent

150

His master's child, as worshipfully he terms it,
Shall lose the royalty of England's throne.

Cousin Buckingham, a word with you.
[Takes him aside]
Catesby has sounded out Hastings with regard to our business,
and finds that the impetuous gentleman is so passionate
that he will lose his head before he agrees to
his master's child, as he respectfully calls it,
losing the throne of England.

BUCKINGHAM.
Withdraw yourself awhile; I'll go with you.
Exeunt RICHARD and BUCKINGHAM

Let's make ourselves absent for a while.

DERBY.
We have not yet set down this day of triumph.
To-morrow, in my judgment, is too sudden;
For I myself am not so well provided
As else I would be, were the day prolong'd.

We haven't yet agreed on a day for the correlation.
In my opinion tomorrow is too soon;
I am not so well prepared
as I would be, if it were further off.

Re-enter the BISHOP OF ELY

BISHOP OF ELY.
Where is my lord the Duke of Gloucester?
I have sent for these strawberries.

Where is my lord the Duke of Gloucester?
I have sent for the strawberries.

HASTINGS.
His Grace looks cheerfully and smooth this
morning;
There's some conceit or other likes him well
When that he bids good morrow with such spirit.
I think there's never a man in Christendom
Can lesser hide his love or hate than he;

For by his face straight shall you know his heart.

His Grace looks calm and happy this morning;
there's something or other going on that he is pleased with,
when he says good morning so cheerfully.
I don't think there's any man in Christendom
who is less able to hide his love or his hate;
you can tell what he's feeling at once by looking in his face.

DERBY.
What of his heart perceive you in his face
By any livelihood he show'd to-day?

What did you think he was feeling
by looking at his face today.

HASTINGS.
Marry, that with no man here he is offended;
For, were he, he had shown it in his looks.

Well, that there is nobody here who has offended him;
if there was, he would have shown it in his looks.

Re-enter RICHARD and BUCKINGHAM

RICHARD.
I pray you all, tell me what they deserve
That do conspire my death with devilish plots
Of damned witchcraft, and that have prevail'd
Upon my body with their hellish charms?

I beg you all to tell me, how should I punish
people who plot my death with devilish plans
of hellish witchcraft, who have affected
my body with their hellish charms?

HASTINGS.
The tender love I bear your Grace, my lord,
Makes me most forward in this princely presence
To doom th' offenders, whosoe'er they be.
I say, my lord, they have deserved death.

The very great love I have for your Grace, my lord,
gives me the nerve to speak in the presence of a Prince

to say that whomever the offenders are they should be doomed.
I say, my lord, they deserve death.

RICHARD.
Then be your eyes the witness of their evil.
Look how I am bewitch'd; behold, mine arm
Is like a blasted sapling wither'd up.
And this is Edward's wife, that monstrous witch,
Consorted with that harlot strumpet Shore,
That by their witchcraft thus have marked me.

Then let your eyes witness the evil they have done.
Look how I have been bewitched; look, my arm
has withered up like a blasted sapling.
This has been done by Edward's wife, that monstrous witch,
in league with that harlot strumpet Shore,
they have marked me with their witchcraft.

HASTINGS.
If they have done this deed, my noble lord-

If they have done this deed, my noble Lord–

RICHARD.
If?-thou protector of this damned strumpet,
Talk'st thou to me of ifs? Thou art a traitor.
Off with his head! Now by Saint Paul I swear
I will not dine until I see the same.
Lovel and Ratcliff, look that it be done.
The rest that love me, rise and follow me.

If? You protector of this damned strumpet,
are you talking about ifs to me? You are a traitor.
Off with his head! Now by St Paul, I swear
I shall not eat until I see it's done.
Lovel and Ratcliff, see that it's done.
The rest, if you love me, get up and follow me.

Exeunt all but HASTINGS, LOVEL, and RATCLIFF

HASTINGS.
Woe, woe, for England! not a whit for me;
For I, too fond, might have prevented this.
 Stanley did dream the boar did raze our helms,

And I did scorn it and disdain to fly.
Three times to-day my foot-cloth horse did stumble,
And started when he look'd upon the Tower,
As loath to bear me to the slaughter-house.
O, now I need the priest that spake to me!
I now repent I told the pursuivant,
As too triumphing, how mine enemies
To-day at Pomfret bloodily were butcher'd,
And I myself secure in grace and favour.
O Margaret, Margaret, now thy heavy curse
Is lighted on poor Hastings' wretched head!

Woe, woe, for England! Not for me;
for I was too foolish, I could have stopped this.
Stanley dreams that the boar tore at our helmets,
and I mocked him and refused to flee.
three times today my decorated horse stumbled,
and started when he looked at the Tower,
as if he hated to carry me to the slaughterhouse.
Oh, now I need the priest who spoke to me!
Now I regret telling the herald,
to triumphantly, how my enemies
were to be bloodily butchered today at Pomfret,
and how I was safe in grace and favour.
Oh Margaret, Margaret, now your heavy curse
has landed on the wretched head of poor Hastings!

RATCLIFF.
Come, come, dispatch; the Duke would be at
dinner.
Make a short shrift; he longs to see your head.

Come, come, hurry up; the Duke wants his dinner.
Make a quick confession; he's longing to see your head.

HASTINGS.
O momentary grace of mortal men,
Which we more hunt for than the grace of God!
Who builds his hope in air of your good looks
Lives like a drunken sailor on a mast,
Ready with every nod to tumble down
Into the fatal bowels of the deep.

How fleeting the grace of mortal men is,

which we look for more than we do than the grace of God!
Someone who bases his hopes on it
lives his life like a drunken sailor on top of the mast,
living every second with the risk of falling down
into the fatal drowning ocean.

LOVEL.
Come, come, dispatch; 'tis bootless to exclaim.

Come on, hurry up; it's useless to complain.

HASTINGS.
O bloody Richard! Miserable England!
I prophesy the fearfull'st time to thee
That ever wretched age hath look'd upon.
Come, lead me to the block; bear him my head.
They smile at me who shortly shall be dead.

O bloody Richard! Miserable England!
I predict the worst time is coming to you
that any age has ever seen.
Come, take me to the block; take in my head.
These people who smile at me will shortly be dead.

Exeunt

SCENE 5.

London. The Tower-walls

Enter RICHARD and BUCKINGHAM in rotten armour, marvellous
ill-favoured

RICHARD.
Come, cousin, canst thou quake and change
thy colour,
Murder thy breath in middle of a word,
And then again begin, and stop again,
As if thou were distraught and mad with terror?

Come, cousin,can you shake and change colour,
cut off your breath in the middle of the word,
and then begin again, and stop again,
as if you were madly confused with terror?

BUCKINGHAM.
Tut, I can counterfeit the deep tragedian;
Speak and look back, and pry on every side,
Tremble and start at wagging of a straw,
Intending deep suspicion. Ghastly looks
Are at my service, like enforced smiles;
And both are ready in their offices
At any time to grace my stratagems.
But what, is Catesby gone?

Tut, I can play like a great tragic actor;
speak, look around, searching on every side,
trembling and jumping when a blade of grass moves,
pretending to be very suspicious. I can put on
ghastly looks, like Folsom I'll is;
and I have both prepared
to use in my plans at any time.
But what, has Catesbygone?

RICHARD.
He is; and, see, he brings the mayor along.

He has; and, look, he's bringing the mayor with him.

Enter the LORD MAYOR and CATESBY

BUCKINGHAM.
Lord Mayor-

Lord Mayor–

RICHARD.
Look to the drawbridge there!

Make sure that drawbridge is up!

BUCKINGHAM.
Hark! a drum.

Listen! A drum.

RICHARD.
Catesby, o'erlook the walls.

Catesby, look over the walls.

BUCKINGHAM.
Lord Mayor, the reason we have sent-

Lord Mayor, the reason we have sent–

RICHARD.
Look back, defend thee; here are enemies.

Look back, defend yourself; here are the enemies.

BUCKINGHAM.
God and our innocence defend and guard us!

May God and our innocence defend and guard us!

Enter LOVEL and RATCLIFF, with HASTINGS' head

RICHARD.
Be patient; they are friends-Ratcliff and Lovel.

Calm yourself; they are friends–Ratcliff and Lovel.

LOVEL.
Here is the head of that ignoble traitor,
The dangerous and unsuspected Hastings.

Here is the head of that despicable traitor,
the dangerous and unsuspected Hastings.

RICHARD.
So dear I lov'd the man that I must weep.
I took him for the plainest harmless creature
That breath'd upon the earth a Christian;
Made him my book, wherein my soul recorded
The history of all her secret thoughts.
So smooth he daub'd his vice with show of virtue
That, his apparent open guilt omitted,
I mean his conversation with Shore's wife-
He liv'd from all attainder of suspects.

I love that man so dearly that I must weep.
I thought he was the most simple harmless creature
out of all the Christians on earth;
he was my confidant, to whom I told all the
deepest secret thoughts of my soul.
He covered over his evil with a show of goodness so well
that, leaving aside the obvious evidence of his guilt,
I mean his conversation with Shore's wife–
he lived free of all taint of suspicion.

BUCKINGHAM.
Well, well, he was the covert'st shelt'red
traitor
That ever liv'd.
Would you imagine, or almost believe-
Were't not that by great preservation
We live to tell it-that the subtle traitor
This day had plotted, in the council-house,
To murder me and my good Lord of Gloucester.

Well, well, he was the most secret hidden traitor
that ever lived.
Could you imagine, could you even believe–

it's only through divine intervention
where alive to tell it–that the cunning traitor
was planning to murder myself and my good
Lord of Gloucester at today's meeting.

MAYOR.
Had he done so?

Would he have done it?

RICHARD.
What! think you we are Turks or Infidels?
Or that we would, against the form of law,
Proceed thus rashly in the villain's death
But that the extreme peril of the case,
The peace of England and our persons' safety,
Enforc'd us to this execution?

What! Do you think we are Turks or infidels?
Do you think we would illegally
rush this villain to his death
if it wasn't for the great danger of the matter,
the risk to the peace of England and ourselves,
which forced us to execute him?

MAYOR.
Now, fair befall you! He deserv'd his death;
And your good Graces both have well proceeded
To warn false traitors from the like attempts.
I never look'd for better at his hands
After he once fell in with Mistress Shore.

Now, may you have good luck! He deserved to die;
and your good graces have both done well
in warning. It is not to try the same thing.
I didn't expect any better from him
once he had fallen in with Mistress Shore.

BUCKINGHAM.
Yet had we not determin'd he should die
Until your lordship came to see his end-
Which now the loving haste of these our friends,
Something against our meanings, have prevented-
Because, my lord, I would have had you heard

The traitor speak, and timorously confess
The manner and the purpose of his treasons:
That you might well have signified the same
Unto the citizens, who haply may
Misconstrue us in him and wail his death.

But we had decided that he should not die
until your Lordship came to see him finished–
but the loving host of our friends here has
prevented that, somewhat against our intentions bash
because, my lord, I wanted you to hear
the traitors speak, and cringingly confess
the type and purpose of his treason:
then you could have reported the same
to the systems, who perhaps might
misunderstand the case and mourn for his death.

MAYOR.
But, my good lord, your Grace's words shall serve
As well as I had seen and heard him speak;
And do not doubt, right noble Princes both,
But I'll acquaint our duteous citizens
With all your just proceedings in this cause.

But, my good lord, your Grace's words will do
just as well as if I had seen and heard him speak;
and do not doubt, truly noble princes as you both are,
that I shall inform our loyal citizens
of how correctly you acted in this case.

RICHARD.
And to that end we wish'd your lordship here,
T' avoid the the the censures of the carping world.

That is why we wanted your lordship here,
to stop the sniping world from criticising us.

BUCKINGHAM.
Which since you come too late of our intent,
Yet witness what you hear we did intend.
And so, my good Lord Mayor, we bid farewell.

You came too late to see what we did,
but you can tell them the reasons for it.

And so, my good Lord Mayor, we bid farewell.

Exit LORD MAYOR

RICHARD.
Go, after, after, cousin Buckingham.
The Mayor towards Guildhall hies him in an post.
There, at your meet'st advantage of the time,
Infer the bastardy of Edward's children.
Tell them how Edward put to death a citizen
Only for saying he would make his son
Heir to the crown-meaning indeed his house,
Which by the sign thereof was termed so.
Moreover, urge his hateful luxury
And bestial appetite in change of lust,
Which stretch'd unto their servants, daughters, wives,
Even where his raging eye or savage heart
Without control lusted to make a prey.
Nay, for a need, thus far come near my person:
Tell them, when that my mother went with child
Of that insatiate Edward, noble York
My princely father then had wars in France
And, by true computation of the time,
Found that the issue was not his begot;
Which well appeared in his lineaments,
Being nothing like the noble Duke my father.
Yet touch this sparingly, as 'twere far off;
Because, my lord, you know my mother lives.

Follow him, cousin Buckingham:
the mayor is rushing towards the Guildhall.
There, when you get a chance,
imply that Edward's children are illegitimate;
tell them how he put a citizen to death
just for saying that he would make his son
heir to the Crown–when all he meant was his house,
which was called by that name.
What's more, mention his horrible lustfulness
and his bestial appetite for new sexual adventures,
which made him approach their servants, daughters, wives,
wherever his angry eye or savage heart
lasted without control afternew prey.
If you have to, you may talk about me:
tell them that when my mother was pregnant

by the insatiable Edward, noble York,
my princely father, was then at war in France,
and by calculating the time
he found that he was not the father;
it showed obviously in his face,
he was nothing like the noble duke, my father–
but only speak of this a little, just hint at it;
because, my lord, you know my mother is still alive.

BUCKINGHAM.
Doubt not, my lord, I'll play the orator
As if the golden fee for which I plead
Were for myself; and so, my lord, adieu.

Don't worry, my lord, I'll speak
as if the golden prize I am asking for
work for myself; and so, my lord, goodbye.

RICHARD.
If you thrive well, bring them to Baynard's
Castle;
Where you shall find me well accompanied
With reverend fathers and well learned bishops.

If you do well, bring them to Baynard's Castle;
there you will find me in good company
with reverend fathers and well learned bishops.

BUCKINGHAM.
I go; and towards three or four o'clock
Look for the news that the Guildhall affords.

I'm going; and about three or four o'clock
look out for news from the Guildhall.

Exit
RICHARD.
Go, Lovel, with all speed to Doctor Shaw.
[To CATESBY]Go thou to Friar Penker. Bid them both
Meet me within this hour at Baynard's Castle.
Exeunt all but RICHARD
Now will I go to take some privy order
To draw the brats of Clarence out of sight,
And to give order that no manner person

Have any time recourse unto the Princes.

Go, Lovel, as quick as you can to Doctor Shaw.
[To Catesby] You go to Friar Penker. Tell them both
to meet me within the hour at Baynard's Castle.

Now I shall make arrangements
to get the brats of Clarence out of sight,
and to give orders that absolutely nobody
can see the Princes at any time.

Exit

SCENE 6.

London. A street

Enter a SCRIVENER

SCRIVENER.
Here is the indictment of the good Lord Hastings;
Which in a set hand fairly is engross'd
That it may be to-day read o'er in Paul's.
And mark how well the sequel hangs together:
Eleven hours I have spent to write it over,
For yesternight by Catesby was it sent me;
The precedent was full as long a-doing;
And yet within these five hours Hastings liv'd,
Untainted, unexamin'd, free, at liberty.
Here's a good world the while! Who is so gros
That cannot see this palpable device?
Yet who's so bold but says he sees it not?
Bad is the world; and all will come to nought,
When such ill dealing must be seen in thought.

Here is the indictment of the good Lord Hastings;
which has been written out in large letters
and it can be read today at St Paul's.
And make a note of how things have worked out:
I took 11 hours writing it out,
for Catesby sent it to me yesterday night;
the original took that long again to write.
And yet less than five hours ago Hastings was alive,
untainted, unexamined, free, at liberty.
What a fine world this is! Who is so stupid
that they can't see this obvious trick?
Who's so shameless that he says he can't see it?
It's a bad world, and we'll all come to a bad end
when we can only think about these things, and don't say them.

Exit

SCENE 7.

London. Baynard's Castle

Enter RICHARD and BUCKINGHAM, at several doors

RICHARD.
How now, how now! What say the citizens?

Hello there, hello! What do the citizens say?

BUCKINGHAM.
Now, by the holy Mother of our Lord,
The citizens are mum, say not a word.

By the holy mother of our Lord,
the citizens are silent, they don't say a word.

RICHARD.
Touch'd you the bastardy of Edward's
children?

Did you mention how Edward's children are bastards?

BUCKINGHAM.
I did; with his contract with Lady Lucy,
And his contract by deputy in France;
Th' insatiate greediness of his desire,
And his enforcement of the city wives;
His tyranny for trifles; his own bastardy,
As being got, your father then in France,
And his resemblance, being not like the Duke.
Withal I did infer your lineaments,
Being the right idea of your father,
Both in your form and nobleness of mind;
Laid open all your victories in Scotland,
Your discipline in war, wisdom in peace,
Your bounty, virtue, fair humility;
Indeed, left nothing fitting for your purpose
Untouch'd or slightly handled in discourse.

And when mine oratory drew toward end
I bid them that did love their country's good
Cry 'God save Richard, England's royal King!'

I did, and his engagement to Lady Lucy,
and his other engagement in France;
the insatiable greed of his desires,
and the way he forces himself on the wives of the townsmen;
his tyrannous behaviour in small matters; the fact that he himself was illegitimate,
having been conceived when your father was in France,
and how he did not look like the Duke.
Furthermore, I mentioned your looks–
saying that you were the image of your father,
both in your body and the nobleness of your mind–
I spoke of your victories in Scotland,
your discipline in war, wisdom in peace,
your generosity, goodness, sweet modesty;
indeed, I left nothing to your advantage
unmentioned, neither did I only mention it fleetingly.
And when my speech came to an end,
I called on those who wanted the best for their country
to shout, 'God save Richard, England's Royal King!'

RICHARD.
And did they so?

And did they?

BUCKINGHAM.
No, so God help me, they spake not a word;
But, like dumb statues or breathing stones,
Star'd each on other, and look'd deadly pale.
Which when I saw, I reprehended them,
And ask'd the Mayor what meant this wilfull silence.
His answer was, the people were not used
To be spoke to but by the Recorder.
Then he was urg'd to tell my tale again.
'Thus saith the Duke, thus hath the Duke inferr'd'–
But nothing spoke in warrant from himself.
When he had done, some followers of mine own
At lower end of the hall hurl'd up their caps,
And some ten voices cried 'God save King Richard!'
And thus I took the vantage of those few–
'Thanks, gentle citizens and friends,' quoth I

'This general applause and cheerful shout
Argues your wisdoms and your love to Richard.'
And even here brake off and came away.

No, God help me, they didn't say a word;
they just stared at each other and looked deathly pale,
like dumb statues or living stones.
When I saw this, I reprimanded them,
and asked the mayor what the deliberate silence meant.
He answered that the people were not used
to being spoken to by anybody but the magistrate.
So I told him to repeat what I have said,
'The Duke has said this, the Duke has explained'–
but he didn't say anything on his own behalf.
When he had finished, some of my followers
at the far end of the hall threw up their caps,
and some ten voices cried 'God save King Richard!'
And so I used those few for my purposes:
'Thank you kind citizens and friends,' I said;
'this universal applause and happy shouting
shows your intelligence and your love for Richard.'
And I stopped there, and came away.

RICHARD.
What, tongueless blocks were they? Would
they not speak?
Will not the Mayor then and his brethren come?

What, lost their tongues had they? Would they not speak?
So will the mayor and his associates not come?

BUCKINGHAM.
The Mayor is here at hand. Intend some fear;
Be not you spoke with but by mighty suit;
And look you get a prayer-book in your hand,
And stand between two churchmen, good my lord;
For on that ground I'll make a holy descant;
And be not easily won to our requests.
Play the maid's part: still answer nay, and take it.

The mayor is right here.Pretend to be afraid;
only listen to powerful entreaties;
take a prayer book in your hand
and stand between two churchmen, my good lord;

I'll build a good fantasy on those foundations;
don't be easily won over by our requests.
Act like a woman: keep refusing, but take what is offered.

RICHARD.
I go; and if you plead as well for them
As I can say nay to thee for myself,
No doubt we bring it to a happy issue.

I shall go; and if you speak for them
as well as I can pretend to refuse,
no doubt we shall get a good outcome.

BUCKINGHAM.
Go, go, up to the leads; the Lord Mayor
knocks.

Go, go, up to the gallery; the Lord Mayor is knocking.

Exit RICHARD

Enter the LORD MAYOR, ALDERMEN, and citizens

Welcome, my lord. I dance attendance here;
I think the Duke will not be spoke withal.

Enter CATESBY

Now, Catesby, what says your lord to my request?

Welcome, my lord. I'm kicking my heels here.
I don't think the Duke wants to speak with you.

Now, Catesby, what does your lord say to my request?

CATESBY.
He doth entreat your Grace, my noble lord,
To visit him to-morrow or next day.
He is within, with two right reverend fathers,
Divinely bent to meditation;
And in no worldly suits would he be mov'd,
To draw him from his holy exercise.

He begs your Grace, my noble lord,

to visit him tomorrow or the next day.
He's inside, with two very holy priests,
in divine meditation;
he will not allow any earthly things
to distract him from his devotions.

BUCKINGHAM.
Return, good Catesby, to the gracious Duke;
Tell him, myself, the Mayor and Aldermen,
In deep designs, in matter of great moment,
No less importing than our general good,
Are come to have some conference with his Grace.

Good Catesby, go back to the gracious Duke;
tell him that myself, the Mayor and aldermen,
have all come to speak to his Grace about
weighty matters, extremely important things,
which are most important for the general good.

CATESBY.
I'll signify so much unto him straight.

I'll go and let himknow at once.

Exit

BUCKINGHAM.
Ah ha, my lord, this prince is not an Edward!
He is not lolling on a lewd love-bed,
But on his knees at meditation;
Not dallying with a brace of courtezans,
But meditating with two deep divines;
Not sleeping, to engross his idle body,
But praying, to enrich his watchful soul.
Happy were England would this virtuous prince
Take on his Grace the sovereignty thereof;
But, sure, I fear we shall not win him to it.

Ah ha, my lord, this prince is not like Edward!
He is not lying around on a lustful bed,
but is on his knees praying;
not playing with a pair of tarts,
but praying with two holy men;
not sleeping as his idle body gets fatter,

but praying, to expand his holy soul.
England would be very lucky if this good prince
agreed to become its monarch;
but I'm afraid I'm certain we won't persuade him.

MAYOR.
Marry, God defend his Grace should say us nay!

Well, heaven forbid that he should refuse us!

BUCKINGHAM.
I fear he will. Here Catesby comes again.

Re-enter CATESBY

Now, Catesby, what says his Grace?

I'm afraid he will. Here comes Catesby again.

Now, Catesby, what does his Grace say?

CATESBY.
My lord,
He wonders to what end you have assembled
Such troops of citizens to come to him.
His Grace not being warn'd thereof before,
He fears, my lord, you mean no good to him.

My Lord,
he is asking why you have gathered
such an army ofcitizens to come to him.
As his Grace was not told they were coming,
he is afraid, my lord, that you mean him harm.

BUCKINGHAM.
Sorry I am my noble cousin should
Suspect me that I mean no good to him.
By heaven, we come to him in perfect love;
And so once more return and tell his Grace.
Exit CATESBY
When holy and devout religious men
Are at their beads, 'tis much to draw them thence,
So sweet is zealous contemplation.

I'm sorry my noble cousin can
suspect me of intending to harm him.
By heaven, we come to him out of perfect love;
please go back and tell his Grace that.

When holy and devout religious men
are praying, it's very difficult to get them away,
their holy meditations are so sweet.

 Enter RICHARD aloft, between two BISHOPS.
CATESBY returns

MAYOR.
See where his Grace stands 'tween two clergymen!

Look where his Grace is standing between two clergymen!

BUCKINGHAM.
Two props of virtue for a Christian prince,
To stay him from the fall of vanity;
And, see, a book of prayer in his hand,
True ornaments to know a holy man.
Famous Plantagenet, most gracious Prince,
Lend favourable ear to our requests,
And pardon us the interruption
Of thy devotion and right Christian zeal.

Two good supports for a Christian prince,
to stop him turning to sin;
and, see, a prayer book in his hand,
a true sign of a holy man.
Famous Plantagenet, most gracious prince,
look favourably on our requests,
and excuse us for interrupting
your devotions and your proper Christian passion.

RICHARD.
My lord, there needs no such apology:
I do beseech your Grace to pardon me,
Who, earnest in the service of my God,
Deferr'd the visitation of my friends.
But, leaving this, what is your Grace's pleasure?

My lord, there is no need for an apology:

I beg your Grace to pardon me,
for, in my deep devotion to God,
making my friends wait.
But forget that, what can I do for your Grace?

BUCKINGHAM.
Even that, I hope, which pleaseth God above,
And all good men of this ungovern'd isle.

Something that, I hope, will please God above,
and all good men on this leaderless island.

RICHARD.
I do suspect I have done some offence
That seems disgracious in the city's eye,
And that you come to reprehend my ignorance.

I suspect I have done something wrong
which seems displeasing to the city,
and that you have come to criticise my ignorance.

BUCKINGHAM.
You have, my lord. Would it might please
your Grace,
On our entreaties, to amend your fault!

You have, my lord. We hope it will please your Grace,
when we ask you, to make things right!

RICHARD.
Else wherefore breathe I in a Christian land?

Why else am I here in this Christian land?

BUCKINGHAM.
Know then, it is your fault that you resign
The supreme seat, the throne majestical,
The scept'red office of your ancestors,
Your state of fortune and your due of birth,
The lineal glory of your royal house,
To the corruption of a blemish'd stock;
Whiles in the mildness of your sleepy thoughts,
Which here we waken to our country's good,
The noble isle doth want her proper limbs;

Her face defac'd with scars of infamy,
Her royal stock graft with ignoble plants,
And almost should'red in the swallowing gulf
Of dark forgetfulness and deep oblivion.
Which to recure, we heartily solicit
Your gracious self to take on you the charge
And kingly government of this your land-
Not as protector, steward, substitute,
Or lowly factor for another's gain;
But as successively, from blood to blood,
Your right of birth, your empery, your own.
For this, consorted with the citizens,
Your very worshipful and loving friends,
And by their vehement instigation,
In this just cause come I to move your Grace.

Know then that your fault is your rejection
of the highest seat, the majestic throne,
the ruling office of your ancestors,
your lucky state, and your birthright,
the ancestral glory of your royal house,
to allow a perverted line to take it;
while you indulge your mild unearthly thoughts–
which we now arouse for the good of the country–
the noble island is lacking her limbs;
her face is scarred with shame,
her royal stock has had low plants grafted to it,
and she has almost been pushed into the consuming gulf
of dark forgetfulness and deep oblivion;
to make things better, we earnestly ask
your gracious self to assume the responsibility
of governing this land of yours as a king,
not as Protector, steward, substitute,
or a low agent for someone else's profit,
but as your birthright, your territory, your own,
handed down through your bloodline.
Along with these citizens–
your very worshipful and loving friends,
and at their strong insistence–
I have come to persuade your Grace in this just cause.

RICHARD.
I cannot tell if to depart in silence
Or bitterly to speak in your reproof

Best fitteth my degree or your condition.
If not to answer, you might haply think
Tongue-tied ambition, not replying, yielded
To bear the golden yoke of sovereignty,
Which fondly you would here impose on me;
If to reprove you for this suit of yours,
So season'd with your faithful love to me,
Then, on the other side, I check'd my friends.
Therefore-to speak, and to avoid the first,
And then, in speaking, not to incur the last-
Definitively thus I answer you:
Your love deserves my thanks, but my desert
Unmeritable shuns your high request.
First, if all obstacles were cut away,
And that my path were even to the crown,
As the ripe revenue and due of birth,
Yet so much is my poverty of spirit,
So mighty and so many my defects,
That I would rather hide me from my greatness-
Being a bark to brook no mighty sea-
Than in my greatness covet to be hid,
And in the vapour of my glory smother'd.
But, God be thank'd, there is no need of me-
And much I need to help you, were there need.
The royal tree hath left us royal fruit
Which, mellow'd by the stealing hours of time,
Will well become the seat of majesty
And make, no doubt, us happy by his reign.
On him I lay that you would lay on me-
The right and fortune of his happy stars,
Which God defend that I should wring from him.

I can't decide if to leave in silence
or to bitterly reprimand you
would be most suited to my rank and your position.
If I didn't answer you might think
my ambition, by not replying, made me agree
to assume the golden burden of kingship
which you foolishly want to place on me;
if I reprimanded you for your request,
inspired as it is by your faithful love for me,
then, on the other hand, I might be insulting my friends.
So, I shall speak, and avoid the first accusation
and by speaking I shall avoid the last,

so I give you this definitive answer:
I must thank you for your love, but my
lack of merit rejects your great request.
Firstly, if there were no obstacles
to my taking the crown and I followed
my birthright to my inheritance,
my spirit is so poor,
I have so many great defects,
that I would rather reject my greatness–
I am a ship not made for the great oceans–
than cover my faults with greatness,
hide them beneath my glory.
But, thank God, you do not need me–
and I can't help you if you did.
The King has left descendants,
who, as they ripen over time,
will be well suited to the throne,
and no doubt make us happy in their reign.
I give to him what you want to give to me:
his rightful inheritance,
and God forfend that I should take it from him.

BUCKINGHAM.
My lord, this argues conscience in your
Grace;
But the respects thereof are nice and trivial,
All circumstances well considered.
You say that Edward is your brother's son.
So say we too, but not by Edward's wife;
For first was he contract to Lady Lucy-
Your mother lives a witness to his vow-
And afterward by substitute betroth'd
To Bona, sister to the King of France.
These both put off, a poor petitioner,
A care-craz'd mother to a many sons,
A beauty-waning and distressed widow,
Even in the afternoon of her best days,
Made prize and purchase of his wanton eye,
Seduc'd the pitch and height of his degree
To base declension and loath'd bigamy.
By her, in his unlawful bed, he got
This Edward, whom our manners call the Prince.
More bitterly could I expostulate,
Save that, for reverence to some alive,

I give a sparing limit to my tongue.
Then, good my lord, take to your royal self
This proffer'd benefit of dignity;
If not to bless us and the land withal,
Yet to draw forth your noble ancestry
From the corruption of abusing times
Unto a lineal true-derived course.

My Lord, this shows good feeling in your Grace;
but all things considered your objections
are slight and trivial.
You say that Edward is your brother's son:
and we agree—but not the son of his wife.
For he was first engaged to Lady Lucy
(your mother is a living witness to his promise),
and afterwards he was, through a stand-in, engaged
to Bona, sister of the King of France.
Avoiding both of these, a poor beggar,
the mother of many sons, mad through care,
a faded beauty, a distressed widow,
with her best days behind her,
managed to capture his lusty eye,
and seduce his great position
to low things and horrible bigamy.
In his unlawful bed he conceived through her
this Edward, whom we politely call the Prince.
I could speak more bitterly,
but respect for some people still alive
makes me curb my tongue.
So, my good lord, take to your royal self
the position which we offer you:
if not to do both us and the country good,
to lead your noble bloodline away
from the corruption of these bad times
back to the proper course of its descent.

MAYOR.
Do, good my lord; your citizens entreat you.

Do, my good lord; your citizens are begging you.

BUCKINGHAM.
Refuse not, mighty lord, this proffer'd love.

Don't refuse the love we offer you, mighty lord.

CATESBY.
O, make them joyful, grant their lawful suit!

Oh, give them joy, agree to their lawful requests!

RICHARD.
Alas, why would you heap this care on me?
I am unfit for state and majesty.
I do beseech you, take it not amiss:
I cannot nor I will not yield to you.

Alas, why do you want to load this burden on me?
I am not fit for kingship and for rule.
I beg you not to be offended:
I cannot and I will not agree.

BUCKINGHAM.
If you refuse it-as, in love and zeal,
Loath to depose the child, your brother's son;
As well we know your tenderness of heart
And gentle, kind, effeminate remorse,
Which we have noted in you to your kindred
And equally indeed to all estates-
Yet know, whe'er you accept our suit or no,
Your brother's son shall never reign our king;
But we will plant some other in the throne
To the disgrace and downfall of your house;
And in this resolution here we leave you.
Come, citizens. Zounds, I'll entreat no more.

If you refuse it–through love and piety,
not wanting to overthrow the child, the son of your brother;
we are well aware of your tender heart
and your gentle, kind, womanish penitence,
which we have seen you show to your family
and indeed just as much to all people–
you should know that whether you agree or not,
your brother's son shall never reign as our King;
we shall put someone else on the throne
which will lead to the disgrace and downfall of your house;
we shall leave you here and do this.
Come, citizens. By God, I shall beg no more.

RICHARD.
O, do not swear, my lord of Buckingham.

Oh, do not swear, my Lord of Buckingham!

Exeunt BUCKINGHAM, MAYOR, and citizens

CATESBY.
Call him again, sweet Prince, accept their suit.
If you deny them, all the land will rue it.

Call him back, sweet prince, accept their request.
If you refuse them, the whole country will regret it.

RICHARD.
Will you enforce me to a world of cares?
Call them again. I am not made of stones,
But penetrable to your kind entreaties,
Albeit against my conscience and my soul.

Re-enter BUCKINGHAM and the rest

Cousin of Buckingham, and sage grave men,
Since you will buckle fortune on my back,
To bear her burden, whe'er I will or no,
I must have patience to endure the load;
But if black scandal or foul-fac'd reproach
Attend the sequel of your imposition,
Your mere enforcement shall acquittance me
From all the impure blots and stains thereof;
For God doth know, and you may partly see,
How far I am from the desire of this.

Do you want me to accept a world of trouble?
Call them back. I am not made of stone,
but I am affected by your kind requests,
even though they are against my conscience and my soul.

My cousin Buckingham, and you wise respected men,
since you insist on placing this burden of fate
on my back, whether I want it or not,
I must be strong enough to accept it;
but if scandal or criticism comes my way

as a result of your imposition,
the fact that you have forced me shall make me
innocent of the dark stain of that;
for God knows, and you can partly see,
how much I do not want this.

MAYOR.
God bless your Grace! We see it, and will say it.

God bless your Grace! We can see it, and will tell everyone.

RICHARD.
In saying so, you shall but say the truth.

If you say it, you will only be telling the truth.

BUCKINGHAM.
Then I salute you with this royal title-
Long live King Richard, England's worthy King!

Then I salute you with this royal title–
Long live King Richard, England's worthy King!

ALL.
Amen.

Amen.

BUCKINGHAM.
To-morrow may it please you to be crown'd?

Will you agree to be crowned tomorrow?

RICHARD.
Even when you please, for you will have it so.

Whenever you want, it's you who wants it.

BUCKINGHAM.
To-morrow, then, we will attend your Grace;
And so, most joyfully, we take our leave.

Then tomorrow we will come to your Grace;
and so, with great joy, we shall leave you.

RICHARD.
[To the BISHOPS]Come, let us to our holy
work again.
Farewell, my cousin; farewell, gentle friends.

Come, let us return to our holy work.
Farewell, my cousin; farewell,kind friends.

Exeunt

ACT IV.

SCENE 1.

London. Before the Tower

Enter QUEEN ELIZABETH, DUCHESS of YORK, and MARQUIS of DORSET, at one door;
ANNE, DUCHESS of RICHARD, leading LADY MARGARET PLANTAGENET,
CLARENCE's young daughter, at another door

DUCHESS.
Who meets us here? My niece Plantagenet,
Led in the hand of her kind aunt of Gloucester?
Now, for my life, she's wand'ring to the Tower,
On pure heart's love, to greet the tender Princes.
Daughter, well met.

Who is this who meets us here? My niece Plantagenet,
led by the hand by her kind aunt Gloucester?
Now, I swear, she's going to the Tower,
out of pure love, to greet the young Princes.
Daughter, good to see you.

ANNE.
God give your Graces both
A happy and a joyful time of day!

May God give both your Graces
comfort and joy!

QUEEN ELIZABETH.
As much to you, good sister! Whither
away?

The same to you, good sister! Where are you going?

ANNE.
No farther than the Tower; and, as I guess,
Upon the like devotion as yourselves,
To gratulate the gentle Princes there.

182

Just as far as the Tower; and, I'm guessing,
on the same errand as yourselves,
to salute the young princes there.

QUEEN ELIZABETH.
Kind sister, thanks; we'll enter
all together.

Enter BRAKENBURY

And in good time, here the lieutenant comes.
Master Lieutenant, pray you, by your leave,
How doth the Prince, and my young son of York?

Thank you, kind sister; we'll all go in together.

And right on time, here comes the lieutenant.
Master Lieutenant, would you please tell me
how is the Prince, and my young son York?

BRAKENBURY.
Right well, dear madam. By your patience,
I may not suffer you to visit them.
The King hath strictly charg'd the contrary.

Very well, dear madam. If you'll excuse me,
I can't let you visit them.
The King has given strict orders.

QUEEN ELIZABETH.
The King! Who's that?

The King! Who's that?

BRAKENBURY.
I mean the Lord Protector.

I mean the Lord Protector.

QUEEN ELIZABETH.
The Lord protect him from that kingly
title!
Hath he set bounds between their love and me?
I am their mother; who shall bar me from them?

May the Lord protect him from taking the title of King!
Is he setting limits on the love between them and me?
I am their mother; who will keep me from them?

DUCHESS.
I am their father's mother; I will see them.

I am their father's mother; I insist on seeing them.

ANNE.
Their aunt I am in law, in love their mother.
Then bring me to their sights; I'll bear thy blame,
And take thy office from thee on my peril.

I am legally their aunt, but I love them like a mother.
Take me to see them; I'll take the blame for you,
and absolve you from any responsibility.

BRAKENBURY.
No, madam, no. I may not leave it so;
I am bound by oath, and therefore pardon me.

No, madam, no. This cannot be;
I am bound by oath, and so you must excuse me.

Exit

Enter STANLEY

STANLEY.
Let me but meet you, ladies, one hour hence,
And I'll salute your Grace of York as mother
And reverend looker-on of two fair queens.
[To ANNE]Come, madam, you must straight to Westminster,
There to be crowned Richard's royal queen.

If I only met you one hour later, ladies,
I would salute your Grace of York as mother
and revered observer of two lovely queens.
[To Anne] Come, madam, you must go straight to Westminster,
where you will be crowned as Richard's royal queen.

QUEEN ELIZABETH.
Ah, cut my lace asunder
That my pent heart may have some scope to beat,
Or else I swoon with this dead-killing news!

Oh, unlace my corset
so that my imprisoned heart can have room to beat,
otherwise I will faint at this fatal news.

ANNE.
Despiteful tidings! O unpleasing news!

Horrible report! Unpleasant news!

DORSET.
Be of good cheer; mother, how fares your Grace?

Be happy; mother, how are you?

QUEEN ELIZABETH.
O Dorset, speak not to me, get thee
gone!
Death and destruction dogs thee at thy heels;
Thy mother's name is ominous to children.
If thou wilt outstrip death, go cross the seas,
And live with Richmond, from the reach of hell.
Go, hie thee, hie thee from this slaughter-house,
Lest thou increase the number of the dead,
And make me die the thrall of Margaret's curse,
Nor mother, wife, nor England's counted queen.

Oh Dorset, do not speak to me, go away!
Death and destruction are pursuing you;
your mother's name is dangerous to children.
If you want to escape death, cross the sea,
go and live with Richmond, out of reach of hell.
Go, get away, get away from this slaughterhouse,
in case you increase the number of dead,
and make me die the way Margaret's curse predicted,
neither mother, wife, nor recognised Queen of England.

STANLEY.
Full of wise care is this your counsel, madam.
Take all the swift advantage of the hours;

You shall have letters from me to my son
In your behalf, to meet you on the way.
Be not ta'en tardy by unwise delay.

Your advice is full of loving wisdom, madam.
You should act as quickly as you can;
I shall give you letters of recommendation
to my son, I'll send them after you.
Don't be caught out by any foolish delay.

DUCHESS.
O ill-dispersing wind of misery!
O my accursed womb, the bed of death!
A cockatrice hast thou hatch'd to the world,
Whose unavoided eye is murderous.

Oh scattering wind of misery!
Oh my cursed womb, the bed of death!
You have released a basilisk into the world,
and to look him in the eye is death.

STANLEY.
Come, madam, come; I in all haste was sent.

Come, madam, come; I was told to hurry.

ANNE.
And I with all unwillingness will go.
O, would to God that the inclusive verge
Of golden metal that must round my brow
Were red-hot steel, to sear me to the brains!
Anointed let me be with deadly venom,
And die ere men can say 'God save the Queen!'

And I will go as unwillingly as you could imagine.
Oh, I wish to God that the circle of
gold metal that will surround my head
was red-hot steel, to burn my brains!
Let me be anointed with deadly poison,
so I can die before men can say 'God save the Queen!'

QUEEN ELIZABETH.
Go, go, poor soul; I envy not thy glory.
To feed my humour, wish thyself no harm.

Go, go, poor soul; I do not envy your glory.
For my sake, do not wish harm upon yourself.

ANNE.
No, why? When he that is my husband now
Came to me, as I follow'd Henry's corse;
When scarce the blood was well wash'd from his hands
Which issued from my other angel husband,
And that dear saint which then I weeping follow'd-
O, when, I say, I look'd on Richard's face,
This was my wish: 'Be thou' quoth I 'accurs'd
For making me, so young, so old a widow;
And when thou wed'st, let sorrow haunt thy bed;
And be thy wife, if any be so mad,
More miserable by the life of thee
Than thou hast made me by my dear lord's death.'
Lo, ere I can repeat this curse again,
Within so small a time, my woman's heart
Grossly grew captive to his honey words
And prov'd the subject of mine own soul's curse,
Which hitherto hath held my eyes from rest;
For never yet one hour in his bed
Did I enjoy the golden dew of sleep,
But with his timorous dreams was still awak'd.
Besides, he hates me for my father Warwick;
And will, no doubt, shortly be rid of me.

Why not? When the one who is now my husband
came to me as I followed Henry's body,
when the blood has hardly been washed from his hands
which came from my other angelic husband,
that dear saint whom I was following, weeping;
when, I tell you, I looked on Richard's face
this is what I wished: 'May you', I said, 'be cursed
for making me, so young, such an old widow;
and when you marry, may sorrow attend your bed;
and may your wife–if anyone is mad enough to marry you–
be made more miserable by you
then you have made me through killing my dear Lord.'
Then in the time it took me to say this curse,
such a short time, my woman's heart
was disgracefully taken in by his sweet words,
and made myself the subject of my own soul's curse,

and I have never had a moment's sleep since then;
for there hasn't been a single hour in his bed
when I was enjoying the golden blessing of sleep
that I have been awoken by his evil dreams.
Besides, he hates me because my father was Warwick,
and he will no doubt shortly rid himself of me.

QUEEN ELIZABETH.
Poor heart, adieu! I pity thy complaining.

Poor dear, goodbye! I sympathise with your sorrow.

ANNE.
No more than with my soul I mourn for yours.

No more than I mourn for your soul with mine.

DORSET.
Farewell, thou woeful welcomer of glory!

Farewell, you sad recipient of glory!

ANNE.
Adieu, poor soul, that tak'st thy leave of it!

Goodbye, poor soul, who is leaving it!

DUCHESS.
[To DORSET]Go thou to Richmond, and good
fortune guide thee!
[To ANNE]Go thou to Richard, and good angels tend
thee![To QUEEN ELIZABETH]Go thou to sanctuary, and good
thoughts possess thee!
I to my grave, where peace and rest lie with me!
Eighty odd years of sorrow have I seen,
And each hour's joy wreck'd with a week of teen.

[To Dorset] Go to Richmond, and may good fortune guide you!
[To Anne] You go to Richard, and may good angels watch over you!
[To Queen Elizabeth] You seek sanctuary, and may you be
full of good thoughts!
I am going to my grave, and let peace and rest find me there!
I have seen eighty odd years of sorrow,
and every hour of joy has been matched by a week of misery.

QUEEN ELIZABETH.
Stay, yet look back with me unto the
Tower.
Pity, you ancient stones, those tender babes
Whom envy hath immur'd within your walls,
Rough cradle for such little pretty ones.
Rude ragged nurse, old sullen playfellow
For tender princes, use my babies well.
So foolish sorrows bids your stones farewell.

Wait, look back at the Tower with me.
You ancient stones, pity those tender children
whom envy has imprisoned within your walls,
a rough cradle for such pretty little ones.
Rough and rugged nurse, sullen old play fellow
for tender Princes, treat my babies well.
And so foolish sorrow says farewell to your stones.

Exeunt

SCENE 2.

London. The palace

Sound a sennet. Enter RICHARD, in pomp, as KING; BUCKINGHAM,
CATESBY,
RATCLIFF, LOVEL, a PAGE, and others

KING RICHARD.
Stand all apart. Cousin of Buckingham!

Everyone stand aside. Cousin Buckingham!

BUCKINGHAM.
My gracious sovereign?

My sweet King?

KING RICHARD.
Give me thy hand.
[Here he ascendeth the throne. Sound]
Thus high, by thy advice
And thy assistance, is King Richard seated.
But shall we wear these glories for a day;
Or shall they last, and we rejoice in them?

Give me your hand.
[He climbs onto the throne. Trumpets.]
So King Richard is seated on high
on your advice and with your help.
But shall I have this glory for a day,
or will it last for me to enjoy it?

BUCKINGHAM.
Still live they, and for ever let them last!

They are still living, and let them live forever!

KING RICHARD.
Ah, Buckingham, now do I play the touch,

To try if thou be current gold indeed.
Young Edward lives-think now what I would speak.

Ah, Buckingham, now I'm going to test
you to see if you are really true.
Young Edward is alive–what do you think I'm going to say?

BUCKINGHAM.
Say on, my loving lord.

Keep talking, my dear lord.

KING RICHARD.
Why, Buckingham, I say I would be King.

Why, Buckingham, I say I want to be king.

BUCKINGHAM.
Why, so you are, my thrice-renowned lord.

Well, you are, my triply famous lord.

KING RICHARD.
Ha! am I King? 'Tis so; but Edward lives.

Ha! Am I king? I am; but Edward is alive.

BUCKINGHAM.
True, noble Prince.

True, noble Prince.

KING RICHARD.
O bitter consequence:
That Edward still should live-true noble Prince!
Cousin, thou wast not wont to be so dull.
Shall I be plain? I wish the bastards dead,
And I would have it suddenly perform'd.
What say'st thou now? Speak suddenly, be brief.

This is what I find so horrible:
that Edward should still be alive, a true noble Prince!
Cousin, you're not usually so dull-witted.
Shall I be clear? I want the bastards dead,

and I want it done quickly.
Now what you say? Speak quickly, be brief.

BUCKINGHAM.
Your Grace may do your pleasure.

Your grace may do as he wishes.

KING RICHARD.
Tut, tut, thou art all ice; thy kindness freezes.
Say, have I thy consent that they shall die?

Tut tut, you are like ice; your kindness is freezing.
Tell me if you agree that they shall die?

BUCKINGHAM.
Give me some little breath, some pause,
dear Lord,
Before I positively speak in this.
I will resolve you herein presently.

Give me a little breathing space, a pause, dear lord,
before I give you a definitive answer.
I shall do that shortly.

Exit

CATESBY.
[Aside to another]The King is angry; see, he
gnaws his lip.

The King is angry; look, he's chewing his lip.

KING RICHARD.
I will converse with iron-witted fools
[Descends from the throne]
And unrespective boys; none are for me
That look into me with considerate eyes.
High-reaching Buckingham grows circumspect.
Boy!

I have to talk to stupid fools
and disrespectful boys; there's nobody on my side
who looks at me with prudent eyes.

Haughty Buckingham is becoming cautious.
Boy!

PAGE.
My lord?

My lord?

KING RICHARD.
Know'st thou not any whom corrupting
gold
Will tempt unto a close exploit of death?

Don't you know anyone who can be bribed with gold
to commit murder?

PAGE.
I know a discontented gentleman
Whose humble means match not his haughty spirit.
Gold were as good as twenty orators,
And will, no doubt, tempt him to anything.

I know a discontented gentleman
who does not have the money to match his arrogant spirit.
To him gold is as persuasive as
twenty orators, and I've nodoubt he'll do anything for it.

KING RICHARD.
What is his name?

What is his name?

PAGE.
His name, my lord, is Tyrrel.

His name, my lord, is Tyrrel.

KING RICHARD.
I partly know the man. Go, call him hither,
boy. Exit PAGE
The deep-revolving witty Buckingham
No more shall be the neighbour to my counsels.
Hath he so long held out with me, untir'd,
And stops he now for breath? Well, be it so.

Enter STANLEY

How now, Lord Stanley! What's the news?

I know something of the man. Go and summon him here, boy.

The plotting and clever Buckingham
shall no longer be my confidant.
How has he kept up with me for so long, without tiring,
that now he wants to pause for breath? Well, so be it.

Hello there, Lord Stanley! What's the news?

STANLEY.
Know, my loving lord,
The Marquis Dorset, as I hear, is fled
To Richmond, in the parts where he abides.

You should know, my dear lord,
that the Marquis Dorset, so I hear, has run
to Richmond, in the country where he lives.

[Stands apart]

KING RICHARD.
Come hither, Catesby. Rumour it abroad
That Anne, my wife, is very grievous sick;
I will take order for her keeping close.
Inquire me out some mean poor gentleman,
Whom I will marry straight to Clarence' daughter-
The boy is foolish, and I fear not him.
Look how thou dream'st! I say again, give out
That Anne, my queen, is sick and like to die.
About it; for it stands me much upon
To stop all hopes whose growth may damage me.
Exit CATESBY
I must be married to my brother's daughter,
Or else my kingdom stands on brittle glass.
Murder her brothers, and then marry her!
Uncertain way of gain! But I am in
So far in blood that sin will pluck on sin.
Tear-falling pity dwells not in this eye.

Re-enter PAGE, with TYRREL

Is thy name Tyrrel?

Come here, Catesby. Put round a rumour
that Anne, my wife, is very seriously ill;
I will order her to be confined.
Find me some lowborn gentleman,
and I will marry him at once to Clarence's daughter–
the boy is stupid, and I am not afraid of him.
Pull yourself together! I'm telling you, tell people
that Anne, my queen, is ill and looks like dying.
Get on with it; it's very necessary for me
to nip in the bud the hopes of anyone who can damage me.

I must marry my brother's daughter,
or otherwise my kingdom is on quicksand.
To murder her brothers, and then marry her–
it's not a certain way of winning! But I have shed
so much blood that one sin will assist another;
there are no tears of pity in these eyes.

Is your name Tyrrel?

TYRREL.
James Tyrrel, and your most obedient subject.

James Tyrrel, and your most obedient subject.

KING RICHARD.
Art thou, indeed?

Are you, really?

TYRREL.
Prove me, my gracious lord.

Test me, my gracious lord.

KING RICHARD.
Dar'st'thou resolve to kill a friend of mine?

Would you dare to agree to kill a friend of mine?

TYRREL.
Please you;
But I had rather kill two enemies.

If you wanted;
but I would rather kill two enemies.

KING RICHARD.
Why, then thou hast it. Two deep enemies,
Foes to my rest, and my sweet sleep's disturbers,
Are they that I would have thee deal upon.
Tyrrel, I mean those bastards in the Tower.

Well, then you have your wish. Two great enemies,
disturbers of my sleep, enemies of my rest,
are the ones I want you to do this to.
Tyrrel, I mean those bastards in the tower.

TYRREL.
Let me have open means to come to them,
And soon I'll rid you from the fear of them.

Give me the opportunity to get at them,
and soon you won't have to worry about them any more.

KING RICHARD.
Thou sing'st sweet music. Hark, come
hither, Tyrrel.
Go, by this token. Rise, and lend thine ear.[Whispers]
There is no more but so: say it is done,
And I will love thee and prefer thee for it.

You're singing sweet music. Listen, come here, Tyrrel.
Go, with this token. Get up, and listen. [Whispers]
That's all there is to it: once you tell me it's done
I will love you and promote you for it.

TYRREL.
I will dispatch it straight.

I'll do it at once.

Exit

Re-enter BUCKINGHAM

BUCKINGHAM.
My lord, I have consider'd in my mind
The late request that you did sound me in.

*My Lord, I have been thinking about
the matter you recently asked me about.*

KING RICHARD.
Well, let that rest. Dorset is fled to
Richmond.

Don't worry about that. Dorset has fled to Richmond.

BUCKINGHAM.
I hear the news, my lord.

I heard the news, my lord.

KING RICHARD.
Stanley, he is your wife's son: well, look
unto it.

Stanley, Richmond is your wife's son: deal with it.

BUCKINGHAM.
My lord, I claim the gift, my due by promise,
For which your honour and your faith is pawn'd:
Th' earldom of Hereford and the movables
Which you have promised I shall possess.

*My lord, I claim the gift, which you promised to me,
the price of your honour and your faith:
the earldom of Hereford and the portable possessions
which you promised I should have.*

KING RICHARD.
Stanley, look to your wife; if she convey
Letters to Richmond, you shall answer it.

*Stanley, watch out for your wife; if she sends
letters to Richmond, you shall pay for it.*

BUCKINGHAM.
What says your Highness to my just request?

What does your Highness say to my fair request?

KING RICHARD.
I do remember me: Henry the Sixth
Did prophesy that Richmond should be King,
When Richmond was a little peevish boy.
A king!-perhaps-

I call to mind that Henry the sixth
prophesied that Richmond should be king,
when Richmond was just a little brat.
A king!–Perhaps–

BUCKINGHAM.
My lord-

My lord–

KING RICHARD.
How chance the prophet could not at that
time
Have told me, I being by, that I should kill him?

Why didn't the prophet tell me at that time
as I was standing by, that I would kill him?

BUCKINGHAM.
My lord, your promise for the earldom-

My lord, you promised me the earldom–

KING RICHARD.
Richmond! When last I was at Exeter,
The mayor in courtesy show'd me the castle
And call'd it Rugemount, at which name I started,
Because a bard of Ireland told me once
I should not live long after I saw Richmond.

Richmond! Last time I was at Exeter
the mayor, out of courtesy, showed me the castle
and called it Rougemont, and the name made me jump,

because an Irish poet once told me
that I would not live for long after I had seen Richmond.

BUCKINGHAM.
My lord-

My Lord–

KING RICHARD.
Ay, what's o'clock?

Yes, what's the time?

BUCKINGHAM.
I am thus bold to put your Grace in mind
Of what you promis'd me.

I should like to remind your Grace
of what you promised me.

KING RICHARD.
Well, but o'clock?

Yes, but what's the time?

BUCKINGHAM.
Upon the stroke of ten.

Just coming up to ten.

KING RICHARD.
Well, let it strike.

Well, let it strike.

BUCKINGHAM.
Why let it strike?

Why let it strike?

KING RICHARD.
Because that like a Jack thou keep'st the stroke
Betwixt thy begging and my meditation.

I am not in the giving vein to-day.

Because you're like a bell that's ringing
between your begging and my thoughts.
I am not in the mood for giving today.

BUCKINGHAM.
May it please you to resolve me in my suit.

Could you please grant what I ask.

KING RICHARD.
Thou troublest me; I am not in the vein.

You're bothering me; I'm not in the mood.

Exeunt all but Buckingham

BUCKINGHAM.
And is it thus? Repays he my deep service
With such contempt? Made I him King for this?
O, let me think on Hastings, and be gone
To Brecknock while my fearful head is on!

That's it, is it? He's repaying my great service
with contempt? Did I make him king for this?
O, let me remember Hastings, and go
to Brecknock while I still have my fearful head!

Exit

SCENE 3.

London. The palace

Enter TYRREL

TYRREL.
The tyrannous and bloody act is done,
The most arch deed of piteous massacre
That ever yet this land was guilty of.
Dighton and Forrest, who I did suborn
To do this piece of ruthless butchery,
Albeit they were flesh'd villains, bloody dogs,
Melted with tenderness and mild compassion,
Wept like two children in their deaths' sad story.
'O, thus' quoth Dighton 'lay the gentle babes'-
'Thus, thus,' quoth Forrest 'girdling one another
Within their alabaster innocent arms.
Their lips were four red roses on a stalk,
And in their summer beauty kiss'd each other.
A book of prayers on their pillow lay;
Which once,' quoth Forrest 'almost chang'd my mind;
But, O, the devil'-there the villain stopp'd;
When Dighton thus told on: 'We smothered
The most replenished sweet work of nature
That from the prime creation e'er she framed.'
Hence both are gone with conscience and remorse
They could not speak; and so I left them both,
To bear this tidings to the bloody King.

Enter KING RICHARD

And here he comes. All health, my sovereign lord!

The terrible and bloody act is done;
the most shocking deed of pitiful slaughter
that this country has ever seen.
Dighton and Forrest, whom I employed
to commit this act of ruthless luxury–
even though they were hardened villains, bloody dogs–

broke down with tenderness and soft compassion,
they wept like two children, telling the story of their deaths.
Dighton said, 'The gentle babies lay like this';
'Like this, like this', said Forrest, 'hugging one another
with their innocent spotless arms;
their lips were like four red roses on a stalk
kissing each other in their summer beauty.
There was a book of prayers lying on their pillow,
which almost', Forrest said, 'changed my mind.
But oh, the devil–' the villain stopped there,
and Dighton continued: 'We smothered the most perfect thing
that nature ever made from the perfection of creation.'
They have both gone away full of conscience and remorse;
they could not speak, and so I left them both
to bring the murderous King the news;

and here he comes. Your health, your Majesty.

KING RICHARD.
Kind Tyrrel, am I happy in thy news?

Kind Tyrrel, do you have news to make me happy?

TYRREL.
If to have done the thing you gave in charge
Beget your happiness, be happy then,
For it is done.

If having done the thing you ordered
will make you happy, then be happy,
for it is done.

KING RICHARD.
But didst thou see them dead?

But did you see them dead?

TYRREL.
I did, my lord.

I did, my lord.

KING RICHARD.
And buried, gentle Tyrrel?

And buried, kind Tyrrel?

TYRREL.
The chaplain of the Tower hath buried them;
But where, to say the truth, I do not know.

The chaplain of the Tower has buried them;
but to tell the truth I don't know where.

KING RICHARD.
Come to me, Tyrrel, soon at after supper,
When thou shalt tell the process of their death.
Meantime, but think how I may do thee good
And be inheritor of thy desire.
Farewell till then.

Come to me, Tyrrel, after supper,
and you shall tell me how they died.
In the meantime, just think of what you'd like me to do for you,
and you shall have it.
Farewell until then.

TYRREL.
I humbly take my leave.

I humbly take my leave.

Exit

KING RICHARD.
The son of Clarence have I pent up close;
His daughter meanly have I match'd in marriage;
The sons of Edward sleep in Abraham's bosom,
And Anne my wife hath bid this world good night.
Now, for I know the Britaine Richmond aims
At young Elizabeth, my brother's daughter,
And by that knot looks proudly on the crown,
To her go I, a jolly thriving wooer.

I have got Clarence's son in custody;
I have matched his daughter in a mean marriage;
the sons of Edward dead,
and my wife Anne has said good night to the world.

Now, as I know that Richmond from Brittany has intentions
upon the young Elizabeth, the daughter of my brother,
and hopes through that marriage to gain the crown,
then off I go to see her, a jolly prosperous suitor.

Enter RATCLIFF

RATCLIFF.
My lord!

My lord!

KING RICHARD.
Good or bad news, that thou com'st in so
bluntly?

Is it good or bad news that has you barging in?

RATCLIFF.
Bad news, my lord: Morton is fled to Richmond;
And Buckingham, back'd with the hardy Welshmen,
Is in the field, and still his power increaseth.

Bad news, my lord: Morton has fled to Richmond;
and Buckingham, supported by the strong Welshmen,
is threatening battle, and his forces are increasing.

KING RICHARD.
Ely with Richmond troubles me more near
Than Buckingham and his rash-levied strength.
Come, I have learn'd that fearful commenting
Is leaden servitor to dull delay;
Delay leads impotent and snail-pac'd beggary.
Then fiery expedition be my wing,
Jove's Mercury, and herald for a king!
Go, muster men. My counsel is my shield.
We must be brief when traitors brave the field.

Ely allied to Richmond worries me more
than Buckingham and his quickly raised forces.
Come: I have learned that nervous discussion
is what leads to stupid delay;
delay leads to powerless slow defeat:
so let me take fiery swift action,

which will announce the arrival of the king into battle!
Go, gather forces. My weapons will be my advisers.
We must hurry when traitors are on the attack.

Exeunt

SCENE 4.

London. Before the palace

Enter old QUEEN MARGARET

QUEEN MARGARET.
So now prosperity begins to mellow
And drop into the rotten mouth of death.
Here in these confines slily have I lurk'd
To watch the waning of mine enemies.
A dire induction am I witness to,
And will to France, hoping the consequence
Will prove as bitter, black, and tragical.
Withdraw thee, wretched Margaret. Who comes here?

So now the fruit of summer begins to mellow
and drop into the rotten mouth of death.
I have cunningly hidden round these parts
to watchmy enemies fall.
I have seen a terrible prologue,
and shall go to France, hoping the outcome
will be as bitter, black and tragic as the beginning.
Hide yourself, wretched Margaret. Who is this coming?

[Retires]

Enter QUEEN ELIZABETH and the DUCHESS OF YORK

QUEEN ELIZABETH.
Ah, my poor princes! ah, my tender
babes!
My unblown flowers, new-appearing sweets!
If yet your gentle souls fly in the air
And be not fix'd in doom perpetual,
Hover about me with your airy wings
And hear your mother's lamentation.

Ah, my poor Princes! Ah, my tender babies!
My immature flowers, my newly opened blossoms!

If your gentle souls are still flying in the air
and have not yet been allocated their place in the afterlife,
hover around me with your fairy wings
and hear your mother's lamentation.

QUEEN MARGARET.
Hover about her; say that right for right
Hath dimm'd your infant morn to aged night.

Hover around her; say that tit for tat
is what has made a night out of your infant morning.

DUCHESS.
So many miseries have craz'd my voice
That my woe-wearied tongue is still and mute.
Edward Plantagenet, why art thou dead?

So many miseries have cracked my voice
that my sorrowful tongue is mute.
Edward Plantagenet, why are you dead?

QUEEN MARGARET.
Plantagenet doth quit Plantagenet,
Edward for Edward pays a dying debt.

Plantagenet has paid back Plantagenet,
Edward has paid a dying debt for Edward.

QUEEN ELIZABETH.
Wilt thou, O God, fly from such gentle
lambs
And throw them in the entrails of the wolf?
When didst thou sleep when such a deed was done?

Will you, O God, abandon such gentle lambs
and allow them to be eaten by the wolf?
When were you sleeping when this deed was done?

QUEEN MARGARET.
When holy Harry died, and my sweet
son.

When holy Harry died, and my sweet son.

DUCHESS.
Dead life, blind sight, poor mortal living ghost,
Woe's scene, world's shame, grave's due by life usurp'd,
Brief abstract and record of tedious days,
Rest thy unrest on England's lawful earth,[Sitting down]
Unlawfully made drunk with innocent blood.

Life is dead, sight is blind, poor mortal living ghost,
the picture of woe, the shame of the world, what should be in the grave still living,
symbol of these terrible days,
rest your misery on the lawful earth of England,
made unlawfully drunk with innocent blood.

QUEEN ELIZABETH.
Ah, that thou wouldst as soon afford a
grave
As thou canst yield a melancholy seat!
Then would I hide my bones, not rest them here.
Ah, who hath any cause to mourn but we?

Ah, I wish you could as easily provide a grave
as you can a seat of sadness!
Then I would hide my bones away, not just rest them here.
Ah, who has any reason to mourn but us?

[Sitting down by her]

QUEEN MARGARET.
[Coming forward]If ancient sorrow be
most reverend,
Give mine the benefit of seniory,
And let my griefs frown on the upper hand.
If sorrow can admit society,[Sitting down with them]
Tell o'er your woes again by viewing mine.
I had an Edward, till a Richard kill'd him;
I had a husband, till a Richard kill'd him:
Thou hadst an Edward, till a Richard kill'd him;
Thou hadst a Richard, till a Richard kill'd him.

If the oldest sorrow is the most respected,
give mine the benefits of seniority,
and let my grief look down on yours from above.
If sorrow can cope with company,
you can see all yours again in mine.

208

I had an Edward, until a Richard killed him;
I had a husband, until a Richard killed him;
you had an Edward, until a Richard killed him;
you had a Richard, until a Richard killed him.

DUCHESS.
I had a Richard too, and thou didst kill him;
I had a Rutland too, thou holp'st to kill him.

I had a Richard too, and you killed him;
I had a Rutland too, you helped to kill him.

QUEEN MARGARET.
Thou hadst a Clarence too, and Richard
kill'd him.
From forth the kennel of thy womb hath crept
A hell-hound that doth hunt us all to death.
That dog, that had his teeth before his eyes
To worry lambs and lap their gentle blood,
That foul defacer of God's handiwork,
That excellent grand tyrant of the earth
That reigns in galled eyes of weeping souls,
Thy womb let loose to chase us to our graves.
O upright, just, and true-disposing God,
How do I thank thee that this carnal cur
Preys on the issue of his mother's body
And makes her pew-fellow with others' moan!

You also have a Clarence, and Richard killed him.
From out of the kennel of your womb there has crept
a hell hound that is hunting us all to death.
That dog, that grew teeth before it grew eyes,
to worry lambs and drink their gentle blood,
that foul vandaliser of God's handiwork,
that unparalleled earthly tyrant
who rules in the sore eyes of weeping souls,
that was what your womb unleashed to chase us to our graves.
O upright, just and fair dealing God,
how I thank you that this lusty cur
is preying on his mother's other children
and makes her sit down with her fellow sufferers.

DUCHESS.
O Harry's wife, triumph not in my woes!

God witness with me, I have wept for thine.

Oh wife of Harry, do not rejoice in my sorrow!
As God is my witness, I wept for yours.

QUEEN MARGARET.
Bear with me; I am hungry for revenge,
And now I cloy me with beholding it.
Thy Edward he is dead, that kill'd my Edward;
The other Edward dead, to quit my Edward;
Young York he is but boot, because both they
Match'd not the high perfection of my loss.
Thy Clarence he is dead that stabb'd my Edward;
And the beholders of this frantic play,
Th' adulterate Hastings, Rivers, Vaughan, Grey,
Untimely smother'd in their dusky graves.
Richard yet lives, hell's black intelligencer;
Only reserv'd their factor to buy souls
And send them thither. But at hand, at hand,
Ensues his piteous and unpitied end.
Earth gapes, hell burns, fiends roar, saints pray,
To have him suddenly convey'd from hence.
Cancel his bond of life, dear God, I pray,
That I may live and say 'The dog is dead.'

Bear with me; I am hungry for revenge,
and I am feeding myself as I see it.
Your Edward who killed my Edward is dead;
the other Edward is dead, to pay for my Edward;
young York is just small change, because together
they did not add up to the high perfection of the one I lost.
Your Clarence is dead who stabbed my Edward;
and the ones who looked on at this vicious event,
the adulterous Hastings, Rivers, Vaughan, Grey,
have found early deaths in their dark graves.
Richard, the black spy of hell, is still alive;
hell keeps him as its agent to buy souls
and send them there. But soon, soon,
he will meet his terrible and un-pitied end.
Earth is opening, hell burns, devils roar, saints pray,
all wanting him to be suddenly carried away from here.
Don't permit him any more life, dear God, I pray,
so that I can live and say 'The dog is dead.'

QUEEN ELIZABETH.
O, thou didst prophesy the time would
come
That I should wish for thee to help me curse
That bottled spider, that foul bunch-back'd toad!

Oh, you did prophesy that the time would come
when I would ask for you to help me curse
that swollen spider, that foul hunchbacked toad!

QUEEN MARGARET.
I Call'd thee then vain flourish of my
fortune;
I call'd thee then poor shadow, painted queen,
The presentation of but what I was,
The flattering index of a direful pageant,
One heav'd a-high to be hurl'd down below,
A mother only mock'd with two fair babes,
A dream of what thou wast, a garish flag
To be the aim of every dangerous shot,
A sign of dignity, a breath, a bubble,
A queen in jest, only to fill the scene.
Where is thy husband now? Where be thy brothers?
Where be thy two sons? Wherein dost thou joy?
Who sues, and kneels, and says 'God save the Queen'?
Where be the bending peers that flattered thee?
Where be the thronging troops that followed thee?
Decline an this, and see what now thou art:
For happy wife, a most distressed widow;
For joyful mother, one that wails the name;
For one being su'd to, one that humbly sues;
For Queen, a very caitiff crown'd with care;
For she that scorn'd at me, now scorn'd of me;
For she being fear'd of all, now fearing one;
For she commanding all, obey'd of none.
Thus hath the course of justice whirl'd about
And left thee but a very prey to time,
Having no more but thought of what thou wast
To torture thee the more, being what thou art.
Thou didst usurp my place, and dost thou not
Usurp the just proportion of my sorrow?
Now thy proud neck bears half my burden'd yoke,
From which even here I slip my weary head
And leave the burden of it all on thee.

Farewell, York's wife, and queen of sad mischance;
These English woes shall make me smile in France.

At that time I called you a vain imitation of what I should be;
I called you a poor shadow, a painted queen,
just an imitation of what I had been;
a predictive prologue to the pageant of terrible things to come;
you were one lifted up high, to be hurled down;
a mother mocked by being given two fair babies;
a dream of what you were; a gaudy flag
for every dangerous shot to aim at;
a symbol of dignity; a breath, a bubble;
a joke Queen, just to complete the picture.
Where is your husband now? Where are your brothers?
Where are your two sons? Where do you get happiness?
Who begs, and kneels, and says 'God save the Queen'?
Where are the bowing peers who flattered you?
Where are the crowds of troops who followed you?
Think about all this, and see what you are now:
the huppy wife is now a terribly distressed widow;
the joyful mother who wails for her children;
someone who was begged who is now a humble beggar;
a queen who has become an outcast, her only crown is sorrow;
the one who scorned me is now scorned by me;
the one who was feared by everyone is now afraid of one;
she who used to command everything is now obeyed by no one.
So the wheel of justice has spun around
and left you a victim of time,
left with nothing but memories of what you were
to torture you more, being what you are.
You stole my place, and now do you not
steal your fair share of my sorrow?
Now your proud neck carries half of my burden,
and right now I take away my tired head
and leave you to manage all of it.
Farewell, York's wife, the Queen of sorrowful bad luck;
your English woes will make me smile in France.

QUEEN ELIZABETH.
O thou well skill'd in curses, stay awhile
And teach me how to curse mine enemies!

You are so good at curses, stay a while
and teach me how to curse my enemies!

212

QUEEN MARGARET.
Forbear to sleep the nights, and fast the
days;
Compare dead happiness with living woe;
Think that thy babes were sweeter than they were,
And he that slew them fouler than he is.
Bett'ring thy loss makes the bad-causer worse;
Revolving this will teach thee how to curse.

Do not sleep at night, and do not eat in the day;
compare your dead happiness with your living sorrows;
imagine that your babies were sweeter than they were,
and the one who killed them is fouler than he is.
Making your loss seem greater makes the one who caused it seem worse;
thinking of this will teach you how to curse.

QUEEN ELIZABETH.
My words are dull; O, quicken them
with thine!

My words are dull; oh, sharpen them with yours!

QUEEN MARGARET.
Thy woes will make them sharp and
pierce like mine.

Your sorrows will sharpen them and make them stab like mine.

Exit

DUCHESS.
Why should calamity be full of words?

Why must disaster be full of words?

QUEEN ELIZABETH.
Windy attorneys to their client woes,
Airy succeeders of intestate joys,
Poor breathing orators of miseries,
Let them have scope; though what they will impart
Help nothing else, yet do they ease the heart.

They are the windy lawyers of their client sorrows,

airy inheritors of intestate happiness,
the poor breathing speakers of misery,
let them run free; even if what they say
helps nothing else, they can ease the heart.

DUCHESS.
If so, then be not tongue-tied. Go with me,
And in the breath of bitter words let's smother
My damned son that thy two sweet sons smother'd.
The trumpet sounds; be copious in exclaims.

If that's true, then let your speech out. Come with me,
and with a gale of bitter words let's smother
my damned son who smothered your two sweet sons.
The trumpet sounds; be profligate with your curses.

Enter KING RICHARD and his train, marching with
drums and trumpets

KING RICHARD.
Who intercepts me in my expedition?

Who intercepts me on my journey?

DUCHESS.
O, she that might have intercepted thee,
By strangling thee in her accursed womb,
From all the slaughters, wretch, that thou hast done!

Oh, she who might have intercepted you
by strangling you in her cursed womb,
and prevented all the slaughters, wretch, you have committed!

QUEEN ELIZABETH.
Hidest thou that forehead with a golden
crown
Where't should be branded, if that right were right,
The slaughter of the Prince that ow'd that crown,
And the dire death of my poor sons and brothers?
Tell me, thou villain slave, where are my children?

Are you hiding your forehead with a golden crown,
where you should be branded, if there was any justice,
with the slaughter of the Prince who owned that Crown,

and the terrible death of my poor sons and brothers?
Tell me, you slavish villain, where are my children?

DUCHESS.
Thou toad, thou toad, where is thy brother
Clarence?
And little Ned Plantagenet, his son?

You toad, you toad, where is your brother Clarence?
And little Ned Plantagenet, his son?

QUEEN ELIZABETH.
Where is the gentle Rivers, Vaughan,
Grey?

Where are the gentle Rivers, Vaughan and Grey?

DUCHESS.
Where is kind Hastings?

Where is kind Hastings?

KING RICHARD.
A flourish, trumpets! Strike alarum, drums!
Let not the heavens hear these tell-tale women
Rail on the Lord's anointed. Strike, I say!
[Flourish. Alarums]
Either be patient and entreat me fair,
Or with the clamorous report of war
Thus will I drown your exclamations.

Blow the trumpets! Sound the alarm, drums!
Don't let the heavens hear these tell-tale women
insulting the Lord's anointed. Sound, I say!

Either be calm and speak to me nicely,
or I will drown out everything you say
with these warlike noises.

DUCHESS.
Art thou my son?

Are you my son?

KING RICHARD.
Ay, I thank God, my father, and yourself.

Yes, I thank God, I am made from my father and yourself.

DUCHESS.
Then patiently hear my impatience.

Then listen patiently to my anger.

KING RICHARD.
Madam, I have a touch of your condition
That cannot brook the accent of reproof.

*Madam, I have some of your characteristic
of not being able to listen to reprimands.*

DUCHESS.
O, let me speak!

O, let me speak!

KING RICHARD.
Do, then; but I'll not hear.

Speak then, but I won't listen.

DUCHESS.
I will be mild and gentle in my words.

I will be sweet and kind with my words.

KING RICHARD.
And brief, good mother; for I am in haste.

And brief, good mother, for I am in a hurry.

DUCHESS.
Art thou so hasty? I have stay'd for thee,
God knows, in torment and in agony.

*Are you in such a hurry? I waited for you,
God knows, in tortured agony.*

KING RICHARD.
And came I not at last to comfort you?

And didn't I come in the end to comfort you?

DUCHESS.
No, by the holy rood, thou know'st it well
Thou cam'st on earth to make the earth my hell.
A grievous burden was thy birth to me;
Tetchy and wayward was thy infancy;
Thy school-days frightful, desp'rate, wild, and furious;
Thy prime of manhood daring, bold, and venturous;
Thy age confirm'd, proud, subtle, sly, and bloody,
More mild, but yet more harmful-kind in hatred.
What comfortable hour canst thou name
That ever grac'd me with thy company?

No, by the holy blood, you know well
that you came on earth to make it hell for me.
Your birth was a terrible burden for me;
as a child you were tetchy and disobedient;
your school days were terrible, desperate, wild and furious;
in the prime of your manhood you were daring, bold and adventurous;
as you got older you became proud, cunning, sly and bloodthirsty,
less aggressive, but more deceitfully spiteful in your hatred.
Can you name me one hour
that you ever gave me of your company?

KING RICHARD.
Faith, none but Humphrey Hour, that call'd
your Grace
To breakfast once forth of my company.
If I be so disgracious in your eye,
Let me march on and not offend you, madam.
Strike up the drum.

Only Humphrey Hour, a member of my company
who once called your Grace to come to breakfast.
If I am so unpleasing to your eye,
let me march on and not offend you, madam.
Strike up the drum.

DUCHESS.
I prithee hear me speak.

I pray you to listen to me.

KING RICHARD.
You speak too bitterly.

You speak too bitterly.

DUCHESS.
Hear me a word;
For I shall never speak to thee again.

Just listen to a word from me;
For I shall never speak to you again.

KING RICHARD.
So.

Very well.

DUCHESS.
Either thou wilt die by God's just ordinance
Ere from this war thou turn a conqueror;
Or I with grief and extreme age shall perish
And never more behold thy face again.
Therefore take with thee my most grievous curse,
Which in the day of battle tire thee more
Than all the complete armour that thou wear'st!
My prayers on the adverse party fight;
And there the little souls of Edward's children
Whisper the spirits of thine enemies
And promise them success and victory.
Bloody thou art; bloody will be thy end.
Shame serves thy life and doth thy death attend.

Either you shall die by God's just orders
before you triumph in this war,
or I shall perish from grief and old age
and never see your face again.
So take with you my most terrible curse,
and on the day of battle may it tire you more
than all the full suit of armour you wear!
My prayers go with your adversaries;
and the little souls of Edward's children

whisper to the ghosts of your enemies
and promise them success and victory.
You are bloodthirsty; your death will be bloody.
Shame follows your life and will be with you in your death.

Exit

QUEEN ELIZABETH.
Though far more cause, yet much less
spirit to curse
Abides in me; I say amen to her.

Although I have far more cause to curse you,
I have less ability at it; I second what she has said.

KING RICHARD.
Stay, madam, I must talk a word with you.

Wait, madam, I must speak to you.

QUEEN ELIZABETH.
I have no moe sons of the royal blood
For thee to slaughter. For my daughters, Richard,
They shall be praying nuns, not weeping queens;
And therefore level not to hit their lives.

I have no other royal sons
for you to slaughter. As from my daughters, Richard,
they shall be praying nuns, not weeping queens;
and so don't plan to take their lives.

KING RICHARD.
You have a daughter call'd Elizabeth.
Virtuous and fair, royal and gracious.

You have a daughter called Elizabeth.
Good and beautiful, royal and gracious.

QUEEN ELIZABETH.
And must she die for this? O, let her
live,
And I'll corrupt her manners, stain her beauty,
Slander myself as false to Edward's bed,
Throw over her the veil of infamy;

So she may live unscarr'd of bleeding slaughter,
I will confess she was not Edward's daughter.

And she must die for that? O, let her live,
and I will corrupt her manners, spoil her beauty,
lie and say that I betrayed Edward,
I will make her ill thought of;
if it means she can escape bloody slaughter,
I will swear that she was not Edward's daughter.

KING RICHARD.
Wrong not her birth; she is a royal
Princess.

Do not lie about her birth; she is a royal princess.

QUEEN ELIZABETH.
To save her life I'll say she is not so.

To save her life I'll say she isn't.

KING RICHARD.
Her life is safest only in her birth.

Her birth is the only thing saving her life.

QUEEN ELIZABETH.
And only in that safety died her
brothers.

It was their birth that killed her brothers.

KING RICHARD.
Lo, at their birth good stars were opposite.

Well, the stars werecontrary when they were born.

QUEEN ELIZABETH.
No, to their lives ill friends were
contrary.

No, it was poor friends who were contrary to their lives.

KING RICHARD.

All unavoided is the doom of destiny.

Fate cannot be avoided.

QUEEN ELIZABETH.
True, when avoided grace makes destiny.
My babes were destin'd to a fairer death,
If grace had bless'd thee with a fairer life.

Truth, when avoiding grace brings destiny.
My babies were destined to have a sweeter death,
if grace had blessed you with a sweeter life.

KING RICHARD.
You speak as if that I had slain my cousins.

You speak as if it was I who killed my cousins.

QUEEN ELIZABETH.
Cousins, indeed; and by their uncle
cozen'd
Of comfort, kingdom, kindred, freedom, life.
Whose hand soever lanc'd their tender hearts,
Thy head, an indirectly, gave direction.
No doubt the murd'rous knife was dull and blunt
Till it was whetted on thy stone-hard heart
To revel in the entrails of my lambs.
But that still use of grief makes wild grief tame,
My tongue should to thy ears not name my boys
Till that my nails were anchor'd in thine eyes;
And I, in such a desp'rate bay of death,
Like a poor bark, of sails and tackling reft,
Rush all to pieces on thy rocky bosom.

They were indeed your cousins; and you their uncle cheated them
of comfort, kingdom, family, freedom, life.
Whoever's hand it was which stabbed their tender hearts
it was you who gave the orders.
No doubt the murderous knife was dull and blunt
until it was sharpened on your stony heart
before it went to tear around the innards of my lambs.
But this calm talk of grief calms my wild grief,
my tongue should not be speaking the names of my boys to you
until my nails were scratching out your eyes;

and I, a poor ship with all its tackle gone,
smash myself to pieces on your rocky heart
in this desperate bay of death.

KING RICHARD.
Madam, so thrive I in my enterprise
And dangerous success of bloody wars,
As I intend more good to you and yours
Than ever you or yours by me were harm'd!

Madam, if I succeed in this business
of dangerous and bloody war,
I plan for you and yours to receive more good
from me than you ever got harm.

QUEEN ELIZABETH.
What good is cover'd with the face of
heaven,
To be discover'd, that can do me good?

What good is hiding behind the clouds,
that when revealed could do me good?

KING RICHARD.
Advancement of your children, gentle
lady.

Advancement of your children, gentle lady.

QUEEN ELIZABETH.
Up to some scaffold, there to lose their
heads?

Advancement up some scaffold, where they will lose their heads?

KING RICHARD.
Unto the dignity and height of Fortune,
The high imperial type of this earth's glory.

Up to the greatest position available,
the greatest glory available on earth.

QUEEN ELIZABETH.
Flatter my sorrow with report of it;

Tell me what state, what dignity, what honour,
Canst thou demise to any child of mine?

Please my sorrow by telling me about it;
tell me what position, what dignity, what honour
you can award to any child of mine?

KING RICHARD.
Even all I have-ay, and myself and all
Will I withal endow a child of thine;
So in the Lethe of thy angry soul
Thou drown the sad remembrance of those wrongs
Which thou supposest I have done to thee.

I will give all I have, myself as well,
to the child of yours;
so drown your sad memory of the wrongs
which you imagine I have done to you
in the river of forgetfulness of your angry soul.

QUEEN ELIZABETH.
Be brief, lest that the process of thy
kindness
Last longer telling than thy kindness' date.

Speak quickly, in case your actual kindness doesn't last
as long as the time it takes you to tell it.

KING RICHARD.
Then know, that from my soul I love thy
daughter.

Then know that I love your daughter with all my soul.

QUEEN ELIZABETH.
My daughter's mother thinks it with her
soul.

My daughter's mother thinks it with her soul.

KING RICHARD.
What do you think?

What do you think?

QUEEN ELIZABETH.
That thou dost love my daughter from
thy soul.
So from thy soul's love didst thou love her brothers,
And from my heart's love I do thank thee for it.

That you love my daughter something other than your soul.
The same soulful love you had for her brothers,
and I thank you for it with something other than my heart's love.

KING RICHARD.
Be not so hasty to confound my meaning.
I mean that with my soul I love thy daughter
And do intend to make her Queen of England.

Don't be so quick to misunderstand me.
I mean that with my soul I love your daughter
and I intend to make her Queen of England.

QUEEN ELIZABETH.
Well, then, who dost thou mean shall be
her king?

Well who do you intend to be her king?

KING RICHARD.
Even he that makes her Queen. Who else
should be?

The person who makes her queen. Who else would it be?

QUEEN ELIZABETH.
What, thou?

What, you?

KING RICHARD.
Even so. How think you of it?

That's right. What do you think of it?

QUEEN ELIZABETH.
How canst thou woo her?

How can you woo her?

KING RICHARD.
That would I learn of you,
As one being best acquainted with her humour.

That's what I want you to tell me,
you knowing her personality best.

QUEEN ELIZABETH.
And wilt thou learn of me?

And will you learn from me?

KING RICHARD.
Madam, with all my heart.

Madam, with all my heart.

QUEEN ELIZABETH.
Send to her, by the man that slew her
brothers,
A pair of bleeding hearts; thereon engrave
'Edward' and 'York.' Then haply will she weep;
Therefore present to her-as sometimes Margaret
Did to thy father, steep'd in Rutland's blood-
A handkerchief; which, say to her, did drain
The purple sap from her sweet brother's body,
And bid her wipe her weeping eyes withal.
If this inducement move her not to love,
Send her a letter of thy noble deeds;
Tell her thou mad'st away her uncle Clarence,
Her uncle Rivers; ay, and for her sake
Mad'st quick conveyance with her good aunt Anne.

Send her, via the man who killed her brothers,
a pair of bleeding hearts; scratch on them
'Edward' and 'York.' Then maybe she will weep;
so give her—as sometimes Margaret
did to your father, soaked in Rutland's blood—
a handkerchief; tell her that it mopped up
the blood from her sweet brother's body,
and tell her to wipe her weeping eyes with it.

If this doesn't make her love you,
send a letter telling her of your noble deeds;
tell her that you killed her uncle Clarence,
her uncle Rivers; yes, and for her sake
you quickly got rid of her good aunt Anne.

KING RICHARD.
You mock me, madam; this is not the way
To win your daughter.

You're mocking me, madam; this isn't the way
to win over your daughter.

QUEEN ELIZABETH.
There is no other way;
Unless thou couldst put on some other shape
And not be Richard that hath done all this.

There is no other way;
unless you can assume some other shape
and not be the Richard who has done all these things.

KING RICHARD.
Say that I did all this for love of her?

What if I did all these things out of love for her?

QUEEN ELIZABETH.
Nay, then indeed she cannot choose but
hate thee,
Having bought love with such a bloody spoil.

No, then she would have no choice but to hate you,
as you had bought her love with such bloody coin.

KING RICHARD.
Look what is done cannot be now amended.
Men shall deal unadvisedly sometimes,
Which after-hours gives leisure to repent.
If I did take the kingdom from your sons,
To make amends I'll give it to your daughter.
If I have kill'd the issue of your womb,
To quicken your increase I will beget
Mine issue of your blood upon your daughter.

A grandam's name is little less in love
Than is the doating title of a mother;
They are as children but one step below,
Even of your metal, of your very blood;
Of all one pain, save for a night of groans
Endur'd of her, for whom you bid like sorrow.
Your children were vexation to your youth;
But mine shall be a comfort to your age.
The loss you have is but a son being King,
And by that loss your daughter is made Queen.
I cannot make you what amends I would,
Therefore accept such kindness as I can.
Dorset your son, that with a fearful soul
Leads discontented steps in foreign soil,
This fair alliance quickly shall can home
To high promotions and great dignity.
The King, that calls your beauteous daughter wife,
Familiarly shall call thy Dorset brother;
Again shall you be mother to a king,
And all the ruins of distressful times
Repair'd with double riches of content.
What! we have many goodly days to see.
The liquid drops of tears that you have shed
Shall come again, transform'd to orient pearl,
Advantaging their loan with interest
Of ten times double gain of happiness.
Go, then, my mother, to thy daughter go;
Make bold her bashful years with your experience;
Prepare her ears to hear a wooer's tale;
Put in her tender heart th' aspiring flame
Of golden sovereignty; acquaint the Princes
With the sweet silent hours of marriage joys.
And when this arm of mine hath chastised
The petty rebel, dull-brain'd Buckingham,
Bound with triumphant garlands will I come,
And lead thy daughter to a conqueror's bed;
To whom I will retail my conquest won,
And she shall be sole victoress, Caesar's Caesar.

Whatever has been done cannot now be changed:
men sometimes do the wrong thing,
which they may later regret.
If I took the kingdom from your sons,
to make amends I'll give it to your daughter;

if I have killed your children,
to revive your family tree I shall create
children of your blood with your daughter.
The name of grandmother is loved almost as much
as the sweet title of mother;
grandchildren are children just one step removed;
they will be of the same substance as you, of your blood;
you will take the same trouble for them, apart from a night of labour
which she will suffer, which you previously suffered for her.
Your children were troublesome in your youth,
but mine shall comfort you in your old-age;
all you have lost is having a king as a son,
and through that loss your daughter will become Queen.
I can't make it up to you as I would like:
so accept what kindness I can offer.
Your son Dorset, who with a fearful soul
is walking unhappily in foreign lands,
will be quickly summoned home by this sweet alliance
to be given high promotion and great dignity.
The King who calls your beautiful daughter his wife
shall in friendship call Dorset his brother;
you will be mother to a king again,
and all the damage of sorrowful times
will be repaired with a double helping of happiness.
What! There are many happy days ahead.
The liquid drops of tears that you have shared
will be returned, changed into Oriental pearls,
the loan being repaid with interest
of ten times a double sum of happiness.
Go then, my mother; go to your daughter:
make her coy youth strong through your experience;
tell her how to listen to a wooer;
make her tender heart aspire to
golden monarchy; tell the Princess
about the sweet silent hours of joy marriage will bring,
and when I have beaten
the petty rebel, the dullard Buckingham,
I shall return in triumph
and take your daughter to a conqueror's bed;
I shall tell her of how I won my victory
and she will triumph, winning over the greatest.

QUEEN ELIZABETH.
What were I best to say? Her father's

brother
Would be her lord? Or shall I say her uncle?
Or he that slew her brothers and her uncles?
Under what title shall I woo for thee
That God, the law, my honour, and her love
Can make seem pleasing to her tender years?

What would be the best thing for me to say? That her father's brother
wants to marry her? Or should I say her uncle?
Or the one who killed her brothers and her uncles?
What title shall I use to speak for you
so that God, the law, my honour and her love
can make this business seem pleasant to her youth?

KING RICHARD.
Infer fair England's peace by this alliance.

Tell her that this marriage will bring peace to fair England.

QUEEN ELIZABETH.
Which she shall purchase with
still-lasting war.

Which will be bought with this ongoing war.

KING RICHARD.
Tell her the King, that may command,
entreats.

Tell her that the King, who could order her, begs her.

QUEEN ELIZABETH.
That at her hands which the King's
King forbids.

For something which the law of God forbids.

KING RICHARD.
Say she shall be a high and mighty queen.

Say that she will be a high and mighty Queen.

QUEEN ELIZABETH.
To wail the title, as her mother doth.

To wish she never had the title, like her mother.

KING RICHARD.
Say I will love her everlastingly.

Say I will love her for ever.

QUEEN ELIZABETH.
But how long shall that title 'ever' last?

But for how long will 'forever' last?

KING RICHARD.
Sweetly in force unto her fair life's end.

It will last as long as her sweet life does.

QUEEN ELIZABETH.
But how long fairly shall her sweet life
last?

But how long will her sweet life last?

KING RICHARD.
As long as heaven and nature lengthens it.

As long as heaven and nature allows it.

QUEEN ELIZABETH.
As long as hell and Richard likes of it.

As long as hell and Richard still like her.

KING RICHARD.
Say I, her sovereign, am her subject low.

Tell her that I, her monarch, am her low subject.

QUEEN ELIZABETH.
But she, your subject, loathes such
sovereignty.

But she, your subject, loathes your monarchy.

KING RICHARD.
Be eloquent in my behalf to her.

Speak eloquently to her on my behalf.

QUEEN ELIZABETH.
An honest tale speeds best being plainly
told.

The best thing to do with honest tale is to speak plainly.

KING RICHARD.
Then plainly to her tell my loving tale.

Then tell her plainly about my love.

QUEEN ELIZABETH.
Plain and not honest is too harsh a style.

To be plain when you're not honest would sound too harsh.

KING RICHARD.
Your reasons are too shallow and too quick.

Your reasoning is to shallow and too quick.

QUEEN ELIZABETH.
O, no, my reasons are too deep and
dead-
Too deep and dead, poor infants, in their graves.

Oh no, it's too deep and dead—
deep and dead, like the poor infants in their graves.

KING RICHARD.
Harp not on that string, madam; that is past.

Don't keep playing that old tune, madam; that's in the past.

QUEEN ELIZABETH.
Harp on it still shall I till heartstrings
break.

I shall play that tune until my heartstrings break.

KING RICHARD.
Now, by my George, my garter, and my
crown-

Now, by my decorations and my crown–

QUEEN ELIZABETH.
Profan'd, dishonour'd, and the third
usurp'd.

Stained, dishonoured, and the third one stolen.

KING RICHARD.
I swear-

I swear–

QUEEN ELIZABETH.
By nothing; for this is no oath:
Thy George, profan'd, hath lost his lordly honour;
Thy garter, blemish'd, pawn'd his knightly virtue;
Thy crown, usurp'd, disgrac'd his kingly glory.
If something thou wouldst swear to be believ'd,
Swear then by something that thou hast not wrong'd.

By nothing; this is no promise:
your title of St George, blasphemed, has lost its lordly honour;
your garter, stained, has sold its knightly virtue;
your crown, stolen, has lost its kingly glory.
If you want to have your oaths believed,
then swear by something you have not insulted.

KING RICHARD.
Then, by my self-

Then, by myself–

QUEEN ELIZABETH.
Thy self is self-misus'd.

You have abused yourself.

KING RICHARD.
Now, by the world-

Now, by the world–

QUEEN ELIZABETH.
'Tis full of thy foul wrongs.

Which is full of your foul misdeeds.

KING RICHARD.
My father's death-

By my father's death–

QUEEN ELIZABETH.
Thy life hath it dishonour'd.

Your life has dishonoured it.

KING RICHARD.
Why, then, by God-

Why then, by God–

QUEEN ELIZABETH.
God's wrong is most of all.
If thou didst fear to break an oath with Him,
The unity the King my husband made
Thou hadst not broken, nor my brothers died.
If thou hadst fear'd to break an oath by Him,
Th' imperial metal, circling now thy head,
Had grac'd the tender temples of my child;
And both the Princes had been breathing here,
Which now, two tender bedfellows for dust,
Thy broken faith hath made the prey for worms.
What canst thou swear by now?

The wrong done to God is worst of all.
If you were afraid to break an oath with God,
you would not have broken the unity
my husband the King made, and my brothers would not have died.
If you had feared to break an oath to God
then the crown which is now on your head

233

would be on the tender head of my child;
both princes would still be alive instead
of lying side-by-side in their graves,
made worm food by your broken promises.
What can you swear by now?

KING RICHARD.
The time to come.

The future.

QUEEN ELIZABETH.
That thou hast wronged in the time
o'erpast;
For I myself have many tears to wash
Hereafter time, for time past wrong'd by thee.
The children live whose fathers thou hast slaughter'd,
Ungovern'd youth, to wail it in their age;
The parents live whose children thou hast butchered,
Old barren plants, to wail it with their age.
Swear not by time to come; for that thou hast
Misus'd ere us'd, by times ill-us'd o'erpast.

You have wronged that by your behaviour in the past;
I have many tears to be cried
in the future, for your wrongs in the past.
There are children alive whose fathers you have slaughtered,
leaderless youths, who will mourn it when they are older;
there are parents alive whose children you have butchered,
old barren plants, who will mourn it when they're older.
Don't swear by the future; you have already
abused it, by your behaviour in the past.

KING RICHARD.
As I intend to prosper and repent,
So thrive I in my dangerous affairs
Of hostile arms! Myself myself confound!
Heaven and fortune bar me happy hours!
Day, yield me not thy light; nor, night, thy rest!
Be opposite all planets of good luck
To my proceeding!-if, with dear heart's love,
Immaculate devotion, holy thoughts,
I tender not thy beauteous princely daughter.
In her consists my happiness and thine;

Without her, follows to myself and thee,
Herself, the land, and many a Christian soul,
Death, desolation, ruin, and decay.
It cannot be avoided but by this;
It will not be avoided but by this.
Therefore, dear mother-I must call you so-
Be the attorney of my love to her;
Plead what I will be, not what I have been;
Not my deserts, but what I will deserve.
Urge the necessity and state of times,
And be not peevish-fond in great designs.

Only let me prosper in the dangerous affairs
of this war if I intend to repent! May I damn myself!
May heaven and fate keep me from happiness!
Day, do not give me your light; night do not give me rest!
May all planets which bring good luck be opposed
to my business! –if, with the love of a sweet heart,
perfect devotion, holy thoughts,
I do not win your beautiful princely daughter.
My happiness and yours rests in her;
without her death, desolation, ruin and decay
will come to you and to me, to her,
the country, and many Christian souls.
This is the only way it can be avoided;
nothing else will do.
Therefore, dear mother–that's what I must call you–
be the advocate of my love to her;
urge what I will be, not what I have been;
not what I deserve, but what I will deserve in future.
Speak of what is needed in this time,
and make sure you emphasise the importance of these matters.

QUEEN ELIZABETH.
Shall I be tempted of the devil thus?

Shall I let the devil tempt me like this?

KING RICHARD.
Ay, if the devil tempt you to do good.

Yes, if the devil tempts you to do good.

QUEEN ELIZABETH.

Shall I forget myself to be myself?

Shall I not be true to myself?

KING RICHARD.
Ay, if your self's remembrance wrong
yourself.

Yes, if doing that will do you harm.

QUEEN ELIZABETH.
Yet thou didst kill my children.

But you killed my children.

KING RICHARD.
But in your daughter's womb I bury them;
Where, in that nest of spicery, they will breed
Selves of themselves, to your recomforture.

But I will bury them in your daughter's womb;
and in that phoenix nest they will breed
copies of themselves, for your consolation.

QUEEN ELIZABETH.
Shall I go win my daughter to thy will?

Will I go and win your daughter over to your wishes?

KING RICHARD.
And be a happy mother by the deed.

And make yourself a happy mother by doing so.

QUEEN ELIZABETH.
I go. Write to me very shortly,
And you shall understand from me her mind.

I shall go. Write to me very soon,
and I will tell you what she's thinking.

KING RICHARD.
Bear her my true love's kiss; and so, farewell.

Kissing her. Exit QUEEN ELIZABETH

Relenting fool, and shallow, changing woman!

 Enter RATCLIFF; CATESBY following

How now! what news?

Take her my kiss of true love; and so, farewell.

Forgiving fool, and shallow, changeable woman!

Hello there! What's the news?

RATCLIFF.
Most mighty sovereign, on the western coast
Rideth a puissant navy; to our shores
Throng many doubtful hollow-hearted friends,
Unarm'd, and unresolv'd to beat them back.
'Tis thought that Richmond is their admiral;
And there they hull, expecting but the aid
Of Buckingham to welcome them ashore.

Your great Majesty, on the western coast
there is a strong navy; many frightened
and weak hearted friends have gone to the shore,
unarmed and without the resolution to repel them.
It is thought that Richmond is leading them;
they are riding at anchor, just waiting for the help
of Buckingham to welcome them ashore.

KING RICHARD.
Some light-foot friend post to the Duke of
Norfolk.
Ratcliff, thyself-or Catesby; where is he?

Somebody ride quickly to the Duke of Norfolk.
Ratcliff, you–or Catesby; where is he?

CATESBY.
Here, my good lord.

Here, my good lord.

KING RICHARD.
Catesby, fly to the Duke.

Catesby, hurry to the Duke.

CATESBY.
I will my lord, with all convenient haste.

I will, my lord, as quickly as I can.

KING RICHARD.
Ratcliff, come hither. Post to Salisbury;
When thou com'st thither-[To CATESBY]Dull,
unmindfull villain,
Why stay'st thou here, and go'st not to the Duke?

Ratcliff, come here. Hurry to Salisbury;
when you get there–[to Catesby] you dull, stupid villain,
why are you staying here, and not going to the Duke?

CATESBY.
First, mighty liege, tell me your Highness' pleasure,
What from your Grace I shall deliver to him.

First, great King, tell me what your Highness wants,
what message I should give him from your Grace.

KING RICHARD.
O, true, good Catesby. Bid him levy straight
The greatest strength and power that he can make
And meet me suddenly at Salisbury.

That's true, good Catesby. Tell him to raise the greatest
force that he can as quickly as possible
and meet me at once at Salisbury.

CATESBY.
I go.

I'm going.

Exit

RATCLIFF.

What, may it please you, shall I do at Salisbury?

What, if you please, shall I do at Salisbury?

KING RICHARD.
Why, what wouldst thou do there before I
go?

Why, what would you be doing them before I get there?

RATCLIFF.
Your Highness told me I should post before.

Your Highness told me I should ride ahead.

KING RICHARD.
My mind is chang'd.

Enter LORD STANLEY

Stanley, what news with you?

I've changed my mind.

Stanley, what news have you got?

STANLEY.
None good, my liege, to please you with
the hearing;
Nor none so bad but well may be reported.

No good news, my lord, to please your ears;
but no news so bad I can't tell you it.

KING RICHARD.
Hoyday, a riddle! neither good nor bad!
What need'st thou run so many miles about,
When thou mayest tell thy tale the nearest way?
Once more, what news?

Hello, a riddle! Not good or bad!
Why do you need to go such a roundabout way
when you can tell me your tale directly?
I ask you again, what news?

STANLEY.
Richmond is on the seas.

Richmond is on the sea.

KING RICHARD.
There let him sink, and be the seas on him!
White-liver'd runagate, what doth he there?

Let him sink there, and have the sea on him!
Lily livered runaway, what's he doing there?

STANLEY.
I know not, mighty sovereign, but by guess.

I don't know, great King, I can only guess.

KING RICHARD.
Well, as you guess?

Well, what do you guess?

STANLEY.
Stirr'd up by Dorset, Buckingham, and Morton,
He makes for England here to claim the crown.

That he has been encouraged by Dorset, Buckingham and Morton,
and is coming here to England to claim the crown.

KING RICHARD.
Is the chair empty? Is the sword unsway'd?
Is the King dead, the empire unpossess'd?
What heir of York is there alive but we?
And who is England's King but great York's heir?
Then tell me what makes he upon the seas.

Is the throne empty? Does no one hold the sword?
Is the king dead, does nobody own the empire?
What heir of York is alive apart from me?
And who is the King of England apart from the heir of great York?
So tell me what he's doing on the sea.

STANLEY.

Unless for that, my liege, I cannot guess.

Unless it's for that, my lord, I can't guess.

KING RICHARD.
Unless for that he comes to be your liege,
You cannot guess wherefore the Welshman comes.
Thou wilt revolt and fly to him, I fear.

Unless he's coming to be your Lord,
you cannot guess why the Welshman is coming.
You will revolt and fly to him, I fear.

STANLEY.
No, my good lord; therefore mistrust me not.

No, my good lord; do not mistrust me.

KING RICHARD.
Where is thy power then, to beat him back?
Where be thy tenants and thy followers?
Are they not now upon the western shore,
Safe-conducting the rebels from their ships?

Where are your forces then, to beat him back?
Where are your tenants and your followers;
aren't they now on the western shore,
helping the rebels to disembark?

STANLEY.
No, my good lord, my friends are in the north.

No, my good lord, my friends are in the North.

KING RICHARD.
Cold friends to me. What do they in the
north,
When they should serve their sovereign in the west?

They are no use to me. What are they doing in the North
when they should be serving their king in the West?

STANLEY.
They have not been commanded, mighty King.

Pleaseth your Majesty to give me leave,
I'll muster up my friends and meet your Grace
Where and what time your Majesty shall please.

They have not had their orders, mighty king.
If your Majesty will give me permission,
I will gather up my friends and meet your Grace
at any place and time your Majesty orders.

KING RICHARD.
Ay, ay, thou wouldst be gone to join with
Richmond;
But I'll not trust thee.

I see, you would go and join Richmond;
but I won't trust you.

STANLEY.
Most mighty sovereign,
You have no cause to hold my friendship doubtful.
I never was nor never will be false.

Most mighty King,
you have no reason to doubt my friendship.
I was never, nor will I ever be, false.

KING RICHARD.
Go, then, and muster men. But leave behind
Your son, George Stanley. Look your heart be firm,
Or else his head's assurance is but frail.

Then go and gather your men. But leave your son,
George Stanley, behind. Make sure you stay loyal,
or his head will pay the price.

STANLEY.
So deal with him as I prove true to you.

Treat him according to my behaviour.

Exit

Enter a MESSENGER

MESSENGER.
My gracious sovereign, now in Devonshire,
As I by friends am well advertised,
Sir Edward Courtney and the haughty prelate,
Bishop of Exeter, his elder brother,
With many moe confederates, are in arms.

My gracious king, I have been told by friends
that in Devonshire Sir Edward Courtney and the arrogant priest
the Bishop of Exeter, his older brother,
with many other confederates, have taken up arms.

Enter another MESSENGER

SECOND MESSENGER.
In Kent, my liege, the Guilfords are in
arms;
And every hour more competitors
Flock to the rebels, and their power grows strong.

In Kent, my lord, the Guildfords have taken up arms;
and every hour more forces
flock to the rebels, and they are growing strong.

Enter another MESSENGER

THIRD MESSENGER.
My lord, the army of great Buckingham-

My Lord, the army of great Buckingham–

KING RICHARD.
Out on you, owls! Nothing but songs of
death?[He strikes him]
There, take thou that till thou bring better news.

Get out, owls! Do you have nothing but songs of death?
There, take that until you bring better news.

THIRD MESSENGER.
The news I have to tell your Majesty
Is that by sudden floods and fall of waters
Buckingham's army is dispers'd and scatter'd;
And he himself wand'red away alone,

No man knows whither.

The news I have to tell your majesty
is that due to sudden floods and change of tides
Buckley's army is dispersed and scattered;
and he himself has gone away alone,
no man knows where.

KING RICHARD.
I cry thee mercy.
There is my purse to cure that blow of thine.
Hath any well-advised friend proclaim'd
Reward to him that brings the traitor in?

I beg your pardon.
Take my purse as compensation for that blow.
Has any sensible friend announced
a reward for whoever captures the traitor?

THIRD MESSENGER.
Such proclamation hath been made,
my Lord.

This announcement has been made, my lord.

Enter another MESSENGER

FOURTH MESSENGER.
Sir Thomas Lovel and Lord Marquis
Dorset,
'Tis said, my liege, in Yorkshire are in arms.
But this good comfort bring I to your Highness-
The Britaine navy is dispers'd by tempest.
Richmond in Dorsetshire sent out a boat
Unto the shore, to ask those on the banks
If they were his assistants, yea or no;
Who answer'd him they came from Buckingham
Upon his party. He, mistrusting them,
Hois'd sail, and made his course again for Britaine.

Sir Thomas Lovel and Lord Marquis Dorset
are said, my lord, to have taken up arms in Yorkshire.
But I bring your Highness this consolation–
the navy of Brittany has been split up by storms.

244

In Dorsetshire Richmond sent out a boat
to the shore, to ask those on the banks
if they were his friends or not;
they told him they came from Buckingham
to help him. He, not trusting them,
hoisted his sails and set off back to Brittany.

KING RICHARD.
March on, march on, since we are up in
arms;
If not to fight with foreign enemies,
Yet to beat down these rebels here at home.

March on, march on, We are ready for battle:
if we are not fighting with foreign enemies
we shall beat down these rebels here at home.

Re-enter CATESBY

CATESBY.
My liege, the Duke of Buckingham is taken-
That is the best news. That the Earl of Richmond
Is with a mighty power landed at Milford
Is colder tidings, yet they must be told.

My Lord, the Duke of Buckingham has been captured–
that is the best news. That the Earl of Richmond
has landed with a great force at Milford Haven
is not such good news, but it has to be said.

KING RICHARD.
Away towards Salisbury! While we reason
here
A royal battle might be won and lost.
Some one take order Buckingham be brought
To Salisbury; the rest march on with me.

Off to Salisbury! While we argue here
the battle for the Crown could be won and lost.
Someone make sure Buckingham is brought
to Salisbury; the rest of you march with me.

Flourish. Exeunt

SCENE 5.

LORD DERBY'S house

Enter STANLEY and SIR CHRISTOPHER URSWICK

STANLEY.
Sir Christopher, tell Richmond this from me:
That in the sty of the most deadly boar
My son George Stanley is frank'd up in hold;
If I revolt, off goes young George's head;
The fear of that holds off my present aid.
So, get thee gone; commend me to thy lord.
Withal say that the Queen hath heartily consented
He should espouse Elizabeth her daughter.
But tell me, where is princely Richmond now?

Sir Christopher, tell Richmond this from me:
that my son George Stanley is imprisoned
in the sty of the most deadly boar;
if I rebel, he loses his head;
the fear of that stops me from helping.
So, go; my best wishes to your Lord.
Also say that the Queen has given full agreement
that he should marry her daughter Elizabeth.
But tell me, where is the princely Richmond now?

CHRISTOPHER.
At Pembroke, or at Ha'rford west in Wales.

At Pembroke, or at Haverfordwest in Wales.

STANLEY.
What men of name resort to him?

Who are the men who have gone to him?

CHRISTOPHER.
Sir Walter Herbert, a renowned soldier;
Sir Gilbert Talbot, Sir William Stanley,

Oxford, redoubted Pembroke, Sir James Blunt,
And Rice ap Thomas, with a valiant crew;
And many other of great name and worth;
And towards London do they bend their power,
If by the way they be not fought withal.

Sir Walter Herbert, a famous soldier;
Sir Gilbert Talbot, Sir William Stanley,
Oxford, good Pembroke, Sir James Blunt,
Rice ap Thomas, with a brave force;
and many others of great name and worth;
they are bringing their forces to London,
if they are not fought along the way.

STANLEY.
Well, hie thee to thy lord; I kiss his hand;
My letter will resolve him of my mind. Farewell.

Well, go to your lord; I kiss his hand;
my letter will tell him of my decision.
Farewell.

Exeunt

ACT V.

SCENE 1.

Salisbury. An open place

Enter the SHERIFF and guard, with BUCKINGHAM, led to execution

BUCKINGHAM.
Will not King Richard let me speak with
him?

Won't King Richard let me speak with him?

SHERIFF.
No, my good lord; therefore be patient.

No, my good lord; so calm yourself.

BUCKINGHAM.
Hastings, and Edward's children, Grey, and
Rivers,
Holy King Henry, and thy fair son Edward,
Vaughan, and all that have miscarried
By underhand corrupted foul injustice,
If that your moody discontented souls
Do through the clouds behold this present hour,
Even for revenge mock my destruction!
This is All-Souls' day, fellow, is it not?

Hastings, and Edward's children, Grey, and Rivers,
holy King Henry, and your good son Edward,
Vaughan, and all who have fallen through this
underhand, corrupt, evil injustice,
if your unhappy souls
are seeing this time through the clouds
you may mock my death to take your revenge!
This is All–Souls' day, isn't it, my man?

SHERIFF.
It is, my lord.

It is, my lord.

BUCKINGHAM.
Why, then All-Souls' day is my body's
doomsday.
This is the day which in King Edward's time
I wish'd might fall on me when I was found
False to his children and his wife's allies;
This is the day wherein I wish'd to fall
By the false faith of him whom most I trusted;
This, this All-Souls' day to my fearful soul
Is the determin'd respite of my wrongs;
That high All-Secr which I dallied with
Hath turn'd my feigned prayer on my head
And given in earnest what I begg'd in jest.
Thus doth He force the swords of wicked men
To turn their own points in their masters' bosoms.
Thus Margaret's curse falls heavy on my neck.
'When he' quoth she 'shall split thy heart with sorrow,
Remember Margaret was a prophetess.'
Come lead me, officers, to the block of shame;
Wrong hath but wrong, and blame the due of blame.

Why then, All–Souls' day is judgement day for my body.
This is the day which I wished in King Edward's
time might fall on me when I was discovered to be
false to his children and his wife's allies;
this is the day when I wished to fall
by the treacherous ways of the one whom I most trusted;
this All–Souls' day is the date set for the punishments
of my fearful soul for everything I have done wrong;
the omnipotent God whom I tried to joke with
has turned my pretend prayer back on me
and given for real what I begged for as a joke.
So he forces the swords of wicked men
to turn their points back against their masters.
So Margaret's curse has fallen heavily upon me:
she said, 'When he splits your heart with sorrow,
remember that Margaret predicted it!'
Come, officers, lead me to the shameful place of execution;
wrong has bred wrong, and blame gets the blame it deserves.

Exeunt

SCENE 2.

Camp near Tamworth

Enter RICHMOND, OXFORD, SIR JAMES BLUNT, SIR WALTER HERBERT, and others,
with drum and colours

RICHMOND.
Fellows in arms, and my most loving friends,
Bruis'd underneath the yoke of tyranny,
Thus far into the bowels of the land
Have we march'd on without impediment;
And here receive we from our father Stanley
Lines of fair comfort and encouragement.
The wretched, bloody, and usurping boar,
That spoil'd your summer fields and fruitful vines,
Swills your warm blood like wash, and makes his trough
In your embowell'd bosoms-this foul swine
Is now even in the centre of this isle,
Near to the town of Leicester, as we learn.
From Tamworth thither is but one day's march.
In God's name cheerly on, courageous friends,
To reap the harvest of perpetual peace
By this one bloody trial of sharp war.

My fellow soldiers, and my most loving friends,
bruised beneath the weight of tyranny;
so far we have marched into the centre
of the country without facing opposition;
and I have received from our father Stanley
a message which gives both comfort and encouragement.
The wretched, bloody and thieving boar,
who ruined your summer fields and prospering vines,
who drinks your warm blood like pig swill, and makes your
disembowelled torsos his trough–this foul pig
is right now in the middle of the country,
we have learned, near to the town of Leicester.
From Tamworth to there is just one day's march:
go happily on, brave friends, in the name of God,

so that we can create a lasting peace
through one bloody battle.

OXFORD.
Every man's conscience is a thousand men,
To fight against this guilty homicide.

Every man becomes like a thousand men,
being so determined to fight this guilty murder.

HERBERT.
I doubt not but his friends will turn to us.

I don't doubt that his friends will come over to our side.

BLUNT.
He hath no friends but what are friends for fear,
Which in his dearest need will fly from him.

The only friends he has stay with him out of fear,
when he needs them most they will run from him.

RICHMOND.
All for our vantage. Then in God's name march.
True hope is swift and flies with swallow's wings;
Kings it makes gods, and meaner creatures kings.

This is all to our advantage. So march on in God's name.
Good hope is swift and flies with a swallow's wings;
it makes kings into gods, and lower creatures into kings.

Exeunt

SCENE 3.

Bosworth Field

Enter KING RICHARD in arms, with NORFOLK, RATCLIFF,
the EARL of SURREYS and others

KING RICHARD.
Here pitch our tent, even here in Bosworth
field.
My Lord of Surrey, why look you so sad?

Pitch my tent here, right here on Bosworth Field.
Lord Surrey, why do you look so sad?

SURREY.
My heart is ten times lighter than my looks.

My heart is ten times lighter than I look.

KING RICHARD.
My Lord of Norfolk!

My Lord of Norfolk!

NORFOLK.
Here, most gracious liege.

Here, my most gracious lord.

KING RICHARD.
Norfolk, we must have knocks; ha! must we
not?

Norfolk, we're going to take some blows, we're going to have to, aren't we?

NORFOLK.
We must both give and take, my loving lord.

We're going to have to give them and take them, my loving lord.

KING RICHARD.
Up With my tent! Here will I lie to-night;
[Soldiers begin to set up the KING'S tent]
But where to-morrow? Well, all's one for that.
Who hath descried the number of the traitors?

Put my tent up! I will sleep here tonight;

but where tomorrow? Well, we'll see.
Who has counted the number of the traitors?

NORFOLK.
Six or seven thousand is their utmost power.

Six or seven thousand at most.

KING RICHARD.
Why, our battalia trebles that account;
Besides, the King's name is a tower of strength,
Which they upon the adverse faction want.
Up with the tent! Come, noble gentlemen,
Let us survey the vantage of the ground.
Call for some men of sound direction.
Let's lack no discipline, make no delay;
For, lords, to-morrow is a busy day.

Why, our army is three times that size;
besides, having the King on your side is great strength,
and those on the other side do not have it.
Get the tent up! Come, noble gentlemen,
let us have a look at the battlefield.
Call up some good strategists.
Let's keep our discipline and not waste time;
for, lords, tomorrow is a busy day.
Exeunt

Enter, on the other side of the field,
RICHMOND, SIR WILLIAM BRANDON, OXFORD, DORSET,
and others. Some pitch RICHMOND'S tent

RICHMOND.
The weary sun hath made a golden set,
And by the bright tract of his ficry car

Gives token of a goodly day to-morrow.
Sir William Brandon, you shall bear my standard.
Give me some ink and paper in my tent.
I'll draw the form and model of our battle,
Limit each leader to his several charge,
And part in just proportion our small power.
My Lord of Oxford-you, Sir William Brandon-
And you, Sir Walter Herbert-stay with me.
The Earl of Pembroke keeps his regiment;
Good Captain Blunt, bear my good night to him,
And by the second hour in the morning
Desire the Earl to see me in my tent.
Yet one thing more, good Captain, do for me-
Where is Lord Stanley quarter'd, do you know?

The tired sun has made a golden sunset,
and the bright path of his burning light
says there will be fine weather tomorrow.
Sir William Brandon, you shall carry my banner.
Bring some ink and paper to my tent.
I shall draw out the strategy for our battle,
tell each leader what he has to do,
and divide our small forces up equally.
My Lord of Oxford–you, Sir William Brandon–
and you, Sir Walter Herbert–stay with me.
The Earl of Pembroke is with his regiment;
good Captain Blunt, wish him good night from me,
and say that by the second hour of the morning
I want to see him in my tent.
Just one more thing I'd like you to do for me, good captain:
do you know where Lord Stanley is staying?

BLUNT.
Unless I have mista'en his colours much-
Which well I am assur'd I have not done-
His regiment lies half a mile at least
South from the mighty power of the King.

Unless I have mistaken his banners–
which I'm sure I haven't–
his regiment is at least half a mile
south of the mighty forces of the King.

RICHMOND.

If without peril it be possible,
Sweet Blunt, make some good means to speak with him
And give him from me this most needful note.

If you can do it without danger,
sweet Blunt, find an opportunity to speak with him
and give him this very important note from me.

BLUNT.
Upon my life, my lord, I'll undertake it;
And so, God give you quiet rest to-night!

I swear on my life, my lord, I'll do it;
and so, may God let you sleep peacefully tonight!

RICHMOND.
Good night, good Captain Blunt. Come,
gentlemen,
Let us consult upon to-morrow's business.
In to my tent; the dew is raw and cold.

Good night, good Captain Blunt. Come, gentlemen,
let us discuss tomorrow's business.
Come into my tent; it is a chilly night.

[They withdraw into the tent]

Enter, to his-tent, KING RICHARD, NORFOLK,
RATCLIFF, and CATESBY

KING RICHARD.
What is't o'clock?

What's the time?

CATESBY.
It's supper-time, my lord;
It's nine o'clock.

It's suppertime, my lord;
it's nine o'clock.

KING RICHARD.
I will not sup to-night.

Give me some ink and paper.
What, is my beaver easier than it was?
And all my armour laid into my tent?

I shall not eat tonight.
Give me some ink and paper.
Is my visor moving easier than it was?
And has all my armour been laid out in my tent?

CATESBY.
It is, my liege; and all things are in readiness.

It is, my lord: everything is ready.

KING RICHARD.
Good Norfolk, hie thee to thy charge;
Use careful watch, choose trusty sentinels.

Good Norfolk, go about your duties;
keep a careful watch, use trusty sentries.

NORFOLK.
I go, my lord.

I'm going, my lord.

KING RICHARD.
Stir with the lark to-morrow, gentle Norfolk.

Be up at dawn tomorrow, gentle Norfolk.

NORFOLK.
I warrant you, my lord.

I promise I shall, my lord.

Exit

KING RICHARD.
Catesby!

Catesby!

CATESBY.

My lord?

My lord?

KING RICHARD.
Send out a pursuivant-at-arms
To Stanley's regiment; bid him bring his power
Before sunrising, lest his son George fall
Into the blind cave of eternal night.
Exit CATESBY
Fill me a bowl of wine. Give me a watch.
Saddle white Surrey for the field to-morrow.
Look that my staves be sound, and not too heavy.
Ratcliff!

Send out a Herald
to Stanley's regiment; tell him to bring his forces
before sunrise, to prevent the death
of his son George.

Fill a bowl of wine for me. Give me a candle.
Saddle my white horse Surrey for the battle tomorrow;
check that my lances are in good condition and not too heavy.
Ratcliffe!

RATCLIFF.
My lord?

My lord?

KING RICHARD.
Saw'st thou the melancholy Lord
Northumberland?

Did you see the melancholy Lord Northumberland?

RATCLIFF.
Thomas the Earl of Surrey and himself,
Much about cock-shut time, from troop to troop
Went through the army, cheering up the soldiers.

Thomas the Earl of Surrey and himself,
round about sunset, went from troop to troop
throughout the Army, cheering up soldiers.

KING RICHARD.
So, I am satisfied. Give me a bowl of wine.
I have not that alacrity of spirit
Nor cheer of mind that I was wont to have.
Set it down. Is ink and paper ready?

Well, that's good. Give me a bowl of wine.
I haven't got the same high spirits
or cheerful mind that I am used to having.
Put it down. Is the ink and paper ready?

RATCLIFF.
It is, my lord.

It is, my lord.

KING RICHARD.
Bid my guard watch; leave me.
Ratcliffe, about the mid of night come to my tent
And help to arm me. Leave me, I say.

Tell my sentries to keep guard; leave me.
Ratcliffe, around the middle of the night come to my tent
and help to arm. Leave me, I say.

Exit RATCLIFF. RICHARD sleeps

Enter DERBY to RICHMOND in his tent;
LORDS attending

DERBY.
Fortune and victory sit on thy helm!

May fortune and victory attend you!

RICHMOND.
All comfort that the dark night can afford
Be to thy person, noble father-in-law!
Tell me, how fares our loving mother?

May all the comfort that the dark night can spare
come to you, noble father-in-law!
Tell me, how is my loving mother?

DERBY.
I, by attorney, bless thee from thy mother,
Who prays continually for Richmond's good.
So much for that. The silent hours steal on,
And flaky darkness breaks within the east.
In brief, for so the season bids us be,
Prepare thy battle early in the morning,
And put thy fortune to the arbitrement
Of bloody strokes and mortal-staring war.
I, as I may-that which I would I cannot-
With best advantage will deceive the time
And aid thee in this doubtful shock of arms;
But on thy side I may not be too forward,
Lest, being seen, thy brother, tender George,
Be executed in his father's sight.
Farewell; the leisure and the fearful time
Cuts off the ceremonious vows of love
And ample interchange of sweet discourse
Which so-long-sund'red friends should dwell upon.
God give us leisure for these rites of love!
Once more, adieu; be valiant, and speed well!

As a stand-in for her I give you her blessing,
she prays continually for your good fortune.
Enough of that. The silent hours move on,
and in the east the darkness is starting to fade.
In brief, for that is what the time demands,
prepare for battle early in the morning,
and put your faith to the test
of bloody blows and deadly war.
I'll do what I can–which isn't as much as
I would wish–to deceive the King
and assist you in this uncertain battle.
But I can't be too obvious in my support of you;
if it was seen, your brother, young George,
will be executed in front of his father.
Farewell; our hurry and these desperate times
prevent the usual courtesies of love
and exchange of sweet conversation
which should exist between long parted friends.
May God give us time for this in the future.
Farewell once more: be brave, and good luck.

RICHMOND.
Good lords, conduct him to his regiment.
I'll strive with troubled thoughts to take a nap,
Lest leaden slumber peise me down to-morrow
When I should mount with wings of victory.
Once more, good night, kind lords and gentlemen.
Exeunt all but RICHMOND
O Thou, whose captain I account myself,
Look on my forces with a gracious eye;
Put in their hands Thy bruising irons of wrath,
That they may crush down with a heavy fall
The usurping helmets of our adversaries!
Make us Thy ministers of chastisement,
That we may praise Thee in the victory!
To Thee I do commend my watchful soul
Ere I let fall the windows of mine eyes.
Sleeping and waking, O, defend me still!

Good lords, escort him to his regiment.
I'll fight my troubled thoughts and take a nap,
in case tiredness should weigh me down tomorrow
when I should be climbing on wings of victory.
Once more, good night, kind lords and gentlemen.

Oh God, for whom I am fighting,
look on my forces with a kind eye;
put your bruising weapons of anger in their hands,
so that they can crush down with great blows
the thieving helmets of our adversaries!
Make us the agents of your punishment,
so that we can praise you with victory.
I offer my watchful soul to you
before I close my eyes:
sleeping and waking, always defend me!

[Sleeps]

Enter the GHOST Of YOUNG PRINCE EDWARD,
son to HENRY THE SIXTH

GHOST.
[To RICHARD]Let me sit heavy on thy soul
to-morrow!
Think how thou stabb'dst me in my prime of youth

At Tewksbury; despair, therefore, and die!
[To RICHMOND]Be cheerful, Richmond; for the wronged
souls
Of butcher'd princes fight in thy behalf.
King Henry's issue, Richmond, comforts thee.

[To Richard] Let the guilt of me sit heavy on your soul tomorrow!
Think how you stabbed me in the prime of my youth
at Tewkesbury; therefore, despair, and die!
[To Richmond] Be happy, Richmond; for the wronged souls
of murdered princes are fighting on your side.
The son of King Henry, Richmond, comforts you.

Enter the GHOST of HENRY THE SIXTH

GHOST.
[To RICHARD]When I was mortal, my anointed
body
By thee was punched full of deadly holes.
Think on the Tower and me. Despair, and die.
Harry the Sixth bids thee despair and die.
[To RICHMOND]Virtuous and holy, be thou conqueror!
Harry, that prophesied thou shouldst be King,
Doth comfort thee in thy sleep. Live and flourish!

[To Richard] When I was alive, my sacred body
was punched full of deadly holes by you.
Think of the Tower and me. Despair, and die.
Henry the Sixth orders you to despair and die.
[To Richmond] Good and holy, may you triumph!
Harry, who prophesied that you would be King,
comforts you in your sleep. Live and prosper!

Enter the GHOST of CLARENCE

GHOST.
[To RICHARD]Let me sit heavy in thy soul
to-morrow! I that was wash'd to death with fulsome wine,
Poor Clarence, by thy guile betray'd to death!
To-morrow in the battle think on me,
And fall thy edgeless sword. Despair and die!
[To RICHMOND]Thou offspring of the house of Lancaster,
The wronged heirs of York do pray for thee.
Good angels guard thy battle! Live and flourish!

[To Richard] Let me weigh heavily on your conscience tomorrow!
I am poor Clarence, drowned in that thick wine,
sent to death by your cunning!
Think of me in battle tomorrow,
and fall on your blunted sword. Despair and die!
[To Richmond]
You descendant of the house of Lancaster,
the wronged heirs of York are praying for you.
May good angels stand by you in battle! Live and prosper!

Enter the GHOSTS of RIVERS, GREY, and VAUGHAN

GHOST OF RIVERS.[To RICHARD]Let me sit heavy in thy
soul to-morrow,
Rivers that died at Pomfret! Despair and die!

[To Richard] Let me sit heavily on your conscience tomorrow,
Rivers who died at Pomfret! Despair and die!

GHOST OF GREY.
[To RICHARD]Think upon Grey, and let
thy soul despair!

[To Richard] Think of Grey, and let your soul despair!

GHOST OF VAUGHAN.
[To RICHARD]Think upon Vaughan,
and with guilty fear
Let fall thy lance. Despair and die!

[To Richard] Think of Vaughan, and drop your lance
with guilty fear. Despair and die!

ALL.
[To RICHMOND]Awake, and think our wrongs in
Richard's bosom
Will conquer him. Awake and win the day.

Wake up, and believe that the wrong Richard has done
Will conquer him. Awake and be victorious.

Enter the GHOST of HASTINGS

GHOST.
[To RICHARD]Bloody and guilty, guiltily awake,
And in a bloody battle end thy days!
Think on Lord Hastings. Despair and die.
[To RICHMOND] Quiet untroubled soul, awake, awake!
Arm, fight, and conquer, for fair England's sake!

[To Richard] Bloody and guilty, wake up guilty,
and end your days in a bloody battle!
Think of Lord Hastings. Despair and die.
[to Richmond] Quiet untroubled soul, wake up, wake up!
Arm yourself, fight and conquer for the sake of fair England!

Enter the GHOSTS of the two young PRINCES

GHOSTS.
[To RICHARD]Dream on thy cousins smothered in
the Tower.
Let us be lead within thy bosom, Richard,
And weigh thee down to ruin, shame, and death!
Thy nephews' souls bid thee despair and die.
[To RICHMOND]Sleep, Richmond, sleep in peace, and
wake in joy;
Good angels guard thee from the boar's annoy!
Live, and beget a happy race of kings!
Edward's unhappy sons do bid thee flourish.

Dream of your cousins smothered in the tower.
Let us be like lead inside your heart, Richard,
and weigh you down to cause you ruin, shame and death!
The souls of your nephews order you to despair and die.
[To Richmond] Sleep, Richmond, sleep in peace, and wake happy;
may good angels guard you from the attacks of the boar!
Live, and be father to a happy line of kings!
Edward's unhappy sons order you to prosper.

Enter the GHOST of LADY ANNE, his wife

GHOST.
[To RICHARD]Richard, thy wife, that wretched
Anne thy wife
That never slept a quiet hour with thee
Now fills thy sleep with perturbations.
To-morrow in the battle think on me,

And fall thy edgeless sword. Despair and die.
[To RICHMOND]Thou quiet soul, sleep thou a quiet sleep;
Dream of success and happy victory.
Thy adversary's wife doth pray for thee.

[To Richard] Richard, your wife, wretched Anne your wife,
who never had a quiet hour of sleep with you
now fills your sleep with worry.
Think of me in battle tomorrow,
and let your blunt sword fall. Despair and die.
[to Richmond] You innocent soul, sleep a quiet sleep;
dream of success and happy victory.
Your enemy's wife is praying for you.

Enter the GHOST of BUCKINGHAM

GHOST.
[To RICHARD]The first was I that help'd thee
to the crown;
The last was I that felt thy tyranny.
O, in the battle think on Buckingham,
And die in terror of thy guiltiness!
Dream on, dream on of bloody deeds and death;
Fainting, despair; despairing, yield thy breath!
[To RICHMOND]I died for hope ere I could lend thee aid;
But cheer thy heart and be thou not dismay'd:
God and good angels fight on Richmond's side;
And Richard falls in height of all his pride.

[To Richard] I was the leader in helping you to the Crown;
I was the last one who suffered your tyranny.
Oh, in the battle think of Buckingham,
and die in terror at your guilt!
Dream on, dream of bloody deeds and death;
in your weakness, despair; when you despair, die!
[To Richmond] I died in despair before I could help you;
but be cheerful, do not be dismayed:
God and the good angels are fighting on your side;
and Richard shall fall at the height of his pride.

[The GHOSTS vanish. RICHARD starts out of his dream]

KING RICHARD.
Give me another horse. Bind up my wounds.

Have mercy, Jesu! Soft! I did but dream.
O coward conscience, how dost thou afflict me!
The lights burn blue. It is now dead midnight.
Cold fearful drops stand on my trembling flesh.
What do I fear? Myself? There's none else by.
Richard loves Richard; that is, I am I.
Is there a murderer here? No-yes, I am.
Then fly. What, from myself? Great reason why-
Lest I revenge. What, myself upon myself!
Alack, I love myself. Wherefore? For any good
That I myself have done unto myself?
O, no! Alas, I rather hate myself
For hateful deeds committed by myself!
I am a villain; yet I lie, I am not.
Fool, of thyself speak well. Fool, do not flatter.
My conscience hath a thousand several tongues,
And every tongue brings in a several tale,
And every tale condemns me for a villain.
Perjury, perjury, in the high'st degree;
Murder, stern murder, in the dir'st degree;
All several sins, all us'd in each degree,
Throng to the bar, crying all 'Guilty! guilty!'
I shall despair. There is no creature loves me;
And if I die no soul will pity me:
And wherefore should they, since that I myself
Find in myself no pity to myself?
Methought the souls of all that I had murder'd
Came to my tent, and every one did threat
To-morrow's vengeance on the head of Richard.

Give me another horse! Bandage my wounds!
Have mercy, Jesus!–Wait, I was just dreaming.
You cowardly conscience, how you make me suffer!
The light is burning blue; it is now the stroke of midnight.
Cold sweat stands on my trembling skin.
What do I fear? Myself? There's no one else here;
Richard loves Richard, I am with me.
Is there a murderer here? No. Yes, I am!
Then run. What, from myself? Why should I,
unless I'm taking revenge? What, revenge on myself?
Alas, I love myself. Why? Have I done
myself any good?
Oh no, alas, I actually hate myself
for the hateful things I have done.

I am a villain–I'm lying, I am not!
Fool, speak well of yourself! Fool, do not flatter.
My conscience has several thousand voices,
and every voice has several stories,
and every story shows me to be a villain:
perjury, perjury of the highest order;
murder, terrible murder, of the worst type;
many sins, all explored to the fullest,
bear witness against me, all crying, 'Guilty, guilty!'
I shall despair. There is no creature who loves me,
and if I die, no soul will pity me–
and why should they, since I can find
nothing in myself to pity?
I thought that the souls of all whom I had murdered
came to my tent, and every one threatened
that tomorrow Richard would suffer their revenge.

Enter RATCLIFF

RATCLIFF.
My lord!

My Lord!

KING RICHARD.
Zounds, who is there?

By God, who is there?

RATCLIFF.
Ratcliff, my lord; 'tis I. The early village-cock
Hath twice done salutation to the morn;
Your friends are up and buckle on their armour.

It is I, my lord, Ratcliffe. The early cockerel
has greeted the morning twice;
your friends are up and arming themselves.

KING RICHARD.
O Ratcliff, I have dream'd a fearful dream!
What think'st thou–will our friends prove all true?

Oh Ratcliff, I had a terrible dream!
What do you think—will our friends all be loyal?

RATCLIFF.
No doubt, my lord.

There is no doubt, my lord.

KING RICHARD.
O Ratcliff, I fear, I fear.

Ratcliffe, I am afraid.

RATCLIFF.
Nay, good my lord, be not afraid of shadows.

No, my good lord, do not be afraid of shadows.

KING RICHARD.
By the apostle Paul, shadows to-night
Have stuck more terror to the soul of Richard
Than can the substance of ten thousand soldiers
Armed in proof and led by shallow Richmond.
'Tis not yet near day. Come, go with me;
Under our tents I'll play the eaves-dropper,
To see if any mean to shrink from me.

By the apostle Paul, tonight the shadows
have given the soul of Richard more terror
than the reality of ten thousand soldiers
armed to the teeth and led by pathetic Richmond.
It's not close to daylight yet. Come with me;
I shall listen in around our tents,
to see if anyone intends to fail me.

Exeunt

Enter the LORDS to RICHMOND sitting in his tent

LORDS.
Good morrow, Richmond!

Good day, Richmond!

RICHMOND.
Cry mercy, lords and watchful gentlemen,

That you have ta'en a tardy sluggard here.

Forgive me, lords and watchful gentlemen,
you are following a lazy man.

LORDS.
How have you slept, my lord?

How did you sleep, my lord?

RICHMOND.
The sweetest sleep and fairest-boding dreams
That ever ent'red in a drowsy head
Have I since your departure had, my lords.
Methought their souls whose bodies Richard murder'd
Came to my tent and cried on victory.
I promise you my soul is very jocund
In the remembrance of so fair a dream.
How far into the morning is it, lords?

Since you left me, my lords, I have had
the sweetest sleep and the most propitious dreams
that ever came into a sleepy head.
I thought the souls of those whom Richard had murdered
came to my tent and urged me on to victory.
I promise you my soul is very cheerful
remembering such a good dream.
How far are we into the morning, lords?

LORDS.
Upon the stroke of four.

It's exactly four.

RICHMOND.
Why, then 'tis time to arm and give direction.

His ORATION to his SOLDIERS

More than I have said, loving countrymen,
The leisure and enforcement of the time
Forbids to dwell upon; yet remember this:
God and our good cause fight upon our side;
The prayers of holy saints and wronged souls,

Like high-rear'd bulwarks, stand before our faces;
Richard except, those whom we fight against
Had rather have us win than him they follow.
For what is he they follow? Truly, gentlemen,
A bloody tyrant and a homicide;
One rais'd in blood, and one in blood establish'd;
One that made means to come by what he hath,
And slaughtered those that were the means to help him;
A base foul stone, made precious by the foil
Of England's chair, where he is falsely set;
One that hath ever been God's enemy.
Then if you fight against God's enemy,
God will in justice ward you as his soldiers;
If you do sweat to put a tyrant down,
You sleep in peace, the tyrant being slain;
If you do fight against your country's foes,
Your country's foes shall pay your pains the hire;
If you do fight in safeguard of your wives,
Your wives shall welcome home the conquerors;
If you do free your children from the sword,
Your children's children quits it in your age.
Then, in the name of God and all these rights,
Advance your standards, draw your willing swords.
For me, the ransom of my bold attempt
Shall be this cold corpse on the earth's cold face;
But if I thrive, the gain of my attempt
The least of you shall share his part thereof.
Sound drums and trumpets boldly and cheerfully;
God and Saint George! Richmond and victory!

Why then, it's time to arm and give orders.
There is not time, loving countrymen
to say more than I have said.
But remember this:
God, and our justified cause, fight on our side;
the prayers of holy saints and wronged souls
rise up before us like battlements.
Apart from Richard, those whom we fight
would rather that we won than him.
For who is he that they follow? Truly, gentlemen,
a bloody tyrant and a murderer;
one advanced through bloody deeds, and put in his position by them;
one who made plans to win what he has,
and murdered those who helped him with his plans;

he is a foul pebble, whose only value is the setting
of England's throne, where he has been falsely placed;
someone who has always been an enemy to God.
So, if you fight against the enemy of God,
God will, in his justice, reward you as his soldiers;
if you work hard to destroy a tyrant,
you will sleep in peace, when the tyrant is slain;
if you fight against the enemies of your country,
the wealth of your country shall reward you;
if you fight to protect your wives,
your wives shall welcome home the conquerors;
if you release your children from the threat of the sword,
your grandchildren will pay you back for it when you are old.
So, in the name of God and all these things,
advance your banners, draw your winning swords!
If I fail in my bold attempt
I shall pay for it with my death;
but if I succeed, you shall share in the
proceeds of victory.
Ring out, drums and trumpets, boldly and cheerfully!
For God and St George! Richmond and victory!

Exeunt

Re-enter KING RICHARD, RATCLIFF, attendants,
and forces

KING RICHARD.
What said Northumberland as touching
Richmond?

What did Northumberland say about Richmond?

RATCLIFF.
That he was never trained up in arms.

That he was never trained as a soldier.

KING RICHARD.
He said the truth; and what said Surrey
then?

He was speaking the truth; and what did Surrey reply?

RATCLIFF.
He smil'd, and said 'The better for our purpose.'

He smiled, and said, 'All the better for us.'

KING.
He was in the right; and so indeed it is.
[Clock strikes]
Tell the clock there. Give me a calendar.
Who saw the sun to-day?

He was right; it certainly is.

Count the strokes of the clock. Give me a calendar.
Who saw the sun today?

RATCLIFF.
Not I, my lord.

Not me, my lord.

KING RICHARD.
Then he disdains to shine; for by the book
He should have brav'd the east an hour ago.
A black day will it be to somebody.
Ratcliff!

Then he's refusing to shine; for the book says
he should have risen in the east an hour ago.
It will be a black day for somebody.
Ratcliffe!

RATCLIFF.
My lord?

My lord?

KING RICHARD.
The sun will not be seen to-day;
The sky doth frown and lour upon our army.
I would these dewy tears were from the ground.
Not shine to-day! Why, what is that to me
More than to Richmond? For the selfsame heaven
That frowns on me looks sadly upon him.

The sun will not be seen today;
the sky is frowning and bearing down on our army.
I wish this dew would rise from the ground.
Not shine today! Why, why should that mean more to me
than it does to Richmond? The very same heaven
that frowns on me is looking sadly on him.

Enter NORFOLK

NORFOLK.
Arm, arm, my lord; the foe vaunts in the field.

Arm yourself, my lord; the enemy is in the field.

KING RICHARD.
Come, bustle, bustle; caparison my horse;
Call up Lord Stanley, bid him bring his power.
I will lead forth my soldiers to the plain,
And thus my battle shall be ordered:
My foreward shall be drawn out all in length,
Consisting equally of horse and foot;
Our archers shall be placed in the midst.
John Duke of Norfolk, Thomas Earl of Surrey,
Shall have the leading of this foot and horse.
They thus directed, we will follow
In the main battle, whose puissance on either side
Shall be well winged with our chiefest horse.
This, and Saint George to boot! What think'st thou,
Norfolk?

Come, hurry, hurry; dress my horse;
call up Lord Stanley, tell him to bring his forces.
I will lead my soldiers onto the battlefield,
and this is how we shall fight:
my front line shall be stretched out,
comprised of equal numbers of cavalry and infantry;
our archers shall be placed in the middle.
John, Duke of Norfolk, and Thomas, Earl of Surrey,
shall lead the cavalry and infantry;
with them doing that, I shall follow
with the main force, whose strength shall be
well enforced on either side with our best cavalry.
This, and St George as well! What do you think, Norfolk?

NORFOLK.
A good direction, warlike sovereign.
This found I on my tent this morning.

A good plan, soldierly King.
I found this on my tent this morning.
[He sheweth him a paper]

KING RICHARD.
[Reads]
'Jockey of Norfolk, be not so bold,
For Dickon thy master is bought and sold.'
A thing devised by the enemy.
Go, gentlemen, every man unto his charge.
Let not our babbling dreams affright our souls;
Conscience is but a word that cowards use,
Devis'd at first to keep the strong in awe.
Our strong arms be our conscience, swords our law.
March on, join bravely, let us to it pell-mell;
If not to heaven, then hand in hand to hell.

His ORATION to his ARMY

What shall I say more than I have inferr'd?
Remember whom you are to cope withal-
A sort of vagabonds, rascals, and runaways,
A scum of Britaines, and base lackey peasants,
Whom their o'er-cloyed country vomits forth
To desperate adventures and assur'd destruction.
You sleeping safe, they bring to you unrest;
You having lands, and bless'd with beauteous wives,
They would restrain the one, distain the other.
And who doth lead them but a paltry fellow,
Long kept in Britaine at our mother's cost?
A milk-sop, one that never in his life
Felt so much cold as over shoes in snow?
Let's whip these stragglers o'er the seas again;
Lash hence these over-weening rags of France,
These famish'd beggars, weary of their lives;
Who, but for dreaming on this fond exploit,
For want of means, poor rats, had hang'd themselves.
If we be conquered, let men conquer us,
And not these bastard Britaines, whom our fathers

Have in their own land beaten, bobb'd, and thump'd,
And, in record, left them the heirs of shame.
Shall these enjoy our lands? lie with our wives,
Ravish our daughters?[Drum afar off]Hark! I hear their
drum.
Fight, gentlemen of England! Fight, bold yeomen!
Draw, archers, draw your arrows to the head!
Spur your proud horses hard, and ride in blood;
Amaze the welkin with your broken staves!

Enter a MESSENGER

What says Lord Stanley? Will he bring his power?

'Jockey of Norfolk, don't be so brave:
Dick your master is accounted for.'
Something invented by the enemy.
Go, gentlemen: everyone take your command!
Don't let our foolish dreams worry our souls;
conscience is just a word that cowards use,
invented to control the strong.
Our strong arms are our conscience, our swords are our law.
March on! Fight bravely. Let us go fiercely–
if not to heaven, then hand-in-hand to hell!

What can I say, more than I have already suggested?
Remember whom you are fighting:
vagabonds, rascals and runaways;
a scum of Frenchmen and lowdown peasants,
whom their packed country has vomited out
on desperate adventures and certain destruction.
As you were sleeping safe they brought you disturbances;
as you have lands and beautiful wives,
they want to seize one and dishonour the other.
And who is leading them but some weak fellow,
who has lived long in Brittany at my brother's expense?
A milksop! One who has never suffered the
slightest hardship in his life.
Let's drive the stragglers back over the sea,
whip these arrogant beggars of France back there,
these hungry beggars who are tired of life–
if they didn't have this stupid adventure to dream of
they would have hung themselves for lack of money.
If we are to be conquered, let us be conquered by men!

And not these bastard Frenchman, whom our fathers
thrashed in their own country,
and shamed them throughout history.
Shall these people have our lands? Sleep with our wives?
Rape our daughters?
Listen, I can hear their drum.
Fight, gentlemen of England! Fight, bold yeomen!
Drawback your bows as far as they will go, archers!
Drive on your proud forces, and ride through blood!
Frighten the sky with your broken lances!

What does Lord Stanley say? Will he bring his forces?

MESSENGER.
My lord, he doth deny to come.

My lord, he refuses to come.

KING RICHARD.
Off with his son George's head!

Off with the head of his son George!

NORFOLK.
My lord, the enemy is pass'd the marsh.
After the battle let George Stanley die.

My lord, the enemy has crossed over the marshes.
Let George Stanley die after the battle.

KING RICHARD.
A thousand hearts are great within my
bosom.
Advance our standards, set upon our foes;
Our ancient word of courage, fair Saint George,
Inspire us with the spleen of fiery dragons!
Upon them! Victory sits on our helms.

I have a thousand hearts beating within my chest.
Advance our banners, attack our enemies;
May our ancient example of courage, good St George,
inspire us with the anger of fiery dragons!
Attack them! Victory rides with us.

Exeunt

SCENE 4.

Another part of the field

Alarum; excursions. Enter NORFOLK and forces; to him CATESBY

CATESBY.
Rescue, my Lord of Norfolk, rescue, rescue!
The King enacts more wonders than a man,
Daring an opposite to every danger.
His horse is slain, and all on foot he fights,
Seeking for Richmond in the throat of death.
Rescue, fair lord, or else the day is lost.

To the rescue, my Lord of Norfolk, rescue, rescue!
The King is fighting as if he were more than a man,
throwing himself against every danger.
His horse has been killed, and he is fighting on foot,
looking for Richmond in the most dangerous places.
To the rescue, fair lord, or we have lost the battle.

Alarums. Enter KING RICHARD

KING RICHARD.
A horse! a horse! my kingdom for a horse!

A horse! A horse! I'll give my kingdom for a horse!

CATESBY.
Withdraw, my lord! I'll help you to a horse.

Retreat, my lord! I'll find you a horse.

KING RICHARD.
Slave, I have set my life upon a cast
And I will stand the hazard of the die.
I think there be six Richmonds in the field;
Five have I slain to-day instead of him.
A horse! a horse! my kingdom for a horse!

Slave, I have chanced my life to luck
and I will risk the roll of the dice.
I think there must be six Richmonds in the field;
I have killed five today instead of him.
A horse! A horse! My kingdom for a horse!

Exeunt

SCENE 5.

Another part of the field

Alarum. Enter RICHARD and RICHMOND; they fight; RICHARD is slain.
Retreat and flourish. Enter RICHMOND, DERBY bearing the crown,
with other LORDS

RICHMOND.
God and your arms be prais'd, victorious friends;
The day is ours, the bloody dog is dead.

May God and your weapons be praised, victorious friends;
we have won, the bloody dog is dead.

DERBY.
Courageous Richmond, well hast thou acquit thee!
Lo, here, this long-usurped royalty
From the dead temples of this bloody wretch
Have I pluck'd off, to grace thy brows withal.
Wear it, enjoy it, and make much of it.

Brave Richmond, you have acquitted yourself well!
Look, here, I pulled the stolen crown
from the dead forehead of this bloody wretch
to grace your brow.
Wear it, enjoy it, and do your best with it.

RICHMOND.
Great God of heaven, say Amen to all!
But, tell me is young George Stanley living.

Great God of heaven, amen to all that!
But tell me if young George Stanley is still alive.

DERBY.
He is, my lord, and safe in Leicester town,
Whither, if it please you, we may now withdraw us.

He is, my lord, and safe in the town of Leicester,

to which, if it pleases you, we may now withdraw.

RICHMOND.
What men of name are slain on either side?

What notable men have been killed on either side?

DERBY.
John Duke of Norfolk, Walter Lord Ferrers,
Sir Robert Brakenbury, and Sir William Brandon.

John Duke of Norfolk, Walter Lord Ferrers,
Sir Robert Brackenbury and Sir William Brandon.

RICHMOND.
Inter their bodies as becomes their births.
Proclaim a pardon to the soldiers fled
That in submission will return to us.
And then, as we have ta'en the sacrament,
We will unite the white rose and the red.
Smile heaven upon this fair conjunction,
That long have frown'd upon their emnity!
What traitor hears me, and says not Amen?
England hath long been mad, and scarr'd herself;
The brother blindly shed the brother's blood,
The father rashly slaughter'd his own son,
The son, compell'd, been butcher to the sire;
All this divided York and Lancaster,
Divided in their dire division,
O, now let Richmond and Elizabeth,
The true succeeders of each royal house,
By God's fair ordinance conjoin together!
And let their heirs, God, if thy will be so,
Enrich the time to come with smooth-fac'd peace,
With smiling plenty, and fair prosperous days!
Abate the edge of traitors, gracious Lord,
That would reduce these bloody days again
And make poor England weep in streams of blood!
Let them not live to taste this land's increase
That would with treason wound this fair land's peace!
Now civil wounds are stopp'd, peace lives again-
That she may long live here, God say Amen!

Bury their bodies in a way which fits their nobility.

Announce that all the soldiers who fled who
come back under our orders shall be pardoned;
and then, as I've vowed,
I shall unite the houses of Lancaster and York.
Heaven, smile on this fair union,
as you have long scowled at their opposition.
What traitor listens to me and does not say amen?
England has been mad for a long time, and scarred herself:
brother blindly shed the blood of his brother;
a father rashly slaughtered his own son;
the son was forced to murder the father.
All this divided York and Lancaster–
divided in their terrible conflict.
Oh now let Richmond and Elizabeth,
the true successors of each royal house,
join together under the law of God,
and let their heirs, God, if it is your will,
fill the times to come with beautiful peace,
with happy days of prosperity.
Blunt the swords of traitors, gracious Lord,
who would try to take us back to these bloody days
and make poor England weep streams of blood.
Don't let anyone live to enjoy this prosperity
if they want to harm the peace of this fair land with treason.
The wounds of civil war are staunched; peace thrives again.
May God grant that she lives here a long time.

Exeunt

THE END

25918967R00153

Made in the USA
Lexington, KY
09 September 2013